Karma is back, but this time she's not completely to blame.

After surviving a heart- wrenching tragedy, Lexi Marshall is determined to find happiness with her wacky, new-age family. Stumbling through her first few months of motherhood, she's achieved the perfect balance living with her son, the love of her life, and her best friend and his lover. But happily-ever-after all under the same roof doesn't last long.

For one thing, Rich doesn't exactly agree living with everyone is ideal. With their gay/straight double wedding fast approaching, he wants to find a place of their own instead of continuing to sponge off of Marcus and Kevin. But Lexi isn't ready to give up her easy lifestyle...or the never-ending wisdom of her lifelong best friend, Marcus.

Torn between assured comfort and true happiness, Lexi has to make a choice, and fast. Will she lose everything, or can she trust karma, and have it all?

I0665195

Books by Stephanie Haefner

Karma Series
A Bitch Named Karma
Karma Kameleon

Soap Dreams
Paradise Cove

Published by Kensington Publishing Corporation

Karma Kameleon

Karma Series

Stephanie Haefner

LYRICAL PRESS
Kensington Publishing Corp.
www.kensingtonbooks.com

Lyrical Press books are published by
Kensington Publishing Corp. 119 West 40th Street New York, NY 10018

All Kensington titles, imprints, and distributed lines are available at special quantity discounts for bulk purchases for sales promotion, premiums, fund-raising, and educational or institutional use.

Special book excerpts or customized printings can also be created to fit specific needs. For details, write or phone the office of the Kensington Special Sales Manager:
Kensington Publishing Corp.
119 West 40th Street
New York, NY 10018
Attn. Special Sales Department. Phone: 1-800-221-2647.

First Electronic Edition: January 2010
eISBN-13: 978-1-61650-341-3
eISBN-10: 1-61650-341-6

First Print Edition: January 2010
ISBN-13: 978-1-61650-876-0
ISBN-10: 1-61650-876-0

Printed in the United States of America

To my girls: Amy, Ang, Cara, Jaime, Joleene, Krissy, and Nicole…I love you all and love what we have. Thank you for being the best friends a girl could ever ask for. GNI Forever!

Acknowledgements

I would not be where I am today without the love and support of my husband, Keith. Thank you for helping me follow my dreams. I know that someday we'll get where we want to be.

Thank you to the moms who shared their stories and helped me accurately portray such a heart-breaking experience.

Never-ending thanks to my editor, Piper, and her plethora of knowledge and advice. I would never have become the writer I am without you. One of these days we'll be in the same state and I can buy you a few drinks!

Huge thanks to the Buffalo Writers Meetup Group, for enduring scene after scene and offering your advice for making them better.

Chapter 1

"Rich, I'm pregnant."

The last time I'd said those exact words to him, it had led to our breakup and my entrance to a dark and dreary pit of misery. This time, instead of a dumbfounded, confused expression, a huge grin formed on Rich's face and he kissed me. We laughed and he told me how happy he was and how much he loved me.

"This is perfect." He lay next to me on our bed and combed his hand through my hair. He found his way to the edge of my t-shirt--one of his I wore as a night gown. He lifted it and rubbed his hand across my stomach, then leaned down and kissed it. "Only one thing would make it better."

"Yeah? What's that?"

"You saying 'yes'. Marry me, Lexi."

My heart leapt into my throat and a chaotic flutter of butterflies on speed swirled through my stomach. I stared at Rich, his adoring eyes staring back at me. Was this for real? I'd never been proposed to before.

"Really? Are you sure? You don't have to marry me just 'cause you knocked me up."

His brow furrowed as his lips bowed in a half smile. "You're kinda ruining this moment." He reached into the nightstand drawer next to him. The black velvet box opened with a *pop* and inside sat a princess cut diamond ring--not a small one, either. "I've been trying to find the perfect time for weeks now."

My eyes immediately teared. How could I have doubted his sincerity?

"Will you marry me?" he asked again.

My body shook and I nodded.

"Is that a 'yes'?"

"Yes," I screamed and tackled him, covering his face with kisses.

"Wait," he managed between smooches. "I want to make it official."

"Didn't we just do that?"

"Not yet." Rich plucked the sparkly gem from its box. He slid it onto my left ring finger and I did what all newly engaged women do. I flexed my wrist and held my arm straight, admiring my hand and its brilliant adornment.

"Do you like it?" he asked.

"I love it!" And truly meant it. The square stone appeared flawless, at least a carat and a half, maybe more. I couldn't have picked a more perfect setting myself--simple and elegant platinum, nothing fru-fru about it.

"I know it's not as big as Abby's."

"Uh, there's no need for it to be." I didn't care one bit what my sister had. "And besides, I'm sure your penis is way bigger than Daniel's anyway."

"What?"

"Everybody knows big fat diamond rings are to make up for tiny dicks. Trust me--you have no need whatsoever to buy me a big diamond."

I placed my lips back on his and my hands made their way to his boxers. Rich slipped a hand under my shirt in preparation of removing it.

Thud. Followed by high-pitched wailing.

Rich and I pulled apart. What the heck was that? Before my feet hit the hardwood, Marcus's voice was on the other side of the door.

"Sorry guys. Preston got away from me."

"It's okay. Bring him in," I yelled, still hearing my little man's cries.

Marcus pushed the door open slowly and as soon as Preston's teary eyes met mine, he smiled and reached his arms to me.

"He's getting fast," Marcus said. "I turned around to pick up some toys and he crawled off down the hallway. I think he crashed head first into your door."

Marcus placed my pajama-clad baby in my arms, though I couldn't call him a baby anymore. It had been almost a year since his birth and it seemed like he grew an inch a day. I'd always heard people go on about *how fast time flies*, but had never realized how true it was until I had my own child.

"Should we tell him?" Rich asked, gazing at Preston. I nodded.

"Guess what, my precious boy? Daddy Rich is gonna make an honest woman of me. See?" I wiggled my fingers at him.

He pointed at the diamond and giggled. He had no clue what it meant or how huge a deal it was, but I liked to pretend he did and was happy.

"Wow. Congrats." Marcus smiled and shook Rich's hand, then gave me a hug. "I'm really happy for you."

"There's more."

"Oh?"

"Yeah," I said and turned back to my son. "Preston, you're gonna be a big brother."

"What was that I heard?" Kevin barged in.

"Yep, I'm pregnant."

"Oh my God," Kevin shrieked and skipped over to us. "This is the best news ever!" He plopped onto the bed and pulled Rich, Preston and me into a hug.

"We're getting married, too," Rich added, and Kevin dove in for another hug, shooting me with wedding questions.

"Come on." Marcus playfully yanked Kevin toward the door. "You want us to get Preston out of here so you can, you know, celebrate?"

I looked to Rich, his blue eyes telling me exactly what I wanted to hear. We'd do our celebrating later. I turned back the other half of my new-age family--Marcus in his striped cotton pants and t-shirt, Kevin in silky red pj's. "No. Let's get dressed and celebrate together."

* * * *

I checked my cell after having it off an entire day--a family brunch with Marcus, Kevin and Preston, then a romantic night with Rich, including a stay at the Luxury Inn and Suites for nostalgia's sake. Rich no longer worked for his Uncle Walt full-time, but filled in when he needed someone. He'd worked there even after graduating from NYU, his administrative assistant's job at Big Apple Records not quite paying enough to survive on. But with the step up to promoter, he'd been able to leave the hotel clerk job.

"You have fifteen new messages." A robotic female voice spoke into my ear as we climbed into a cab. What the hell? Can't I be left alone for one day?

"First message...Hey, Lexi! It's Amanda. I got your text and I'm so excited for you guys. Congrats! Call me later."

"Next message...Lexi, dear, it's Mom. I'm putting together a dinner to celebrate your engagement. Oh, this is so wonderful--another wedding to plan! I've already talked with Pastor John and he's ecstatic. He gave me a list of dates the church is available next summer. We can't do May--that's Abigail and Daniel's wedding anniversary. June would be perfect. July and August are too hot--you know how the heat affects your father's hyperhidrosis. So we should book this as soon as possible. Hate to have your heart set on a date and then--"

"Next message... It's Mom again. Geez, they don't give you much time to talk before cutting you off. But anyway, Pastor said many dates next summer are already booked, so we need to pick one soon so you get your first choice. And we need to book the florist and the band, too. Call me when you get this."

I'd been an engaged woman barely twenty-four hours and already the drama had begun.

"Next message... Lexi, it's Sheila. I need your last copy edit for *Mama Drama* ASAP, and we need to go over the schedule for the local book tour. We're trying to book you in a couple other cities--Buffalo, Toronto, maybe Philly. Call me."

I shut the phone off and rested my head on Rich's shoulder with a sigh, not caring about the other messages.

"The real world beckons." He kissed my forehead. "I checked my messages, too. One day away and shit's falling apart at work."

"My mother's already planning our wedding extravaganza."

He laughed. "Honestly, I couldn't care less about the details. I just want to marry you. We could go to City Hall right now for all I care."

"Don't tempt me." I snuggled into him tight, loving that he was just like me. "But don't you want to see me in a gorgeous gown and shove cake in my face?"

"We don't need a big fancy wedding to do that. I'd be happy with something small and intimate, the people who matter."

"If I can wrestle my mom into submission, I'll make it happen."

The cab pulled up in front of the building where I'd been sharing an apartment with Marcus and Kevin for over a year. Rich had moved in right after Preston's birth, and aside from the usual family spats, it had been complete bliss. Every woman should be as lucky--three men to cater to her every need.

The first few months of motherhood had been--for lack of a less profane phrase--pretty damn fucked up. As if cracked, bleeding nipples weren't enough, throw in nights of minuscule sleep, shit explosions--the baby's, not mine--and uncontrollable crying fits--mine, not the baby's. And through it all, my guys were there. Marcus, the tough-as-nails lawyer and my BFF-slash- baby daddy, had morphed into a fluff of bright pink cotton candy when he became a dad. His live-in lover and life partner, Kevin, became the brother I never had, or even knew I wanted.

And then there was Rich, the man I loved and wanted to spend my life with. Our relationship until Preston's birth had been pretty rocky. But once we'd sorted through our feelings, we couldn't live without each other.

Okay, cue the harp music and toss some rose petals over our heads. I know--so not like me.

But never in my life had I found a man who cared for me--not my breasts, my tight ass, or my immeasurable talent for giving head. He did like those attributes, of course, but we had fun together and genuinely wanted the best for each other.

Rich and I held hands and stepped into the apartment amid chaos. Preston screamed, and crawled to the living room wearing nothing. Kevin ran after him, soaked from head to toe. Marcus appeared with a bloodied washcloth held to his nose.

So much for relaxing a bit longer.

"What the hell is going on here?" I picked Preston up and held him close.

"We were giving him a bath, and well, he whacked Marcus in the nose with his tugboat. Then he started splashing me."

All of a sudden, my brand new Diane von Furstenberg maxi sundress got really warm…and wet.

"Son of a bitch." I held Preston away from me by the armpits, pee still trickling from his little fireman's hose.

"Let me have him." Rich took him to the nursery while I headed to the bedroom to change. When I came back to the kitchen, Kevin was cleaning Marcus's face of all traces of blood. After a final wipe, he kissed him on the nose and the two smiled at each other.

I found Rich in the living room with Preston on the couch, an episode of Sesame Street on the flat screen. Peace had been restored.

Chapter 2

"We only have a week until Preston's birthday extravaganza," Kevin stated after taking his seat at the dinner table.

"Can you believe it?" I shoveled a forkful of rice pilaf into my mouth.

"I can't wait to start making all the food. And the decorating! I ordered the cutest centerpiece for the table--it's in a little red wagon! I found the perfect napkins and plates to match and the cake is just adorable. I showed you the picture, right?" Kevin grabbed a folder off the counter and moved a platter of chicken aside.

"I know the party is already planned and all, but I was thinking..." He scattered a few brochures. "We should hire a clown." He picked up a colorful brochure, his head so inflated with ideas it looked like it could explode any second if he didn't let them out. "Or this other company sets up an entire kiddie carnival inside your house."

Marcus and I locked eyes, then turned to Kevin. Poor guy. He was so damn excited.

"I love you for doing this." Marcus put his hand on Kevin's. "But I think it's too much."

"It's only his first birthday," I added. "We can save this cool stuff for when he's older and actually has friends."

"He has friends. Jeanette's kids will be here."

"I know, but don't you think he's a bit young for all this...commotion?" Marcus asked.

There'd be enough commotion as it was with a guest list exceeding fifty, only our closest friends and relatives. I still didn't know where we'd put everyone. Yeah, we had a decent-sized apartment with a formal dining room, huge living room, and even a spacious kitchen, rare for New York, but we'd never tried to fit so many people before.

"Yeah, I guess." The glimmer in Kevin's eyes had faded. "They were just suggestions."

"And we're so appreciative." Marcus smiled and I knew he'd make it up to him later.

* * * *

After kissing Rich goodbye for the day, I showered and readied for my first prenatal appointment with my OBGYN. It seemed odd to be going so soon. With Preston, I hadn't known I was pregnant for months. It made the rest of the pregnancy go really fast. Hopefully this one wouldn't drag by.

I grabbed one of my favorite pairs of skinny jeans and yanked them up over my ass, but zipping was near impossible. Forget about buttoning them. Looked like my body had already been taken over.

Pushing the jeans down, I smiled and rubbed my hand across my stomach. "That's okay, baby." With Preston, I'd not been too happy about my body being invaded, but this time was different. And I reveled in any excuse to go shopping, even for maternity clothes.

I pulled on a pair of black leggings and my knee-high suede boots. Never in my life had I been so thankful stretchy pants were in style.

* * * *

"How far along are we now?" Rich asked, snuggling up to me in bed. His arms curled around my naked body--one hand cupping a breast, the other my stomach.

"Around eight weeks."

One of his hands traveled south. "And you're sure it's okay to fool around?"

"Did you forget the times we did it when I was pregnant with Preston? 'Cause I certainly haven't forgotten." I turned to him and pressed my mouth to his, my tongue dancing inside, twisting with his--a reminder of how hot our sex life was and would always be. I moved my lips to his chest and nibbled one of his pierced nipples, tugging at the metal ring with my teeth.

"Mmm...I could never forget. But I didn't know you were pregnant then. I didn't know I was supposed to be careful."

I climbed on top of his steel-plated god's body and pushed him inside of me--his dick like a surge of electricity. The shock radiated from my G-spot to the tips of my chocolaty curls and the hot pink polish on my toenails.

I began rocking my pelvis against his. "My doctor told me it's fine. And besides, I read that babies in utero love the feeling of orgasm almost as much as the mom."

"Well, in that case..." Rich's seductive smile gazed up at me. He pressed his thumb to my clit while I gyrated. "We better make sure you have more than one. For the baby's sake."

"Oh yes....for the baby's sake."

With the conclusion of fabulous orgasm number one, I yanked on Rich's shoulders and brought him to a sitting position, my legs now encircling his body. I needed the force of his muscled arms to pull my body to his, push his cock deeper into me, hit where I needed it to. After only a few thrusts, orgasm number two shook my body and I clenched every facial muscle in order to hold my euphoric screams inside. We'd made a deal with Marcus and Kevin--we'd keep our orgasmic outbursts to ourselves if they did the same.

I got on all fours, one of Rich's favorite positions, and wiggled my ass. He accepted my invitation and took barely two seconds to connect with me once again, my river of a vagina making the ride a smooth one. I glanced over my shoulder just in time to see his face as he got off, throwing his head back with the last few pumps.

He hunched his sweat-covered body onto my back and together we melted into the sheets. Didn't matter that our heads were on the wrong end of the bed.

* * * *

Knock. Knock. "Lex...Rich? You guys awake?"

I opened my eyes to a room blazing with late spring sun. The air conditioning hadn't been turned on in the apartment yet and it felt like July was upon us. I flung the blanket off, exposing our sweaty naked bodies.

Rich groaned and pulled the pillow over his head. "I can't wait to get our own place."

I laughed. "Yeah, that'll happen."

Knock. Knock. "Can I come in?" Marcus asked.

"Only if you want to see our bare asses."

"Tempting, but no time today. Have you looked at the clock?"

I cast my gaze to the left--eleven twenty-one. "Fuck."

"Okay, I'll take that as a 'yes'. I assume you'll be out soon to help set up the party?"

It was my little man's big day. No time for lounging. I left Rich in bed and headed toward the bathroom. The last year of my life breezed through my brain as the massaging jets rained down from the shower head. This time one year ago, I'd been huge and pregnant, wondering how the hell

I would squish my fat ass into my maid of honor dress for Abby and Daniel's wedding.

Note to self: do not get so fat this time around.

I'd dreaded that day, until it actually happened, anyway. Everything had fallen into place--the bonds with my mother and sister, my reconnection with Rich. It had been the most perfect day ever for Preston to make his debut.

And now here we were, a year later, celebrating my baby boy and the miles we'd traveled since he came into our lives. More than a celebration of his birth, it was a celebration of our family.

An hour later I stood on a ladder in four-inch Pradas hanging a birthday banner on the wall. Marcus and Kevin were in the kitchen putting candles on the cake, while Rich organized the party music playlist. Preston, thank God, had conked out for an early nap.

One o'clock on the dot, the buzzer rang. Grandma and Grandpa Marshall were the first guests to arrive, with Uncle Andy, Aunt Abby, and Uncle Daniel right behind. More guests trickled in: Amanda, Rachel and Brenda, some of Rich's friends, even Sheila. And what party would be complete without at least a few flamboyant homosexuals? Marcus greeted guests while Rich poured drinks. Kevin mingled and served canapes from a silver serving tray.

"Lexi, hon," Kevin yelled to me. "Buzzer's gonna go off any second. Can you take the scallops out of the oven? Thanks, love."

"Um, sure." I turned toward the oven and before I could get there, my mother snagged my arm.

"Dear, where is Pastor John? Didn't you invite him?"

"No, Mom. Hold on, I gotta do something."

"You should have invited him. I bet one of your single girlfriends would be perfect for him. What about the one with the pink sweater and blond hair?"

"I can't think about that right now."

I reached for a potholder off the top of the fridge. Nothing. Searching around, I found one on the island under a bowl of bruschetta. In the meantime, Mom had disappeared and when I cast my gaze to the living room, she was chatting with Rachel. I slipped my hand inside the potholder, ready to open the oven.

"Lexi! So glad I finally got you alone."

I turned and Abby stood behind me.

"I wanted to tell you something before the party got too busy."

"Yeah? What?"

"Well…" Her eyes held a sparkle. "For the first time in my life I can honestly say I'm just like my big sister."

Huh? The kitchen timer started its *beep beep beep*. I didn't have time for one of Abby's guessing games. I fidgeted with the timer, trying to figure out how to stop its incessant noise. After pressing every button on it twice, I finally stopped it. "What are you talking about?"

"Lexi," she said and rubbed her hand over her stomach. "I'm *just* like you."

"Oh my God!" I threw the timer to the counter and hugged my sister. "Congratulations."

"Isn't this great? We're pregnant together."

"You told her?" Mom said, reappearing in the kitchen.

"Yes!" I said, tears in my eyes. I couldn't believe how happy I felt for Abby. Someone close to me was going to experience the joy of motherhood that I had come to cherish.

As if on cue, Preston began to wail.

"Let's go get the birthday boy," Mom said, and we followed her to the nursery.

When we walked in, Preston's cries stopped and his toothy smile beamed. Standing at the crib rail, he looked so damn big. What had happened to my baby?

Mom put him on the changing table and began tickling his feet. Abby grabbed a diaper and wipes while I got his birthday outfit from the closet. After stripping him down and changing his diaper, we dressed him in his brand new clothes--couldn't have him wearing something old on his big day.

As we headed toward the living room, the unmistakable screech of the smoke detector assaulted our ears.

Shit! The scallops.

I handed a screaming Preston to my mother and trotted to the kitchen, where Kevin held a baking pan covered with charred lumps. Marcus opened a window and fanned some of the smoke outside.

"Kevin, I'm so sorry."

"I know. It's okay."

The party guests had congregated near the kitchen to see what the drama was and I felt like a monumental ass. Half an hour into the party and I had already ruined my little man's perfect day. Never in my life had I wanted to be anything like my mother, until that moment. Her parties were always perfect. She never burned a single thing.

I turned toward the bathroom, needing to escape the questioning eyes before my tear ducts erupted. Two months in and the pregnancy hormones were already working overtime. I blew my nose and re-powdered my face. Might as well pee too, since I was already in there. As I pulled on the toilet paper, I noticed a very bright dot on the center of my very plain underwear.

So much for not bursting into tears.

A knock came on the door. "Lex, you okay?"

"Get in here," I yelled to Rich through my sobs, not caring if I sounded hysterical.

"It's okay," he said after closing the door behind him. "No one cares about the food."

"Look!" I showed him my underwear and the pea-sized spot.

His eyes widened like flying saucers. "That's bad, isn't it?"

"Yes...no. I don't know."

He knelt in front of me and pulled me to him. "What can I do?"

Managing to calm myself down and think somewhat rationally, I asked, "Can you get my pregnancy book from the night stand?" I thought I'd read about spotting in the first trimester.

Rich brought the book to me and I flipped to one of the early chapters. "Pink spotting is common during the first trimester, and is usually caused by the egg implanting in the lining of the uterus."

"But this is bright red." Rich stated the obvious.

I scanned further down the page. "The most frightening type of spotting or bleeding during the first trimester is fresh blood, or bright red. While this can be serious, it is not always confirmation that a miscarriage is occurring."

Rich's face turned a vampire shade of pale, without the sparkliness.

"Many things can cause bright red spotting or bleeding. If you are experiencing cramping or clotting, this could signify something serious. Seek medical care immediately."

"Are you cramping?"

"No. I feel fine...normal."

"Then, what should we do?"

"I don't know. We have a house full of people. And my doctor's office is closed."

"We can go to the hospital."

I thought for a minute. "No. It's okay. It's probably nothing."

"Are you sure?"

"This is Preston's big day. I'm not gonna ruin it." I wiped and looked at the toilet paper. Nothing. I held it up. "See. It's done. No more blood."

Chapter 3

I freshened up, hoping no one could tell I'd been crying, and rejoined the party like nothing had happened. I sat with Preston on my lap as we opened fun new toys and clothes and the tricycle Rich and I had picked out. Camera flashes sparked from all over the room with wide smiles behind each and every one.

Cake time, and I sat Preston on the dining room table with a huge sugary confection glowing in front of him. With the smell of butter cream frosting in the air, our family and friends started an off-pitch rendition of *Happy Birthday to You*, and a small pain jabbed at my stomach. I met Rich's gaze on the other side of the table. He noticed my panicked expression and his wide smile went flat.

As the room continued with "Happy birthday dear Preston," the pain sharpened, like a shard of glass being jammed into my mid-section. I gripped one of the dining room chairs and fought to stay on my feet. Me crippling over in pain would only cause mass hysteria. And I didn't want that for my boy's big day.

Rich made it to my side before the song had ended. "Are you okay?"

"No," I answered, cheers erupting.

I grabbed Marcus's arm. "I…um…need to run to the store."

"Right now?"

"Yes."

Maybe he sensed something was wrong. I'm sure the expressions on my face and Rich's were a giveaway. He said, "Okay," and turned his attention back to the table and the birthday boy.

By the time Rich and I got into a cab, my underwear was soaked through. With blood. Intense cramping continued to hammer at my abdomen, in waves, like labor.

Forty-five minutes later, we sat in the ER exam room waiting for the on-call obstetrician to come in. But my pains had slowed considerably. That had to be a good thing, right?

A stout man with graying hair came in, followed by a woman wheeling a machine. I recognized it immediately--an ultrasound machine.

He didn't say much, aside from "Hello. I'm Dr. Leiman," and after sticking his hand inside me, asked if it hurt when he pressed on my stomach. It didn't.

The ultrasound tech lubed the wand and inserted it. She moved it around and fiddled with the machine, and I struggled to interpret the grainy screen. It was dark and blank and silent. I didn't hear the *whump whump whump* of a baby's heartbeat. Maybe this ultrasound machine didn't have sound.

The doctor turned to me. "I'm sorry Ms. Marshall. You've lost your baby."

"No, that can't be right. The pains have weakened. I feel better now."

"I think you're through the worst of it." He turned to the screen and pointed to a gray blob. "See this here?"

I nodded.

"That's most likely the fetus. But there's no heartbeat."

I strained my eyes, praying for something on the screen to move or blink or do something so this nightmare would end.

"You'll continue to bleed for at least a week, maybe longer. And you'll most likely expel some clots."

Rich squeezed my hand so hard I thought he might break it.

The doctor removed his gloves. "We might need to wait a few days, but I don't see the need for a D and C."

"What's that?" I wasn't all up on the miscarriage lingo.

"It stands for dilation and curettage. Basically, if the tissue isn't expelled, we need to go in and scrape your uterus."

"Oh." It sounded horrific.

"You said you were only eight to nine weeks. That's very early in a pregnancy. We'll do a blood test to check your HCG levels, but I want you to follow up with your OB. They'll probably do more bloodwork to make sure the levels are decreasing like they should be. Take it easy a few days." He stood and fidgeted with his white coat--his name embroidered in blue across the left side. "Do you have any questions?"

I shook my head. I couldn't form even one cohesive thought. My body and brain were shutting down. Even my tear ducts had stopped working. Complete numbness had taken over and it wouldn't even allow me to cry.

"Why did this happen?" Rich asked. His voice was strained, the way someone sounded when they were trying to talk and hold back sobs at the same time. The sight of his water-logged eyes jolted mine into perfect working order.

"I wish I had an answer," the doctor said. "Most likely a genetic abnormality. Sometimes these things just happen. But many women go on to have healthy pregnancies after a miscarriage."

He left, with the ultrasound tech right behind, and the room became eerily silent. How could an ER exam room be this crypt-like? On TV there was always some kind of drama, someone running around and breaking the silence.

Rich pulled the chair to the bed and sat down, laying his head on my lap. I stroked his hair as he cried, feeling utterly helpless. Tears cascaded down my own cheeks, but I felt the need to try and be strong. I couldn't let myself break into a million pieces.

"It's my fault," he said through his misery, his body shaking.

"What? You heard the doctor. It's nobody's fault."

He looked up at me. "We shouldn't have had sex last night. I should have stopped."

"Sex doesn't cause miscarriages."

"How do you know? What if I went in too deep?"

I really didn't know.

"I'm so sorry, Lexi."

I pulled him to me and we cried together.

"I loved our baby so much."

* * * *

While we waited for the blood test results, I called Marcus. Thank God the party had ended and everyone had gone home. But not without asking a million questions as to my whereabouts.

"Lex, I didn't know what to tell everyone. What happened?"

I struggled to find the words. "Um, the baby…"

"Is everything okay?"

"No." My hand shook the phone against my ear and fresh tears trickled down my cheeks. "It's gone."

"Oh, Lexi. I'm sorry. What can I do?"

"Give Preston lots of kisses and tell him Mommy loves him. And please make sure he's in bed before we get home. I don't want him to see me like this."

"I will. I love you and we're here for anything you need."

"I know. Thank you."

The phone beeped when I pressed *End*, a piercing sound in such a quiet room. Rich returned, having run to the cafeteria for some strong coffee. His eyes, while dry, still held their red hue and the puffiness from crying.

"Nurse said the results should be back any minute, then we can get out of here."

He just nodded and my heart broke. I wanted to pull him to me and tell him everything was going to be okay, though I wasn't sure I believed it myself. But as devastating as the loss of our baby was for me, it had to be so much more for him. I had Preston at home, a baby I could hug and kiss and snuggle. This would have been Rich's first child--a baby who would only call him *Daddy*.

The nurse came in with some paperwork. "Your blood work came back. The HCG level, which is the hormone produced during pregnancy, is lower than that of a normal healthy pregnancy. It should continue to decrease over the next few days until it's at zero." She gave a sympathetic smile. "I'm so sorry."

I stared at her puppy dog scrubs and the vision began to blur. I'd held onto a small spark of hope that maybe the OB had been wrong. The ultrasound machine had been broken. I wanted the nurse to tell me my levels were exactly where they should be for this stage of my pregnancy. But she didn't. She just confirmed what we already knew.

"I have your discharge papers here. You can leave whenever you feel up to it. No rush."

She left and we were alone again.

Rich stood and tossed his empty Styrofoam cup into the trash. "We should get going."

"Yeah. Can you grab my clothes?"

He reached for the pile and turned to me with another horrid reminder of what we'd gone through. My bloodied underwear, now dried and brown, sat staring at us.

"Please throw those away," I begged and he did without a second of hesitation.

But my dress had a huge blood stain on it too. Without even asking, Rich balled it up and tossed it. He covered his face with his hands and rubbed a few times, then raked his fingers through his hair.

"What do we do now?"

I buzzed the nurse's station and the same compassionate woman came strolling in. After explaining the clothing situation, she brought in a set of pale blue scrubs. I put them on with my beige Prada platforms and searched for my purse. Rich pulled it from under the chair in the corner and set it on the bed. He took me in his arms, squeezing me tight, as if he were holding on for dear life. Like he was falling, his life about to spiral into an endless pit, my body his only way of surviving.

I pulled away and wiped the tears from his cheeks. "I love you."

"I love you too."

* * * *

Seven AM came way too soon. The alarm went off and instead of yawning and stretching and bouncing out of bed to wake my beautiful baby boy, I slammed my hand on the alarm and knocked it on the floor. Which didn't even turn it off. The beeping continued and now I had to get out of bed to turn it off. I threw the comforter and stood, feeling the gush of liquid in my crotch. More blood had oozed out, reminding me the events of the previous day did happen.

I grabbed the alarm clock and beat it into submission, then slammed it on the nightstand, knocking over the picture of Rich, Preston and I. It landed face-side down and after I'd picked it up, relief filled me as I found it unharmed. I sat down on the bed and stared at the picture. Rich came behind me and kissed the back of my neck.

"You okay?"

"Yeah. Sorry I wigged out like that."

"It's understandable. I'd tear the whole place apart if it'd make me feel any better."

"Preston's one-year check up is today. I have to call my doctor too, and see when I can get in. I don't think the receptionist comes in 'til nine though."

"Call me after you make the appointment. I have a couple meetings today, but leave a voicemail. I want to go with you and I'll need to tell my boss so he can guarantee me the day off."

"You're going to work today?"

He sighed and kissed me again. "I thought of calling in sick, but I think staying busy will help, ya know?"

I agreed. I had lots to keep my mind miscarriage-free, or at least, things to try and keep my mind occupied. "I'll call you as soon as I know."

Rich got up and started his morning routine. Many mornings I joined him in the shower and we'd get a quickie in before breakfast. Not today. I got out of bed and headed to Preston's room.

He'd been asleep when Rich and I got home the night before, as requested. I'd peeked in on him, though--his angelic face with a smile, dreaming happy baby dreams. I'd pressed a kiss to his head and felt the emptiness of my womb. Before my sobs could start again, I'd scooted out.

When I'd returned to the living room, Rich sat with Marcus and Kevin, a bottle of Jack on the table. Rich and Kevin had already been sipping on theirs. Marcus had poured another glass and handed it to me. I'd shaken my head at first, but needed something to dull the ache in my gut. I took the glass and snuggled into Rich. Marcus had poured a fourth and sat back, leaving the bottle open. He'd known it would get more use before it needed its cap.

Chapter 4

"He's perfect," Dr. Simon stated after inspecting every crevice of Preston's body. "He needs a few shots before you go--MMR, hib, and chicken pox. Any questions?"

I shook my head and tried to smile.

Her exuberant expression faded. "Lexi, is everything all right?"

I tried to control my tear ducts, but apparently they had a mind of their own. "I'm having a miscarriage."

"Oh no. You should get to the hospital."

"I already went--yesterday. And I'm seeing my OB tomorrow."

Her eyes softened and she placed her hand atop mine. "I'm so sorry."

"Thank you."

The nurse came in and wiped Preston's leg with an alcohol-drenched cotton ball.

I held my boy tight and when he cried, I cried too. It always pained me to see him hurt, but this time my tears were for more than just his shots.

* * * *

I stopped at Smith & Roland on my way home and wheeled Preston down the hall toward Sheila's office. The office employees greeted us with wide smiles and cheery hellos and I plastered on my smile. When we reached Sheila's office, I knocked and waited. Her shrieks blared from behind the closed door. Yikes. I remembered those days. Luckily, Sheila and I were on a whole different level now. I respected her and was certain she had at least a little bit for me too.

When the door opened, a young woman came out, eyes puffy. Our glances met and I tried to smile. "I've been where you are."

She walked off and I pushed the stroller through the door and closed it behind me.

"What happened to you the other day? One minute we're singing and the next you were gone?" She stood and unbuckled Preston's seatbelt, sitting back in her chair with him on her lap. After pulling open a drawer, she sprinkled some goldfish crackers on her desk--treats she kept in her office for him.

"Um...well." No point in lying. She'd see right though it. "I had to go to the hospital. I'm having a miscarriage."

Her eyes met mine and I recognized the hurt. She'd gone through the same thing some fifteen years ago, and still hadn't recovered. I knew by the way she held Preston to her--the way she spoiled him. And how she watched over Amanda and took care of her as if she were her child, rather than just a niece.

"I'm sorry."

I nodded. "Thanks."

She poured a few more fish, then rummaged through a desk drawer. "Here are the cover art options for *Mama Drama*. What do you think?"

Business as usual. Sheila dealt with pain by submerging herself in work.

"Any chance you can get me the first draft of *Which Way to Broadway* by the fifteenth of next month?"

Maybe she thought I needed that too. "Shouldn't be a problem."

Might be a good idea anyway. I needed something to occupy my mind. And this new story, loosely based on Amanda and her experience with moving to New York, was sure to keep my mind baby-free. Unlike my last novel, this one included no babies, aside from a pregnant BFF making an occasional appearance.

* * * *

Kevin's sister Jeanette watched Preston while Rich and I headed to my OB appointment. Right away the nurse took a blood sample, then seated me in a room--paper gown in hand. When the doctor came in, she gave a sympathetic smile.

"How are you, Lexi?"

I was sick of answering that question. Between my mother, and Jeanette, and Amanda, and Rachel, and every other person who had called me over the past two days, my answer of "Okay" had been perfected, regardless of how I actually felt. I wanted to scream, "My baby died. I'm fucking devastated. Why are you asking me such a stupid fucking question?" But no one wanted to hear that.

"I have your blood test results and your HCG levels are lower than the hospital's test, so that's good. May take a few more days to go down to zero." She sat on her rolling stool. "I'm sure the hospital gave you some literature. Is there anything you need clarification on?"

"No, I don't think so."

"Okay, have you--"

"I have a question," Rich interrupted.

"Of course."

He hesitated before asking, his eyes blinking back tears. "Can sex cause a miscarriage?"

The doctor's eyes softened as she looked from Rich to me and back again. "No, it can't. Sex during any stage of pregnancy is more than fine."

"But, um…what if it was different positions? We did it the night before the miscarriage started."

"Having sex did not cause this. Please don't blame yourselves. There is no explanation for why miscarriage happens. And honestly, the baby most liked passed away a week or two ago."

My heart sank to the floor. My baby had been inside me, already dead, and I hadn't noticed? How could I not know there was something wrong?

"Have you passed any clots--large ones?"

I shook my head. "Just a couple small ones."

"I'd like to do another ultrasound, to see what's going on."

We gathered my things and the doctor escorted us to one of the ultrasound rooms. The technician joined us and I already knew the drill. I lay back and she inserted the wand. The gray image of my womb came on the screen, empty.

"Everything is expelling as it should be. But I do see a small sac still attached to the lining of your uterus."

My baby.

"It should come loose in the next few days. It will look like the other clots, only a bit larger. Give me a call when it happens and we'll do another HCG check and ultrasound to make sure everything is as it should be."

This wasn't how it should be. My baby should be alive and growing, not waiting to be "expelled."

I nodded, having no other reaction. The doctor said her goodbye and I redressed. Rich took my hand as we walked home instead of taking a cab. It was a long walk, but the late spring day begged to be taken advantage of. Plus, the walk would do us good.

The sidewalks were filled with businessmen and tourists, all in a hurry to get somewhere. Rich and I walked as if we had nowhere to be and were in no rush to get there. He held my hand in his and we walked on, almost in a daze.

When we reached our building, we both stopped. I had no desire to go home. Jeanette had Preston for the rest of the afternoon--she'd told us to take our time. We had no real need to go home.

Rich looked at me. "Wanna keep walking?"

I nodded.

We walked past a flower shop, the sidewalk out front covered with buckets and pails filled with blooms of all shapes, sizes, and colors. Rich stopped for a minute, caressing the petals of a bright yellow rose.

"Wait here a minute."

He dashed inside the flower shop. What was he doing? Through the front window, I watched him walk up to the counter. A minute later, the woman had brought him a small white box. He handed her some cash and after receiving change, he was back outside.

"What was that all about?"

"I have an idea. Come with me."

He hailed a cab and asked the driver to take us to the Central Park pond. I didn't ask what was in the box or why we were going to the park. Rich had something in his mind and I was along for the ride.

When the cab stopped, Rich paid and I followed him toward the Gapstow Bridge, which curved over the neck of the pond. He stopped at the highest spot of the bridge, facing the water, and placed the small white box on the ledge. Images of tall green trees reflected on the water as ducks swam and dunked their heads for food.

He opened the box and inside sat two perfect gardenias. Lifting them out, he handed one to me, then brought the other to his nose, inhaling its sweet aroma. Our free hands intertwined and I squeezed tight, meeting his gaze, eyes wet with fresh tears.

The warmth of his lips touched mine and then he turned back to his gardenia. "Goodbye," he whispered and tossed his bloom into the water. It landed perfectly, ripples surrounding it.

I did the same, mine landing a few feet from Rich's. He drew in a deep breath and exhaled, taking me into his arms. We stood there for a while before continuing home.

Chapter 5

Back to work. I needed to finish my first draft of *Which Way to Broadway*. But more than that, I needed the distraction. By nine AM, Rich had gone, Kevin and Marcus too, and the babysitter had taken Preston to spend the morning at the children's museum.

Usually I worked at the desk in our bedroom, but with the entire place to myself, I chose the living room love seat instead. We'd hit a cold spell and I couldn't imagine anything more relaxing than my cashmere blanket and a cup of French roast with hazelnut, my legs sprawled in front of me. My laptop sat with its cursor blinking at me. Waiting for me to do something amazing. But my mind kept wandering elsewhere.

It had been a few weeks since I'd added anything new to this story and I'd left it right before the climax, at the part where the main character was practically raped.

I'd already told Amanda about the story. I thought she might have some issues with it, but she didn't. She was flattered, and confessed she'd loosely based her current project on me and my love story with Rich. We'd agreed to change the names, obviously, and decided it a good idea to work on stories near and dear to us.

I sat there, ready to relive one of the worst nights in Amanda's life, just a few days after one of the worst of mine. And once I put my fingers to the keyboard, the story emerged. It felt damn good to have something different to focus on--something that, though sad, was not my personal misery.

A few hours later, my stomach growled and I took a break. Rising from the love seat, I stretched and realized the fullness of my bladder. I sat on the toilet, debating what to make for lunch, and felt something weird. In the toilet water I found a walnut-sized clump--bright red and exactly how my doctor had described.

I'd just *expelled* my baby.

I sank to the frigid tile and hugged the rim of the bowl, my head on the toilet seat. Staring into the water, I cried for the first time that day. There it was--the end of this nightmare. Some women might feel relieved, but not me. Sobs poured out as I let go of the last shred of hope I'd had.

Why had this happened to me? What had I done to deserve this sadistic kind of torture?

And then it hit me. That Karma bitch.

My back straightened and I stood, tears having been replaced with fire. I searched the bathroom and saw nothing. I continued to the hall and the living room, the kitchen. Still nothing.

"Where are you, you fucking bitch?"

I stomped into my bedroom, then into Preston's nursery.

"Show your goddamn face!"

This couldn't be happening--not again. I wasn't the same person I'd been before. I'd reformed and grown a conscience. I was a good person. I didn't deserve any kind of bad karma.

I'd thought Karma and I were good. I'd thought we were friends. Why the hell would she do this to me again? And something so awful? This didn't just hurt me, this hurt Rich. He didn't deserve this kind of pain.

I went back to the bathroom mirror and saw only my bedraggled reflection. I turned and jerked open the shower curtain. "Where the fuck are you hiding?"

As I tore into the linen closet, footsteps came behind me and I swung around to meet Karma's icy gaze.

"Lex, what are you doing?" Rich stood there, staring at me and the pile of towels at my feet--the ones I'd yanked from the closet in search of a paranormal figure only I could see.

"Um, uh…nothing. Just looking for something."

He didn't seem convinced. "Need some help?"

"No." I shook my head as the tears and sadness returned.

He reached to me as I broke down and cradled me in his embrace. "What's going on?" He spoke as if he were talking to Preston. My apparent mind loss was probably freaking him out.

I pulled away and pointed at the toilet.

He peered in and took a second to register the bowl's contents. His arms wrapped around me. "What should we do?"

I shrugged my shoulders. What was there to do?

"Should I, um, flush it?"

My eyes widened in shock. Flush my baby into the New York City sewer system? To be gobbled up by a deformed radioactive alligator? Was he insane?

Sanity was obviously in the eye of the beholder.

"Lexi, we have to let it go."

"I can't."

But I knew it had to be done. Our baby wasn't in the toilet bowl. He or she was floating around somewhere in heaven or whatever. Even at thirty-three years old, I hadn't formed an opinion on what happens after death. But it was easiest to imagine our baby in a white toga, fluttering from cloud to cloud with golden wings.

"Can you do it?" I asked Rich and he nodded. My eyes stayed on our little red blob as he closed the lid and with the *whoosh* of the toilet flushing, I began to cry again. It was finally over.

* * * *

"I'm taking Kevin to dinner tonight. We probably won't come home, okay?" Marcus said while whipping a bowl of eggs for an omelet. Saturday had always been our big homemade breakfast day.

"Okay." I smiled at him. Living together had worked perfectly, except when we wanted to get a little crazy in the bedroom. Every so often Marcus and Kevin would go out and stay the night at a hotel, and we'd do the same. "Have fun."

"That's the plan." He reached into his robe pocket and set a black velvet box on the kitchen island in front of me.

"What's this?"

"Open it." His grin was so big, its brilliance almost blinded me.

After wiping my hands on a kitchen towel, I picked up the box and peeked inside--a men's platinum band with a single diamond in the center.

"Is this what I think it is?"

Marcus nodded. "I drove up to his parents' last weekend to ask for his hand."

I leapt into his arms and hugged him tight. "I'm so happy for you."

"Do you think he'll like it?"

"If he doesn't, there's something wrong with him."

After a few more seconds of congratulatory embrace, we got back to work. Marcus put the ring back in his pocket, having heard Kevin's shower turn off. "I'm nervous."

"What? Why?"

"I've never asked anyone to marry me before. What if he says no?"

"Then he sucks and you kick him to the curb."

He tilted his head and smiled at me. "I know you're kidding, but I'm serious. What if Kevin doesn't want to get married? Or at least not to me."

"He loves you. And he'd be a fool to turn you down."

Before Marcus could allow his anxiety to show any further, Kevin skipped into the room. "Good morning, everyone!" He kissed me on the cheek and Marcus on the lips. "Did I miss anything?"

"Nope, just omelet preparations."

* * * *

The apartment was dark, only the TV flickering as the ending credits rolled on the DVD Rich and I had rented.

"You think Marcus has asked him yet?"

"It's almost midnight." Rich picked up the remote and pressed *Stop,* then turned the DVD player and TV off. "I'm sure they're celebrating by now."

Once he set the remote back down, the darkness of night enveloping us, I pressed my body to his and pushed him down on the couch. My tongue slid past his lips and my hand to the elastic of his Adidas track pants. The tingle of anticipation traveled through my entire body and rested in my clit, throbbing with want.

He pulled away from my hungry kiss. "I think we need to stop."

"No. I'm sure it's fine." My mouth moved to his earlobe and I took hold of his manhood. It hardened in my hand as I stroked it. "It can't hurt anything."

"Lexi." The firmness of his voice startled me. He pushed me away. "I don't want to."

"That's not what your dick is telling me."

"I'm sorry. I just can't."

He stood, walked away, and started the shower.

What? Was I damaged goods now? Was he so repulsed he couldn't make love to me? No way was he getting out of this.

I stomped into the bathroom and ripped the curtain open. Water sprayed all over me and the floor. "Do I disgust you?"

"Of course not." He tilted his head back to rinse the shampoo from his hair. The sight of his naked body, toned and lean--definite perk of being engaged to someone who was twenty-five--took me away from my anger. But not for long.

"Then what is it? Don't want to get your cock a little bloody? How many times have you fucked me on the rag?"

He stared at me.

"And for your information, it's almost stopped anyway."

He shut off the water, grabbed a towel and rubbed his head, then wrapped it around his waist.

I followed him to the bedroom. "What? No comment? No answer for why you can't stomach having sex with me right now?"

"You don't know how off base you are."

He dropped the towel and got into bed.

"Then tell me."

"I'm going to sleep." He flipped off the lamp on the night stand.

"Tell me now." I turned the light back on.

"No! I'm not gonna talk about this," he yelled back.

"Why not? Afraid you're gonna piss me off? Too late."

"I'm tired and I'm going to sleep."

I yanked the covers from the bed.

"What the fuck?"

"I want an explanation."

He pulled the covers back over his body. "Well, you're not getting one."

Preston began to wail.

"Now look what you've done."

I turned and the room went dark. But I could find the way to my baby's room without any lights. When I got there I lifted him out of the crib and held him to me, tears filling my eyes. I hated fighting with Rich. It happened so rarely, and when we did go at it, my whole body shook.

Sitting in the rocker by the window, I sang Preston a song. He loved *You Are My Sunshine* and it seemed to calm us both down. When his eyes stayed closed longer than being open, I laid him in his bed and covered him. I pressed a kiss to my finger and then on his nose.

I headed to Marcus and Kevin's room. No way was I going back to mine. Rich had refused to give me an answer and that pissed me off more than anything. Before the miscarriage, we'd had sex at least three or four times a week, and for him to refuse now was stupid. I at least deserved to know why.

Chapter 6

It took me hours to fall asleep, and when I did, morning came way too soon. It was just before eight when Preston started chatting up Mr. Penguin in his crib. Since he wasn't screaming to get out, I tended to myself first. I used the bathroom and the bleeding had almost stopped. When would this thing be over?

After a diaper change and a new outfit, since his diaper had leaked overnight, I placed Preston in his high chair and grabbed a loaf of bread. Rich was still asleep, and why wouldn't he be? He'd slept in his own bed and it was Sunday. He had no reason to be awake and without the baby monitor squawking in his ear, there would have been no noise distractions to rouse him.

Now, that wasn't fair. I couldn't help it. He still had me pissed off.

I opened a cupboard door, for no apparent reason, and slammed it shut. After taking two slices of bread from the bag, I put them in the toaster slots and pressed the lever as hard as I could. Unfortunately, it made no significant noise. But I needed a plate for Preston's toast, so again opened and slammed the cupboard door. Then I needed a butter knife--opened and slammed that drawer, too.

What a little bitch I was.

But none of it woke him. Truth was, I hated fighting with him and hoped he'd just get out here so we could hash it out and kiss and make up.

It was almost nine by the time Preston had finished his jelly toast and cantaloupe. I cleaned him and set him in his play yard. Right away he grabbed the musical light-up guitar Rich had picked as a Christmas gift. The thing kept him enchanted for at least ten minutes.

I walked to the bedroom, expecting to find Rich's body under the comforter, still miles away in dreamland. But when I got there, the room was empty and the bed even made. I checked the bathroom--nothing.

Back in the kitchen, I scoured the counters for a note or something that had gone unnoticed. Nope again.

He'd left without a word? Not a way to get back into my good graces.

Alone on a Sunday morning and clueless on what to do. Marcus and Kevin were bound to be home soon. Weather was supposed to be nice. Maybe we could go for a picnic or something. And if Rich missed it, oh well.

Preston played contently, so I tried my hand at something domestic. I dusted the living room and vacuumed the kitchen with one of those rechargeable sweeper thingies. Next I wiped down the countertops and began washing the few dishes in the sink. As I rinsed Preston's sippy cup, the front door opened. I knew it was Rich by the crash of keys on the foyer table. Marcus and Kevin always hung theirs on the hook. I kept my eyes on the dishes in the sink. No way would I give him the satisfaction of running and asking where he had been.

He walked into the kitchen and I ignored him. Until he came up behind me and kissed a trail down the side of my neck.

I sighed and used every ounce of restraint I had to stop myself from spinning around and pulling him to me.

"I could hardly sleep last night. By seven o'clock, my eyes were wide open, so I went for a run. I never sleep good without you in my arms."

His hands curled around my waist.

"You should have thought of that when you were rejecting me."

"I wasn't rejecting you."

The anger bubbled up and I turned to him. "Then what the hell do you call pushing me away when I wanted to make love to you? No guy does that--ever."

"Not again," he mumbled and rolled his eyes.

"Yes, again. Until you give me an answer."

"I told you. I didn't want to. Why isn't that good enough?"

"'Cause you're a fucking liar."

"I'm not lying. Please just--"

"Good Morning!" Marcus and Kevin burst into the apartment. Apparently their night had gone well.

Kevin bee-lined toward us, left hand outstretched. "Look, look, look!" He wiggled his fingers.

I smiled, putting my argument with Rich on hold. "You said 'yes?'"

"I said 'Yes,'" he screamed and pulled me and Rich to him in a group hug.

When we pulled apart, Rich gave Marcus a handshake. "Congratulations."

Kevin stayed with me and pulled me to him again. "We're gonna be brides together!" He quickly pulled away. "Or would I still be a groom? Marcus did the asking, so that makes me the bride, though, right? Oh, I don't care. I'm getting married!" He hugged me again.

I let go and moved on to Marcus--my best friend since forever--and hugged him close. When we pulled apart, his smile beamed across his face.

"Were ya nervous?"

"Almost as much as the day I told you I was gay."

I glanced back to Kevin, who was showing his engagement ring to Rich. "I don't think you had anything to worry about."

"I barely got on my knee before he screamed 'Yes.'"

Kevin walked over to me and Marcus. "Let's celebrate."

"I think we celebrated enough last night, don't you think?" Marcus said with a wink.

"Oh, yes." Kevin smiled, eyes turning devilish. "I'm still a little sore."

"TMI," I yelled and covered my ears.

They laughed.

"We did a family brunch to celebrate your engagement," Kevin said, turning to me and Rich. "Let's do something different. Everyone go get ready."

Marcus took Preston, and Rich and I headed to our room. Once the door was closed, I turned to Rich. "Let's enjoy the day and finish our argument later."

"No," he said and stepped to me. He took my hand and brought it to his lips. "I don't want to argue with you later. Can you please let it go?"

I didn't want to fight anymore, either. "Okay."

As he leaned down and kissed me, my anger and frustration melted away.

* * * *

An hour later, we had picked up a picnic lunch from the deli and were in a carriage riding through Central Park. It was a tad on the cliche side, but seemed like the perfect way to celebrate an engagement. The sun shone down on us through leafy tree branches, warming our skin. And warming our insides was the champagne Marcus had popped once we were on our way.

I snuggled against Rich, watching Kevin and Marcus. Preston sat on Kevin's lap as he talked to him about the horse. He seemed very intrigued, for a one-year-old. Marcus beamed with overflowing pride, watching his son and his lover--his fiance. What might be a weird family unit to some, was perfect for us.

"So, Lexi," Kevin started. "Have you guys talked wedding dates yet? 'Cause you know yours and ours can't be too close together."

"Um, no. But we want to keep it as simple as my mother will allow. I managed to talk her out of an engagement party, so that probably means the wedding won't be quite as low key as we'd hoped. But soon...don't want to wait real long."

"We want to get married soon, too. No point in putting it off. We were thinking October. Love the fall foliage."

"Oh, yeah. That will be beautiful." I thought of a possible date for Rich and me and turned to him. "I don't think we want a winter wedding, right?"

He shook his head.

"I guess that pushes us to spring. Wow. Almost a year away. I didn't really want to wait that long."

Silence surrounded us, only the chirp of birds above and a dog barking in the distance.

"I got it," Kevin said, his eyes so full of cheer they might pop out. "A double wedding!"

"What?" the rest of us questioned in unison.

"It's the perfect solution. We'll be inviting virtually the same people to both weddings, right? Give or take a few family members and friends. And this way, we can all be married in the time frame we want without having two separate weddings so close together. It's perfect."

He had some valid points. But we already shared everything--a home, a child, almost every meal. Did we want to share this too?

"Um, I don't know."

"Lexi, it would be fabulous. We have to do it."

I turned to Rich. "You wouldn't want to do it, would you?"

"I don't care. I told you, City Hall is fine with me. As long as it's not crazy and out of control, I'm in."

I hadn't expected Rich to be so agreeable. But it would make the whole thing pretty convenient.

"Come on. Say yes," Kevin begged.

"Marcus, what do you think?"

"I agree with Kevin. Both weddings would have a lot of the same guests. Seems silly to make them come to two separate events."

"Well...okay then. I guess it's unanimous. Double wedding it is."

Kevin clapped. "Yay!"

"The only problem now…" I told him. "Is breaking the news to my mother."

"Oh, you let me handle her."

* * * *

"Are you sure you're okay with this double wedding thing?" I asked Rich as we climbed into bed.

"Yeah. It solves a lot of problems. Plus, we can share the expenses too."

"Money isn't an issue. My parents paid for Abby's entire wedding. And since my mother will insist on planning a fancy shindig, they can pitch in for it, too."

"I wouldn't feel right. And my salary isn't good enough to give you the wedding you deserve." He reached over and turned off the night-stand lamp. "This way we can do something really nice and only have to pay half the cost."

"You know I don't care about the fluff. I just want to be your wife." I crawled to him and kissed him. "Sure you don't care about sharing the spotlight with a gay couple?"

"Nope. Not at all."

I sat up and pulled my nightgown over my head, then pressed my naked body to his bare chest. I kissed him again and started to gyrate on him, an instant rush of moisture between my thighs.

Rich held me tight and kissed me back, his mouth devouring me the way I needed. He hardened beneath me, only a pair of cotton boxer briefs blocking us from satisfaction. I reached my hand down and yanked at the elastic waist band, until he stopped me.

"What are you doing?" I asked, moving my lips to his neck and earlobe.

"We can't."

Not this again. "Are you serious?

"Yes, Lexi. I am." He pushed me off him.

"This is fucking ridiculous."

"Please don't be mad."

We lay there on our backs and I tried to calm myself down. After a few deep breaths, I turned to face him. "Will you please tell me why you won't have sex with me?"

"I…I just don't want to."

What a stupid answer. "That's it? That's your reason?"

"Yeah. That's it."

"Well, it's not all about what *you* want. We're getting married in a few months. What about what *I* want...what I *need*? Did you ever stop to think maybe I need you to make love to me? To touch me and comfort me and remind me you love me and..." Why couldn't I be tear-free for one freakin' moment? "Maybe I need you to show me I'm not broken. Even though this horrible thing happened to us, I'm still...useful."

Rich pulled me to him. "I love you so much. You have to know that. You are everything to me."

I kissed him and my lips traveled to his ear. "Please make love to me."

It took him a few seconds to give his answer. "I...I can't. I'm sorry."

"Fine." I pushed him away, using more force than I really meant to. But I was pissed. "If you won't give me what I need, I'll do it myself.

The full moon shone in through the window and I knew he had a full view of me. I lay back and spread my legs wide, put my finger to my clit and began rubbing.

"What are you doing?"

"Masturbating. What does it look like?"

"Stop...please?"

"No. I need this. And it feels too good to stop."

A fresh flow of moisture came as I worked in tiny circles and big ones, soft moans escaping my lips.

"Come on. Why are you doing this?"

"Shut up. You're ruining it."

He turned his back to me and I kept on going, moving my fingers inside. God, it had been forever since I'd done this. Too bad I'd tossed all my vibrators.

I brought my fingers back to my clit again and gave no mind to my moans. I wanted Rich to hear me enjoying myself--all by myself. I wanted him to hear what he was missing. And when I came, I made sure he knew it.

It was all over and I felt no better than I had before. Shivering, I rolled over and pulled the sheet and comforter to my chin. Tears came to my eyes again, sobs catching in my throat. I couldn't let him hear me cry.

Chapter 7

That's What Friends Are For sounded from my purse and I reached in to answer Amanda's call.

"Hey, what's up?"

"Not much. You?"

"Working, as usual. Sheila wants this first draft in like two weeks."

"Cool. We still on for tonight?"

"Um, yeah. Rich is on my shit list, but we'll be there."

"Oh...well...Glenn isn't coming."

Amanda had been with him a year and they were still in that mushy, inseparable phase, or so I'd thought.

"Can we make it a girl's night instead?"

"Sure. I could definitely use a night to bitch about Rich."

"Okay. Same place, same time. See ya tonight."

A few hours later I walked into Zuni and found Amanda waiting at the bar with a martini in her hand--fake I.D. obviously doing its job--a hot pink belted tube dress on her skinny body. We hugged and said our "hellos," then she waved the bartender over and ordered me a drink. Amazing how comfortable she now was in her NYC gal skin. No one would ever be able to tell how timid, and, well, pathetic, she had been when I'd met her a year and a half ago.

"Thanks," I said to the bartender after he placed some kind of blue concoction in front of me, and turned to Amanda. "I'm gonna need about a dozen more of these tonight."

She frowned. "That bad?"

I explained the sex situation in detail. It took my entire drink to get through it.

"Yeah, that's weird."

"I know, right?" I took a swig of my second cocktail. We were still at the bar and I hadn't eaten since breakfast. My insides already felt tingly.

"Let's talk about something else. Oh, I know. Let's talk about you being one of my bridesmaids."

"Seriously?" Amanda leapt off her bar stool and practically onto my lap. "I'm so excited!"

"I wanted you to be my maid of honor, but I was Abby's so I kinda feel obligated to reciprocate, ya know?"

"Oh, that's okay. I'm honored to be in the wedding party at all." She took her seat and flagged the bartender for two more drinks, this time some wine.

"Well, I hope you're prepared to be a bridesmaid in Marcus and Kevin's wedding too."

Her scrunched nose and furrowed brow said, "Huh?"

"Yeah, Marcus popped the question and we decided to have a double wedding."

"Wow. That is so..." She searched her brain for the right adjective. "Cool!"

"It fits us, don't you think?"

She nodded and smiled. "You know, it really does."

The hostess appeared and showed us to our table. My knees wobbled a bit when I slid off my stool, but I managed to make it to my seat without them buckling. Silence came over us as we read our menus. The text on mine had started to blur. Probably best to slow down a bit and order a glass of water with my meal.

"Don't you want to know why Glenn didn't come tonight?"

"Oh yeah. This was originally a double date."

"We kinda broke up."

"How can you *kinda* break up?"

"Okay, we definitely broke up. Or rather, I dumped him."

Last time we'd talked, which had been at least a few weeks ago, they were happy and in love and she was hoping they could live together this summer and see how it went. "What the hell happened?"

"I met someone else."

"Seriously? I thought he was *the one*?"

"I thought so too, but I don't know. I guess I got bored."

"Like, in bed?"

She giggled. "No. Just in general."

"Who's the new guy?"

The waiter arrived with our salads--a momentary distraction. I dug in, thankful to put something in my stomach.

"How's yours?" Amanda asked.

"Good. Now spill."

"Um." She shoveled in another forkful of arugula. "It's nobody. I'm not sure if it's even going anywhere, so there's no point telling you all about him."

"You ditched your longtime boyfriend for him. He has to be somewhat special."

"Yeah, but I don't want to jinx it."

Now Amanda was the one being weird. I let it go. We talked about wedding stuff and I bitched some more about Rich. I hadn't realized how much I needed to unwind and vent. The past few weeks had been such a roller coaster of emotion and I just wanted my life to get back to normal. And normal included mind-blowing orgasms performed by my soon-to-be husband.

* * * *

The next two weeks, I threw myself into work and stayed on my side of the bed. I stopped asking Rich for answers and masturbated in the shower when necessary. I didn't know what else to do. My questions turned into arguments, and that wasn't helping any.

But the book took my mind off our issues in the bedroom. I focused on my character Melinda's problems instead. And hers seemed much easier to deal with, probably because I'd made them up and solved them. She did what I said and if she started to talk back, I simply hit *Delete* and started again.

What I wouldn't give for a *Delete* button for my life. If I could, I'd erase the last few weeks--I'd still be pregnant and Rich would still make sense to me.

I finished the first draft of the story, even a couple read-throughs, and still got it on Sheila's desk a day early. I managed to pull her away for lunch, and on the way back to the office, we walked past a bridal shop. I glanced in the window, a feeling washing over me, completely different from how I'd felt when I shopped with Abby for her wedding. The only description was giddiness, staring at the dress I knew I had to have.

"I'm going in here," I said to Sheila. "You coming?"

"You want me to go in a bridal shop with you?"

"Not if you don't want to."

She stared at me. "I have nothing better to do at the moment."

We stepped inside and I don't know--the smell of the fabric, maybe the sparkle of rhinestone-encrusted tiaras--something in there turned me into a bubbly bride. My gaze moved from one silk-covered corner to the other, in awe, like the tourists we made fun of every day in Times Square.

"Can I help you?" asked a petite blonde, snapping me out of my bridal coma.

"Yes. I need to try on that dress in the window."

"Do you have an appointment?"

"Well, no. Is that a problem?"

"I'm sorry, but you need an appointment." All my wedding gown dreams faded.

"Oh, okay. Can I--"

"What are you doing right now?" Sheila butted in. "This place is like a mausoleum. You can't tell me every person here is busy."

"Um, no. But you still need an appointment."

"Are you taking care of someone right now?" Sheila persisted.

"Well, no. But--"

"Then you shouldn't have a problem getting the dress for her to try on."

The girl turned and saw there was no one around to rescue her from Sheila's tyranny. "O-okay. Let me set you up in a fitting room."

On the way, she asked my bra size and grabbed a strapless from a drawer. She pulled a crinoline from a rack and took that with us, too. After handing the pile of undergarments to me, she opened the curtain of a small changing room.

"Your mother can sit there." She pointed at a couch near the round pedestal in the center of the room.

My eyes met Sheila's and we burst out laughing. The girl gave a half smile and excused herself from the room. She came back a few minutes later to help me into the dress.

"This is silk razmir with an embellished tulle overlay bodice."

She tugged it down around my body and zipped the back. Its deep lacy v-neck showed off a healthy set of breasts and even with the small mirror in the tiny dressing room, I could tell the dropped waist gave my hips the perfect amount of va-va-voom.

"It has an asymmetrical, floral-embroidered, peplum skirt," she said as she motioned to it.

I had no clue what any of that meant, but I loved the flowy skirt with its ruffled white flowers, something I never would have thought I'd like.

"It's a piece from Monique Lhuillier's fall collection."

Now that was a name I knew.

She opened the curtain and I followed her to the pedestal. Sheila sat on the couch on her cellphone, ending the call when I appeared.

"Wow. You look like a bride."

"That *is* the point."

I turned and caught my reflection in the giant mirror--all of it. The dress girl, Misty, dimmed the lights and flipped on some special ones, making every bead and crystal sparkle. She set a tiara and tulle veil on my head and stepped back.

"What do you think?"

For the first time, maybe ever in my life, there were no words.

"I'll give you a few minutes."

She left and I stared at myself. This was the dress I would be wearing when I married Rich, the love of my life, the only man who had ever completed my world. I remembered our beginning and the moment I knew I loved him. And the moment I knew I couldn't live without him.

I blinked a few times to clear tears before turning and facing Sheila again. "I'm gonna get this dress. What do you think?"

"It's pretty. Too fru-fru for my liking, but it suits you."

"Thanks for bullying the salesgirl into letting me try it on."

"Eh, no problem."

All of a sudden a strange feeling came over me and I had to spit out my thoughts before I lost the nerve. "You wanna be a bridesmaid?"

"Why?"

"I don't know. Seems like a good idea."

She took a second before answering. "Sure. But don't even think about dressing me in anything even remotely like that thing." She pointed to my dress.

"I wouldn't dream of it."

Chapter 8

"I ordered my dress today," I squealed to Kevin later that night. Rich was in the shower and Marcus played with Preston. I pulled a sheet of paper from my purse, an internet picture I'd printed.

He gasped. "A. Maze. Ing."

"I know!"

"Girl, you are so gonna be the prettier bride. How can I possibly compete with that?"

"Oh stop. I'm sure we'll find you something just as fabulous."

Rich came into the kitchen and I scrambled to hide the picture. He kissed me on the cheek. "What's going on?"

"Oh, nothing," Kevin said. "Girl stuff."

* * * *

Summer had just begun and already we were hit with a sweltering heat wave. We were fine in the apartment--central air cooling every square inch. But outside, walking around naked would have done nothing to alleviate the intense heat.

Preston desperately needed summer clothes, especially swim trunks and one of those SPF sun shirts. We'd definitely be working in some days at the pool and the beach. I packed his diaper bag and stroller and set off for the baby store.

When I'd been pregnant with Preston, I never cared to shop for baby stuff. But once he was here, I sometimes couldn't control myself. Good thing the store delivered purchases for a small fee.

We walked into the store, a children's show come to life, with bright colors, cheerful faces, and an annoyingly chipper rendition of *The Wheels on the Bus* blaring from above. There were toys and stuffed animals as far as the eye could see, some human-sized, and right away Preston stretched his hands toward a bright green stuffed dinosaur on a display near the door. I handed it to him, of course, knowing full well there was no way

I'd get it out of his grasp once I did. No biggie. Every boy needs a stuffed dinosaur.

I started in the clothing section, figuring I'd get that taken care of first. Someone once told me girls were much more fun to dress, but boy's stuff was pretty darn cute, too. I grabbed four different pairs of preppy plaid shorts and some khaki cargos. After grabbing the essential polo shirts and some screen printed tees, I spied some adorable rocker-type shirts--had to have those, too. Preston would be oh so adorable in the black one with silver lettering: *I'm with the Band.*

I passed a rack of character tees and tried to zoom by as fast as possible. But Preston had already spotted his favorite--Elmo. I sighed and grabbed one of the shirts and held it up. My baby abandoned his green dinosaur and reached for the white t-shirt with Elmo's face covering the entire thing.

"Do we have to get this?" I asked, not expecting an answer, of course.

I searched the rack and found a red polo with a small embroidered Elmo on the left hand-side, a Sesame Street version of a Lacoste shirt.

"How about this instead?"

Preston seemed somewhat pleased, especially when I shoved the dinosaur back into his hands, along with a stuffed Elmo.

I held up the shirt one more time, shook my head, and added it to my growing pile of purchases.

"I bet you never thought you'd be buying an Elmo shirt." The voice behind me sounded vaguely familiar, but I couldn't place it. When I swung around, there stood Zak--the ex who'd cheated on me with one of my best friends.

It all came swirling back--the day my entire world had fallen apart. I'd walked in on Zak and Brenda screwing on my bed. The morning had already been bad, but after that, it had spiraled into the fiery depths of hell.

"Um, hi."

"How are you?"

"Good. You?"

"Real good, actually." Zak smiled, a cheesy grin. It was then I noticed the blonde next to him--a very pregnant blonde. "Lexi, this is Megan... my wife."

I choked on my saliva. "Excuse me?"

"Hello." She smiled and held out her hand.

I involuntarily pumped it a few times.

Zak spoke again. "Yeah, I'm married. Can you believe it?"

"Uh, no. When did this happen?" I didn't mean to be so blunt. No, that was a lie. Yes I did.

"We've been married ten months. We met last August and..." he turned to her. "It was love at first sight." Cue the harps and angels. "We were married soon as we could arrange it, only a couple weeks later."

"And, you're, um..."

"Yep. We're having a baby. It all happened so fast. We celebrated our two-month anniversary and our positive pregnancy test on the same day."

Zak squatted down to Preston's stroller and held out his hand. Preston giggled and gave him five. "Hi, little guy. Whatcha got there?" He handed over the Elmo. Zak took it and made it dance across the stroller tray. After giving it back, he stood.

"He looks just like you, Lexi."

I could only nod. This was too weird. Zak, married? Zak, talking to a baby and *playing* with him? Zak, having a baby of his own? Wait a minute. That couldn't be possible. He'd had a vasectomy--years ago. Weren't those permanent?

"I have to go," I said to the happy couple.

"Okay. Nice seeing you."

I turned the stroller and bee-lined to the register. I would have rather dashed out the door, but we needed those clothes. The sales clerk rang them up and began folding each item perfectly.

"You don't have to do that. Just throw them in," I said, forcing a smile.

The cashier's eyes bugged out. She placed the remaining clothes in the bag, without folding them, and I practically ran from the place.

Had I awakened in some alternate reality today? This could not be the real world. This pseudo-Zak was nothing like the man I had been with for three years. Even his mid-section bulged a bit. What kind of weird place was this that Zak had abandoned his rock hard abs? He'd cared about those more than anything in his life, even sex. So many nights I'd lain in bed, naked, starting without him so he could pump out a hundred crunches.

God, I needed a drink. Probably not a good idea to take a baby into a bar. I settled for a triple chocolate sundae--extra hot fudge--and some vanilla soft serve with rainbow sprinkles for Preston.

My boy dug into his ice cream without hesitation while I contemplated what had happened. And my brain forced me to think of something I did not want to think about. What if Zak's vasectomy had been botched all those years ago? Preston could be his kid, not Marcus's. Everyone always said he looked like me--nothing like Marcus. Maybe because Zak was his father. We'd never had a DNA test done. And Preston was born a whole month early. I might have gotten pregnant a month before my one-night fling with Marcus.

Oh. My. God. How could this be happening?

No. The doctor had told me vasectomies didn't get screwed up. That was something you only saw on TV.

But couldn't they be reversed? Yes. I think I read that. I pulled out my iPhone and Googled *vasectomy reversal*. I clicked on the first website and after scanning the tiny screen, found what I needed:

> *If the vasectomy reversal procedure is a success, sperm will appear in the semen after a few months, but it could take up to a year. Approximately half of vasectomy reversals are successful.*

Months for the sperm to appear. And only half of the procedures were even successful. If Zak had done a reversal, chances of his wife being pregnant so soon were rare. It had to have been an oopsie.

Which also meant Preston could be Zak's oopsie.

I scanned a few more websites and one caught my eye. A blog post written a year earlier, titled: *My vasectomy reversed itself!*

I clicked on the link right away.

> *Five years after the procedure, my wife got pregnant. Unfortunately, my first thought was that she had an affair. What guy wouldn't think that? After doing the snip, you wouldn't expect to get your wife pregnant ever again. But before I voiced my thoughts to my hormonal wife, who didn't want any more babies either, I went to see my urologist. Tests confirmed it: my vasectomy had reversed itself. The tube had grown back together.*

Oh, fuck.

Zak could have been pumping me with sperm and didn't even know it.

I expected to hear that cackle--the annoying laugh alerting me Karma was back, ready to mess with my life again. But all I heard was ice cream and milk being whipped into a milkshake and the tinkle of the door chime every twenty seconds as sweaty New Yorkers came in for a refreshing treat.

Yeah, once upon a time her meddling had been for the better…but this? How could Zak being Preston's father help anyone? It would destroy my family and screw what Zak now had and was obviously happy with.

And this was so unlike her--hiding like this. She enjoyed showing her face while fucking up my life. Why wasn't she basking in her success?

* * * *

I took the long way home. Preston had fallen asleep in his stroller, so I walked and walked and thought and tried to stop my brain from freaking out. My text message alert sounded as I reached our building.

> *Have you listened to Mom's voicemail yet? We have a wedding, bridal shower and baby shower to plan! Abby*

Her texts were always so perfect--grammar and even proper punctuation. It must take her forever to send a message. And why did she insist on putting her name at the end? I knew it was from her.

> *no. i'll checkk now*

I dialed my voice mail. One new message. I must have missed my phone ringing while I contemplated my child's paternity.

"Lexi, dear, it's Mom. I was thinking, we need to get started on planning all these events, especially if you want the wedding to be this October. And a double wedding, at that. My, this will be a challenge. Can you come to the house this weekend? We'll make a day of it and have dinner. Everyone needs to be here--the bride and the groom, and the other...um, groom and groom. Now, should I call Mrs. Wells and invite her as well? And what about Kevin's mother? I sure can't wait to--"

At least this time when the voicemail cut her off, she didn't call back. I put the phone in my purse and took the elevator to our floor. It was later than I thought. Marcus was already home.

"Oh good. You're here," he said. "Rich ran to pick up dinner and Kevin called. He'll be here soon. We got Chinese--hope that's okay."

Preston began to stir and Marcus picked him up, nuzzling their noses together, both of them smiling.

"Uh, yeah. That's fine."

No way could I tell Marcus that Preston might not be his. It would crush him--no, worse. He might combust right on the spot. I had to keep it a secret until I knew for sure. And even if I did find out Zak was Preston's father, would I even tell him then?

"Lex, hello?"

I shook away my thoughts. "Huh?"

"What's up with you today?"

"Nothing. Hey, I got a voicemail from my mom. She wants to start planning the wedding extravaganza. You up for a Marshall family gathering on Saturday? She wants everyone to be there."

"Not sure how much help I'll be, but I'll go. I figured I'd leave the details to you and Kevin."

"She asked if I wanted her to call your mom and invite her too."

He laughed. "Yeah. It will be a miracle if she even shows for her own son's wedding."

Ever since he'd come out of the closet, Marcus's family hadn't given him much thought.

"Okay. I'll make sure she doesn't call her."

I took out some plates and bowls, getting ready for our food to arrive. Suddenly I was famished.

"Why don't you and Rich stay at that fab bed and breakfast near your folk's on Saturday. Kevin and I can take Preston home. You guys haven't had a night alone in a while."

"What would be the point?"

"So you can, ya know, have some *adult* fun."

"Doubtful. Even a romantic B and B isn't gonna make Rich want to have sex with me."

"What? Why not?"

"Wish I knew. He hasn't touched me since the miscarriage."

"It's been over a month. I thought it was okay to resume normal *activity*."

I sat on one of the stools at the kitchen island. "It was--weeks ago. And I told him that."

"Wow. You guys were always so…what's the right word? Um… insatiable."

I had to laugh. "Yeah, exactly. So you get why I'm frustrated."

"That is just plain weird." He shook his head, then locked eyes with me. "You don't think he's…"

I hadn't thought of it before. A sex-hungry twenty-five-year-old in his prime wouldn't stop having sex. Dread filled me and I fought back tears. "You don't think, do you?"

"Rich? No. He's not a cheater."

"But none of it makes any sense. You know what he says when I ask 'why?' He says he doesn't want to."

Marcus couldn't hide his shock. We both knew no guy on earth, ever in the history of man-kind, casually said "no" to getting laid. There had to be something else going on. And I was damn sure going to find out what.

Chapter 9

Saturday morning, Rich and I were alone in our room as I packed a bag for the day. "Hey, I was gonna surprise you, but maybe I'll tell you now."

"Oh?" He stood at the bed deciding between the two shirts he'd put out.

"I booked us a room tonight at that Cozy Cove Bed and Breakfast not far from my parents' house, the one Marcus and Kevin love."

His head whipped toward me, an expression on his face I'd seen in a few horror films right before the extraneous character had been eaten. "Okay."

Surely my brain had exaggerated his reaction, but that's what it felt like. Geez. So nice that my fiance was terrified to be alone with me.

A knock came on the door and Marcus peeked his head in. "You guys almost ready?"

"Yep." I flung the bag over my shoulder and left the room.

We took the train to my parents' house. Not even ten minutes into the ride, Preston fell asleep on Marcus's shoulder, giving me the opportunity to stare at the scenery as it rushed by. How had my life become so complicated? One thing I knew for sure, I wasn't going to let it go on like this. One way or another, I would get an answer from Rich. Tonight.

And my baby daddy dilemma, well, I already had some ideas on how I would deal with that.

* * * *

"There's the bride-to-be," Mom sang and hugged me when I walked into the house. She then hugged each person after me. When the parade of affection had ended, she led us to the dining room table, covered with bridal barf: *Modern Bride* magazine, invitation samples, catering menus. All there and covered in pixie dust.

Kevin squealed with excitement when he saw the assortment of wedding planning paraphernalia. "Oh, Maryanne, this is perfect. Thank you so much."

She hugged him again. "I wish your mother could've been here today."

"Me too. But you can't pass on theater tickets. She says she'll most definitely be at the next planning meeting."

"Okay," Mom said and clapped her hands together. "Robert, you can take Preston in the yard to play, and everyone else, sit." She pranced into the kitchen and returned twenty seconds later with trays of hors d'oeuvres. After setting them down, she took her seat at the head of the table. "What shall we discuss first?"

"The wedding!" Kevin said at the same time Abby said "The baby shower!"

They smiled politely at each other, and turned away. Yikes. Two divas who wanted the spotlight. Kevin could have that seat.

Mom stepped in. "The wedding is October seventh, and since Abby is not due until mid-January, we've already decided on holding the baby shower in November. It's only logical to discuss the wedding first, seeing it is the biggest of the three events anyway."

Seemed obvious to me, but Abby's slight sneer showed she thought otherwise. Chalk it up to pregnancy hormones--this time.

"I've already spoken with Kevin's aunt and uncle about holding the wedding at their inn in New Paltz. Such a cute little town that is. Here is the brochure." Mom set it on the table, about to explode from sheer joy. "It's so beautiful."

It looked nice enough--a picturesque estate with gardens and ponds, ideal for an outdoor fall wedding. These were the types of details I cared nothing about. As long as it was beautiful and the food was good, Rich and I would be happy. And Marcus only cared what Kevin wanted. The three of us were more than satisfied to sit back and let my mom, Kevin, and his mother take over. And they seemed fine with that, too.

"Auntie June is so excited. I've known since I was a little boy that I wanted to get married there. We used to spend the weekend occasionally, and I'd sneak down to the gardens and watch the weddings. No wonder it was no surprise to my parents when I came out of the closet!" Kevin's eyes glistened. "The day they announced gay marriage had been legalized in New York, I cried. Until that moment, I never thought my dream wedding could happen. But now it is."

Mom's moistened eyes matched his and she reached for his hand and squeezed it. The gay son she never had.

Footsteps echoed above us, then down the staircase. The straight son she did have had decided to make an appearance. Probably smelled the food.

Instead, he strode to the front door.

"Andrew, where are you going?" Mom yelled. "Come say hello to your sisters and everyone."

Andy dragged himself into the dining room and I almost fell off my chair.

"Dear, you look so nice."

He stood there in jeans--that were actually clean, no wrinkles or holes--and a black button-down shirt--again, no wrinkles--with the sleeves rolled a few times. His blond hair was neatly combed, and holy shit! Was there gel in it? The entire table sat speechless.

"Are you going somewhere?" Mom asked, breaking the silence.

"Uh, yeah."

"Oh. Where are you going?"

He sighed and his eyes dropped to the floor. "Just...out."

"You may be an adult, but I still like to know where my children are."

He looked around the table, then back at her. "I have a date, okay?"

I covered my mouth to hold in laughter. Who would ever want to date my brother? Athletic pants and a dirty ball cap were his usual attire, worn to the same pizza place job he'd had since high school. He still lived at home, for God's sake! She had to be pretty desperate, or high, to agree to a date with him. Yeah, the latter was probably more like it.

"How wonderful," Mom exclaimed. "Who is she? You should bring her over for dinner one night. Is it someone from church? Oh, I can't wait to meet her!"

"This is exactly why I don't tell you anything. I'm leaving now."

"Okay, honey. Have fun."

Andy turned and walked away and my mother sucked us all back into wedding talk. Time for decorations and a brochure from a rental company which supplied chairs, arches, gazebos--everything we'd need for the ceremony. As they browsed the brochure, Rich spoke up, finally adding to the conversation.

"I have some ideas for the music. I know a bunch of great bands that could perform during the reception. And it's a little bit different, but we just signed this really awesome neofolk group that could do the ceremony music."

"Oooh, isn't that the CD we listened to last week?" I asked. "They are fantastic. And that singer has such an amazing voice."

"What kind of music does this *neo* band play?" my mother asked, head tilted like an inquisitive dog.

"It comes primarily from Europe and it's an edgy form of folk music. They use an acoustic guitar, violin, flute and horn, sometimes a drum too."

"Oh, well, that certainly sounds…different."

"Maybe a little too different," Marcus added, a crinkle in his nose. "Maybe we should just stick with traditional."

"I know it sounds weird, but it's really beautiful."

Rich and Marcus both turned to me. But Marcus spoke first.

"I think our wedding will be different enough as it is." He gave a little laugh.

I sighed. "You do have a point."

"Wouldn't you rather walk down the aisle to a harpist or string quartet playing *Here Comes the Bride*? Instead of a guitar and flute." Marcus turned to Kevin, who was normally filled with a million wedding opinions. But he hadn't said a word. "What about you?"

"Oh, music isn't my thing. Lexi can do this one."

"Either would be great." I looked back at Rich. "But a harpist would be really pretty."

"Oh yes, I agree," Mom added. "Shirley Stenson's daughter had one for her wedding last year and it was the most angelic music."

Marcus spoke up again. "You remember Donald, one of my partners at the firm. His wife plays the harp and she's phenomenal. They'll be invited to the wedding, and I'm sure she'd love to do it."

"Oh, I remember her. Sweet woman. That would work out great."

"Good. I'll talk to Don about it on Monday."

"So, that's it." Rich said. "The music debate is over?"

Marcus suddenly became engrossed with a hangnail and Kevin had gone back to a brochure my mom had pulled out earlier.

I turned to Rich. "I think it's unanimous. A harpist would be better."

"Sure," he said and took a long drink of his iced tea.

"Okay, so how about flowers?" Kevin said as he set a few internet printouts on the table.

I was so glad for the topic change.

But Rich spoke again. "How is all this going to be paid? I'm sure it's not gonna be cheap."

"Robert and I have some money tucked away," Mom said first. "We've always hoped Lexi would get married one day."

"My parents have a wedding fund too," Kevin said. "They paid for Jeanette's Plaza wedding a decade ago, so of course, they planned on paying for my wedding if and when it happened."

"And I have some money saved," Marcus added.

Rich's gaze locked with Marcus's for a minute then moved around the table. "I need to pay for *something*."

Marcus hated having money conversations with Rich. Everyone knew Rich's salary wasn't huge. But when he'd moved in, he'd insisted on paying his share of expenses, regardless of Marcus's argument against it. There was that whole male pride thing. Rich had taken over the cable and internet bill, water and electricity.

A brilliant idea sprang into my head. "What about the rehearsal dinner? Rich and I can take care of the whole thing."

"I think that's a lovely idea," Mom replied.

I turned to my fiance. "Is that okay with you?"

He nodded. "That's fine."

"Okay, now that that's settled, I need some fresh air." I'd had enough wedding planning for one afternoon. I turned to Rich. "Wanna come?"

He stood and followed me to the patio doors. Outside, Dad pushed Preston in a swing hanging from the branch of a maple tree in the back yard.

"Want me to take over?" I asked.

He stepped back. "I could use a cold one anyway. Rich, you want one?"

"Yeah. Thanks."

I grabbed Preston by the feet and pulled him high, then let go. He giggled the whole way.

Rich came behind me and wrapped both arms around me tight. "Why are we going to that bed and breakfast tonight?"

"Um, why not? It's been ages since we've done anything remotely romantic." I turned to face him. "Don't you want some alone time?"

His lips said, "I guess so," but his eyes said *Hell no*.

I was sick and tired of dealing with this.

* * * *

After helping with the dishes, Rich and I gave our hugs and goodbyes to Preston and the rest of the gang, and climbed into my mother's Volvo. The drive to the Cozy Cove was short, but the silence made it feel like a hundred miles. Rich did not want to go. He looked like he'd rather be anywhere else on the planet than on his way to a romantic getaway with his future wife.

He slung the overnight bag onto his shoulder and followed me up the walkway of an old Victorian home, refurbished and in perfect condition, fronted by a huge porch with white-painted spindles. There were still cast iron horse hitching posts out front and a cross-stitched sign on the door read, *Come In!* We entered an elegant foyer with plush burgundy settees on each side. A small desk stood near a staircase with a green and brass banker's lamp on it.

A petite woman with short curly hair walked in. "Oh, I thought I heard the bell. Welcome to the Cozy Cove."

"Hi. We have a reservation under Lexi Marshall."

"Oh yes," she said, and flipped through a few papers. "I see you're a friend of Marcus Wells and Kevin Jacobs. We just adore those two-- they're always up for a game of charades."

I managed a smile and a laugh.

"I'll show you to your room."

We followed the woman, who'd introduced herself as Peggy, up the wide staircase while she gave us a brief history of the house. It had been built by her great-great-grandfather and turned into a B and B by her mother over thirty years ago. Compelling as it was, I had no desire to learn the home's history. I wanted to get Rich to the room and find out what the hell was going on with him.

She handed me the key. "Wine tasting is in the parlor at eight, with charades at nine. Breakfast is served eight 'til ten on the lanai. Is there anything I can get you?"

"No. Thank you."

"Okay. Hope to see you downstairs in a little while."

I closed the door behind her, ready to puke from all the cheery bubbliness. When I turned to face Rich, he had kicked off his sneakers and flopped on the bed with the remote, pressing the power button on. What normal guy, upon checking into a romantic suite, plops on the bed ready to watch *Sports Center*?

"No, this is not happening." I grabbed the remote and tossed it on the whitewashed antique desk. I pulled my shirt over my head and pushed my jeans down. Standing there in a black lace thong and matching demi bra, my boobs practically throwing themselves out of it, I begged him, "Make love to me."

His gaze met mine, then fell to his lap. "I can't."

"That is fucking bullshit! I need more than that."

"I'm sorry," he said, eyes still on his hands in his lap. "It's all I can give you."

"No. You're not getting off that easy…again." I climbed on top of him, made him look at me. "What is going on with you?"

"Nothing. I just don't want to. I'm not in the mood."

I didn't know whether to be mad as hell or hysterically sad. But I tried to keep my voice calm. "There's someone else, isn't there?"

"Now you're being stupid." He tried to pull his gaze from mine, but I held his head straight.

"Is it stupid to wonder why the man of my dreams--the man who says he loves me--refuses to have sex with me? We did it all the time up until the miscarriage. Now, it's like I disgust you." My voice cracked, but I continued. "It's only logical to think you're fucking someone else."

Rich blinked, his eyes filling with tears, and brought his hand to my cheek. "I could never touch another woman. You have to believe that."

"Then please," I begged, droplets cascading from my eyes. "Tell me why."

He stared at me, his eyes wanting to tell me something. But his head turned to the side. And yet again, he refused to say anything. What more could I do?

I curled around him and rested my forehead on his chest, tears captured in my eyelashes. My body shook as a chill circulated through my veins. This was it--the end. I could not--would not--live my life like this, with a man who shut down and refused to let me in.

I stayed there, unable to move, but wanting to grab my clothes and run away.

"Lexi, I…I'm scared."

I sat up, my half-naked body straddling his, listening to words I didn't expect or understand.

"I'm terrified of us getting pregnant again." A tear trailed down his cheek. "And losing another baby. I don't think I could make it through that again."

I pulled him to me as he cried on my shoulder. This whole time, I'd known the miscarriage had affected him--he'd even blamed himself--but I thought he'd accepted it and moved on. Like I had. Wasn't that what the whole gardenia thing in the park had been?

But even though he'd tried to put it behind him, the miscarriage had left him detrimentally scarred. I was such an asshole. How had I been so lost in my own world that I'd failed to recognize how badly he was hurting?

"I'm so sorry. Please forgive me," I begged.

"No, I'm the one who's sorry. I should have told you."

"You did now. And that's all that matters. We'll get through this. I promise."

I kissed him and put my hands to the edge of his t-shirt. He let me remove it and when I went for his belt buckle, he didn't flinch. Instead, he inched my bra off and continued with the rest of my clothes.

We lay on the bed, both naked, exchanging soft kisses and caresses, until our eyes met. "I love you and I'm not going to push you to do something you don't want to do. But..." I kissed one remaining tear on his cheek. "I ache for you. I need to feel the connection we've always had."

He nodded and brought his lips to mine. A soft kiss intensified by the second as he massaged my body and pulled me on top of him.

"Are you ready?" I asked, knowing his lower region was completely prepared.

He nodded again, fear still filling his eyes.

"Wait." I climbed off him and reached into my purse. Tucked inside the zippered pocket was a lone condom--bought after Preston was born, when I definitely knew I did not want to get pregnant.

I handed it to him and he wasted no time in rolling it onto himself.

"Now are you ready?"

A mischievous smile spread across his face. "You better believe it."

Chapter 10

Rich and I stepped into the elevator and before the door had even closed, he'd cornered me with a hand up the front of my ribbed tank and his lips on my neck. I'd so missed this. A hard bulge pressed into my stomach before we even made it the three floors to our apartment. And when the door opened, Rich didn't stop.

I patted him on the back and giggled. "We're at our floor."

"We can hit the emergency stop button or something," he murmured, moving his lips to my cleavage.

"We're like twenty feet from our front door."

The elevator started to close and I thrust my hand between the doors to stop it.

"Okay." He sighed like a kid who'd been told to go wash his hands before dinner. We walked to our apartment door, where he pinned me to the wall and ravished me with his lips.

"Come on. Let's go inside."

"You said the door. You didn't say anything about going in the apartment."

As Rich covered my neck with more kisses, our door opened and Marcus stepped out. "Oh, sorry guys. Just need to grab the paper. Continue on."

"No, we're coming inside." Rich rolled his eyes as I grabbed him by the hand and we followed Marcus in.

"Hmm. I'm guessing you had a good night."

"*Very.*" We strolled past him to the bedroom, where we stayed until dinner.

* * * *

Rich and I were back where we belonged with only one problem left to deal with--my baby's paternity. Oh, and planning a huge double wedding. And the bridal shower to go with it. And also my sister's baby shower.

Okay, one thing at a time before my brain exploded.

The wedding stuff was in capable hands. I had no doubt it would be beautiful, and as far as the small details went, I didn't care. Same with the bridal shower. And knowing Abby like I did, she'd need to plan her own baby shower.

That left the one problem I had to deal with on my own. How in the world would I find the answers I needed? It was time to do some snooping, I mean, investigating.

I kissed Preston on the head and told the babysitter I was leaving. After a short cab ride, I walked through the doorman-operated doors leading to Jeanette and Jeff's Park Avenue home. Ever since our families had become a big blended smoothie of a family, I'd gotten close with Kevin's sister. She was the perfect mom and I secretly wished I had it as together as she did.

But today I didn't need tips on getting Preston to eat his veggies or suggestions on the best shoes for a just-starting-to-walk toddler--though, I did need that too. But this was more important right now. I needed the scoop on a friend of her husband's--a person we both knew very well.

"Lexi, what a lovely surprise," Jeanette said when she opened the door. The older kids were at day camp, but little Olive came running to see who was there.

"I hope I'm not interrupting anything."

"Of course not."

The house was immaculate and it didn't surprise me one bit when the undeniable aroma of homemade chocolate chip cookies wafted into my nostrils.

"But you'll have to excuse me. I have to get my cookies off the pan before they over-bake."

I followed her to the kitchen. Stainless steel appliances gleamed in every direction. And not one thing with even a dusting of flour. Jeanette had to be some kind of witch or something, like Samantha on *Bewitched*, able to wiggle her nose and clean everything.

"What brings you here today?" she asked and offered a plate of cookies.

I shook my head and tried to formulate my thoughts. Why hadn't I come more prepared? Jeanette wasn't the gossipy type. If I straight asked her about Zak, she'd of course say something to Jeff, and it would get back to Zak.

No, I had to be more sly. "Well, I...I ran into my ex, Zak Young, the other day."

"Oh, yes! I forgot you two knew each other."

"He introduced me to his wife."

"Meg is a great girl and their wedding was amazingly beautiful."

"You were there?" Maybe Jeff and Zak were closer than I thought. When we were together, he'd never mentioned friends. I'd assumed he didn't have any.

"Of course. Jeff was his best man."

Wow. They were close. This would definitely work to my advantage.

She continued. "It was planned so quickly--reminded me of Jeff and I. They fell in love and couldn't wait to be husband and wife. We gathered at her parents' home in The Hamptons. Such a lovely ceremony, right there on the beach at sunset."

"That does sound nice." I didn't need these kinds of details, though. "And now she's pregnant?"

"Isn't it amazing?" she asked with a dreamy sigh. "Just like their romance, it happened so fast."

I needed to get to some kind of point before she caught on that I was pumping her for information. "I'd love to buy them a baby gift. That's why I came here today--to ask you what I should get."

"Oh, that's so sweet. I'm not sure what they still need, but they're registered at Bella Baby."

Yikes. That place was even too pricey for Marcus, and usually he had no trouble parting with his cash for Preston. How would registry info help me find out if Zak was no longer shooting blanks? I needed to buddy up to Megan. But how in the world would I do that?

"Okay. That sounds like a good idea." Then it hit me. "Do you have their home address so I can arrange for the gift to be delivered?"

"Sure." Jeanette retrieved a gold-edged address book and flipped to the Y page. In her perfect penmanship, she wrote on a piece of monogrammed stationery and handed it to me.

"Thanks. This is such a big help."

I left Jeanette's feeling a tad bit guilty. I'd used my friendship with her to extract information about my ex. But I'd had good reasons.

Now that I had their address, what would I do with it? Maybe I could stick with what I'd told Jeanette. It would alleviate a little of my guilt. But I'd have to drop some serious cash on something from Bella Baby. If it got me the answers I needed, though, it would be worth every penny.

* * * *

After their insistence, I met my mother and Abby at the same dress shop I'd visited many times for Abby's wedding--that pukey Peptocolored dress she'd made me wear. Mom needed a dress for the double wedding extravaganza and had decided this was the perfect starting place.

After handing a dozen gowns to the dress coordinator, she turned to me. "I know you're not very interested in the details of the wedding, but as the bride, I do think you should choose the dresses your bridesmaids will be wearing." She led me to one of several racks of bridesmaid's frocks. "Kevin and I chose a beautiful color palette for the fall--espresso, persimmon, and claret."

"I think I can figure out what espresso is, but I need English for the other two."

"Oh, Lexi." Abby laughed and pulled two dresses from the rack, one in a burnt orange color and another in a deep red.

Mom grabbed one in a dark brown and held the three together. "Don't these colors look fantastic together? Which do you like most? We can use it for the bridesmaids' dresses."

They both stared at me with wide smiles and eyes to match.

"Um…" This was not what I had in mind at all. "I thought I'd let each girl buy whatever black cocktail dress she wanted."

Abby's mouth fell open and my mother gasped. No, that's not accurate. She'd sucked in a breath like a Hoover. But which part of my statement had caused their shocked reactions? "Is there something wrong with that?"

Mom stuttered. I knew she was trying to form just the right statement to not piss me off. And I appreciated that.

"Don't you want the wedding party to be formal and unified?"

"No. It doesn't matter to me."

She looked to Abby, then back to me. "But aren't these colors lovely? Abby can try them on and show you. I can already envision the outdoor ceremony surrounded by autumn foliage. Any of these will complement it perfectly."

"They're nice, and I'm sure flowers and decorations in those colors will be beautiful, but I want to keep the dresses casual. And I'd rather the girls buy something they actually like, and can afford, instead of some crazy expensive dress they'll never wear again." My mind flashed to the insanely priced get-up Abby had made me wear and the day I shoved it in a garbage bag. Nothing like throwing away four hundred dollars.

Abby put the dresses back on the rack and both were silent, but I knew my mother wanted to say more. Question was, would she talk, or keep it to herself?

"Why don't you go try on your dresses?" I asked before she could say anything.

* * * *

"Meet me for a drink?" I called Rich at the office after leaving the dress shop. My mother had added three dresses to her file, with appointments at two other boutiques the following week.

"Sure. I can leave in like fifteen minutes. I'll meet you there."

We didn't have to specify the place. Happy Hour was always at Cosmos, the same place I'd been going to for years. Before Preston, and all the drama before that, it was where Marcus, Brenda, Rachel and I had gone every Friday.

I walked in and miraculously found an unoccupied table. Clearly it was Friday and six in the evening--the place was crawling with people ready to start their weekend. Rich walked in before the waitress even made it over to me. He didn't see me at first, and I loved watching him scan the crowd. Unlike most of the male clientele in business suits and power ties, Rich's job required no dress code. He stood there in a pair of semi-faded jeans and a t-shirt from one of the bands he promoted--its tightness in all the right places.

When his blue eyes found mine, a smile bowed his lips. I loved the way my heart still sped a bit when he walked toward me, the eyes of most of the female patrons on him. But his were only on mine.

He leaned down and kissed me square on the mouth. "Everything okay? You sounded stressed on the phone."

"Little bit. I went dress shopping with my mom and Abby today."

"I can see how that would be stressful."

"It wasn't too bad, but I told her I want the bridesmaids to wear black cocktail dresses."

"Ouch. How'd she take it?"

"She didn't say what was on her mind, then anyway. But she's not happy."

"I know your parents are paying for a lot of stuff, but when it comes to dresses, shouldn't your opinion be the one that matters most?"

God, I loved him so much.

"Oh, I wanted to tell you. Marcus picked up a ton of honeymoon brochures. He's pretty sure they're going somewhere European. Paris would be so romantic, don't you think?"

"Yeah, of course. But I don't think we can take a honeymoon."

"Why not?"

"We can't expect your parents to pay thousands of dollars for the wedding and then drop another ten grand on a honeymoon."

"Yeah, probably not." They'd paid for Abby and Daniel's wedding, but the honeymoon to Antigua was a gift from Daniel's parents. "But I'm sure we can save up and at least do something, even if we stay stateside."

"I don't know. Wouldn't you rather save our money so we have a down payment on an apartment?"

"Why?"

"Don't you want to get our own place someday?"

"Not really. I love our weird family, don't you?"

"Yeah, but it gets...*cramped* sometimes."

I laughed. "Cramped? Are you losing your mind? Our place is huge!" I laughed again and stood. "I'm ready for a drink. What do you want?"

"I'll get it," he barked as he stood and walked toward the bar.

What a Crab. He needed to do a few shots and wipe out that mood.

While Rich joined the congregation around the long mahogany bar, I scanned the room. People-watching was a favorite pastime of mine. I saw a group of guys with a bottle of Crown, who erupted in cheers after they'd downed the contents of their shot glasses. A drunk forty-something woman performed a raunchy dance number to the pop song blasting through the speakers. Then I spotted a couple standing in the corner, arms wound around each other.

Wait. I recognized that flat-ironed do and the DKNY eyelet linen dress, because I'd just shopped with her last week. Was this Amanda's new beau with his arms around her and his face buried in her neck?

Rich set my drink on the table. "Hey, is that Amanda? Wow. They're really going at it. Who's the guy?"

"I don't know. All I can see is his hair, but it looks kinda familiar."

"Yeah, it does."

Amanda pulled away, grinning like a maniac, at whom I assumed was her new boyfriend. She gave me full view of his blond hair and the face that went with it. And I most certainly recognized him. Because I had seen him my entire life--even in the womb. Amanda had been making out with my twin brother, Andy.

Chapter 11

"Are we seeing the same thing?" Rich asked.

"If you're seeing my brother swapping spit with Amanda, then yeah."

A booth near them opened and they sat in it on the same side. Andy moved a stray hair from in front of Amanda's eye and kissed the spot where it had been. He then ran his hand through her hair and placed his lips back on hers. The movements were so tender, so sweet--so totally not like Andy at all.

"What should we do?" I asked.

"Um, nothing."

"What do you mean 'nothing'? I can't sit here and watch Andy and Amanda make out and do nothing about it."

"Then don't watch." Rich leaned in and kissed me.

I laughed and pushed him away. "I'm serious. This is my brother and one of my best friends. I need to know what's going on."

They hadn't noticed me and Rich yet. I approached our favorite bartender, ordered a bottle of champagne, and sent it to Amanda and Andy's table.

"What should I say when I take it over?" he asked.

"Tell them 'Lexi and Rich say Congrats.'"

I sat back down with Rich. "What did you do?"

"Watch and see."

The bartender walked over to the corner booth with the champagne in an ice bucket and two flutes. They didn't notice him at first, their faces pressed together and all. And when the bartender delivered my message, both their faces went white. Looks that said *Oh, shit*. Amanda's gaze darted around the room, finally locking with mine.

I waved and mouthed, "Hi."

Amanda and Andy climbed out of their booth and walked over to Rich and me.

"Hi guys," she said, clearly not excited to see us. Andy wouldn't make eye contact at all.

"What's going on?" I asked cheerfully.

"Um…" She looked at Andy, her eyes begging for help.

"Sit," I said and both of them complied. "What's going on here?"

"Well…" Amanda tilted her head, coy little smile. "Remember that night at dinner when I told you I broke up with Glenn 'cause I found someone new?"

"Uh, yeah. You could've mentioned the '*someone new*' was related to me."

"Why does it matter?" Andy asked. "Amanda can be with whoever she wants. She doesn't need your permission."

Did he actually participate in a conversation? I took in my brother's appearance: clean shaven, hair neatly cut and product properly used, nice button-down shirt and dress pants. Was that cologne I smelled? And wait a minute. Did he say "be with?" Were he and Amanda an item, not just some fling?

"So, how did all this start?"

"It was Preston's birthday party and we kinda started talking. It was funny, actually. I told him the bruschetta was good and he said it was just okay. He told me his restaurant makes it way better."

I looked at Andy. "Um, were you referring to the pizza joint you work at?"

"If you came home more than once every six months, you might know that we expanded on the building and made it onto a full service restaurant almost three years ago."

"Oh." I'd had no clue.

"Anyway," Amanda continued, breaking the tension. "I told him I'd love to try it someday and we started talking about other food. He told me how to make a perfect pizza crust."

"Well, he is a pro at it. Been doing it since he was sixteen."

"See," Andy said, turning to Amanda. "This is exactly why I didn't want her to know about us. She always has some smart-ass remark." He stood and took Amanda's hand. "Let's go."

"No, stay. I'm sorry I kinda acted like a bitch."

"*Kinda*?"

"Okay! I was a total bitch. But please stay."

Amanda's eyes pleaded with him. "Let me talk to her."

I followed Amanda outside.

Before the door had even closed, she lit into me. "Why do you treat him like that?"

"What do you mean?"

"Why do you put him down all the time?"

Amanda had never talked to me like that before. It was a whole new side of her and I wasn't sure what to think of it.

"Well, he's kind of a loser. Always has been."

"Lexi, you don't even know how clueless you are."

I was speechless.

"That *pizza joint* is now one of the best restaurants in Westchester. And your brother is the reason. He is the head chef. Has been for over five years. Did you know it was his idea to start serving more than pizza? He was the one who developed the menu and made the place so popular they had to expand the seating area and hire waitresses and take reservations on weekends. You can't get a table there on a Saturday night without one."

What an ass I was. "Why hasn't he said anything?"

"Because everyone thinks he's a screw-up, and what's the point in trying to change people's minds? There's so much you don't know."

Andy had always been a quiet kid--a loner. Aside from insults whispered to each other behind our mother's back, I couldn't recall even one serious conversation between the two of us. "I wish I did."

"He'll probably kill me for telling you this, but I'm gonna anyway. His boss is in the process of having papers drawn making him a partner."

All this time, I'd thought my brother was this uninspired, unmotivated loser who cared about nothing and no one. I stood there staring at Amanda, not knowing what to say.

"I know you don't know this, and who knows if you'll even believe it, but your brother is one of the sweetest guys I have ever met."

"Amanda, I'm so sorry. I had no idea."

"I know." She opened her arms for a hug.

"So you two are kinda serious, huh?"

When Amanda pulled away, her eyes held a sparkle and her lips a demure smile.

"Lexi, I love him."

"What?"

Her smile widened and took up her entire face. "And he loves me too."

"Already? It's only been, like, a month."

"I know. Isn't it amazing?"

"But your ages? There's over ten years between you."

"You are not one to talk about dating and age differences."

She had me there.

"Well, then, congratulations. I'm happy for you--both of you." I hugged her again. Maybe my brother had finally changed for the better. I was living proof that people could successfully re-prioritize their lives. I gave Amanda an extra squeeze before letting go. "Let's go back in and share that bottle of bubbly."

* * * *

"That was bizarre," I said to Rich as we walked home from Cosmos, Amanda and Andy walking in the opposite direction toward the apartment she'd rented for the summer.

"I didn't think so."

"You haven't known Andy as a useless lump of skin for the past thirty-three years."

He just laughed.

"But I have to admit, it was nice to hear him talk for once, a normal conversation, as opposed to the snide remarks he usually throws at me. Maybe my brother has finally grown up. Funny how someone more than a decade younger than him is the one to make him decide to mature."

"I think he started to mature a long time ago, but no one noticed. We talked when you were outside."

"Oooh. Spill!"

"Can't. Guy's oath."

"Uh, there is no 'guy's oath' when it comes to family. I'll tell you what Amanda told me."

"I'm sure it's pretty much the same thing."

"She told me they're in love."

"Well, that's a given."

"Did he say that?"

"Didn't have to. I saw the way he held her hand and the way he looked at her."

I'd seen it too. My brother had never acted like that before. At least not in front of me. He'd had girlfriends, or rather, sex partners. There'd been proof of that leaving our parents' house early in the morning. But an honest to goodness girlfriend? Who he took out and allowed himself to be seen with in public? Someone who also wanted to be seen with him? Weird.

But Rich was right. He did seem to care for Amanda. He'd better. Because if he hurt her--brother or not--I'd kill him.

"What do you think about him becoming a partner in the restaurant?"

"I think it's great. Obviously he enjoys it. It's a tough business to be in."

"Maybe with all the money he'll be making, he'll move out of my parents' house."

"You don't seriously think lack of money was keeping him there?"

"Uh, why else?"

He shook his head and laughed. "I didn't think you were so naive."

"What do you mean?"

"Lexi, your brother, ya know, dealt."

What was he talking about? My cluelessness was apparently funny.

"You really didn't know?"

More laughter.

"Will you spell it out, since I'm so friggin' clueless?"

"Your brother sold weed."

"Andy is not a drug dealer."

"No, not anymore, but he sure used to be."

"I don't believe you. Did he actually tell you that?"

"He didn't have to. You so easily forget that I used to abuse every narcotic on the planet. I can spot a dealer." He put his arm around me and squeezed. "Don't worry. I can tell he's done with it."

I thought back through the last few years, even back to high school. I knew he'd smoked weed. A lot of it. Even scored some from him a few times.

"He better be, if he's serious about being with Amanda." Last thing she needed was to be pulled back into that kind of environment.

Chapter 12

I walked into Bella Baby, ready to drop a wad of cash.

"Can I help you?" a saleswoman asked before I could even check the price tag on a monogrammed burp cloth.

"Yes. I need a registry printed."

"Can I have the name of the mother?"

"Um…" I'd completely forgotten. "The last name is Young."

She tapped away at the keyboard. "Megan and Zachary Young?"

"Yep, that's it."

The printer hummed and within a few seconds, she handed me a list of baby items printed on fancy paper with a hand-and foot-print border. I scanned it. A majority of the items had already been purchased, and I was left with only a few that were outrageously expensive. The handful of things in my price range--under the two-hundred marker--were a ninety-nine dollar Egyptian cotton hooded bath towel, a nursing pillow at a hundred and twenty-nine, or a baby grooming kit for a mere seventy-five bones. Every baby needs a brush, comb and nail clippers, right?

I found it on the shelf--last one. When I took it to the register, the saleswoman scanned the bar code and asked if I wanted it wrapped. Sure, why not?

She measured and cut the shimmery duckie wrapping paper and I waited as patiently as possible. After what felt like an hour, she presented a flawlessly wrapped package topped with a bow and perfect ringlets of curling ribbon.

"Is there anything else I can do for you?"

"Can I have it delivered?"

"Sure." Her fingers tapped away at the keyboard. "Okay, your total after tax, wrapping, and delivery, is one forty-three eighty-eight."

I started to hand over my credit card. Wait a minute. "Excuse me, wasn't the grooming kit seventy-five dollars?" How did we almost double that?

"Yes, it was. But you added wrapping, twenty-five dollars, and then delivery, another thirty-five. And eight point eight seven five percent tax, of course." She smiled at me.

"Thirty-five dollars for delivery?"

"It's guaranteed to be there by five."

I could grab a cab and have it there in twenty minutes for less than half the cost. Was I seriously considering this just to save like twenty bucks? Wait. If I delivered it myself, they'd have to invite me in. And if I went during the day, when Zak was at work, I'd have Meg all to myself.

"You know, maybe it will be more personal if I deliver it myself."

"Oh yes. Absolutely."

She subtracted the delivery charge and I paid the bill. After hailing a cab, I gave the driver the address to Zak's new digs. We pulled up to a building, kind of close to where I lived. But this building was a bit fancier than mine--doorman and all. I walked to the front desk and the clerk asked who I was there to see.

He rang Zak's apartment. After exchanging a few words with the person on the other end, he said to me, "Mrs. Young says you can go up."

The elevator operator took me to the fifth floor and I walked toward Zak and Megan's apartment. All of a sudden my heart sped and my hands got sweaty. What the hell was I doing? There had to be another way to get the info. But I'd already been over all of it. Unless I wanted to tell Marcus, this was it. And confronting Zak wasn't an option either. My only choice was drilling Meg for information. We could become gal pals. There was nothing wrong with her husband's ex wanting to be friends with her, right?

It had been three seconds since I'd knocked and she was already at the door, opening it with a wide smile.

"Lexi! What a surprise."

She was happy to see me? This was going to be easier than I thought.

"Hi. I'm sorry to come by unannounced." I took in her appearance-- low rise capri lounge pants and a ribbed tank that didn't quite cover her huge belly. She was the kind of girl who could get away with that look. I'd been too blobby to show off my naked baby belly.

"It's no problem at all. I was just watching all the baby shows I DVR'd. Only got a couple weeks to go." She rubbed her belly. "I need to be prepared. Please, come in."

I stepped past her and she closed the door behind me.

We walked to the living room, huge floor-to-ceiling windows overlooking the city and fancy leather furniture. Expensive vases and artwork decorated the tables and walls. I laughed inside. They'd learn real quick that that kind of stuff was not baby friendly.

"Here. This is for you," I said and handed the package to her.

"Oh, thank you. That was so sweet of you." She carefully tore the paper, then cooed. "This is perfect."

Uh, it should be. She'd picked it out. It always amused me when brides and moms-to-be acted surprised when opening a gift bought from their registry. But I did appreciate the enthusiasm, even if somewhat fake.

"I'm nervous about trimming those tiny nails, so I hope this will help."

Okay, here was my chance. We could bond over mom stuff and then I'd casually nudge the conversation into how they got pregnant.

"Oh, you'll be fine. I was the last person on this Earth who thought I'd ever be a mom, and it all came naturally. Now I can clip like a pro."

"I hope it's like that for me, too."

I needed to jump in and start digging. "So, you and Zak are still newlyweds? It all happened pretty fast, huh?"

"It did. We both wanted the same things and everything fell right into place."

"You met and got married right away?"

"Yep, pretty much. We did it the first weekend both our families were free."

"Wow. So romantic." Now I needed to get some details of the conception. "And you got pregnant not long after?"

"I did." She stood, taking her time with the weight of her belly, and placed the grooming set on the dining room table. "Can I get you something to drink?"

Hey, come back and talk some more about how you got knocked up. "No thanks."

She went to the kitchen and came back with a glass of water, slowly lowering her body back to the couch. "I am always thirsty."

I needed to get our conversation back to where it was. Did I care if I sounded nosey?

"So, did you get lucky on the first try? You know, getting pregnant?"

She smiled. "We did. We decided we wanted to have a baby right away and *boom* first shot, we got pregnant."

"That is great. Really. I'm so happy for you, but you'll have to excuse my bluntness. This is pretty surreal. When Zak and I were together, he had no interest in having children."

"Yeah, I know. He's told me a lot about his past, and especially about you."

"Oh?" What did she know? My hands turned slimy and a shiver radiated though me like I had stepped outside mid-January in nothing but a bikini.

"He still feels really awful about what he did to you."

This was not what I was expecting. "That's all in the past."

"He knows, but he wishes he would have treated you differently. He says you're a wonderful person and you didn't deserve any of it."

Wow. He'd made me out to be a saint.

"We've all made mistakes in our pasts."

"Oh, I can agree on that one." She laughed and sipped her water.

Back to what was important. "What happened? After he met you, he changed his mind about kids?"

"He did. Until he met me, he didn't want kids. But after our first date, he could see our entire future and it included children. It took him completely by surprise. And next thing we knew, we were married and pregnant."

Okay, so let's figure this out. They met and got married within a month's time. Then they were pregnant right away. No time for a vasectomy reversal procedure. I needed to dig deeper. But I had to control myself or I'd scare her off.

"You didn't get to *practice* making a baby, huh?"

Laughter. That was good. "No practice necessary."

Okay, did this mean they made the baby the old fashioned way? This was not working. I needed to try something else. I needed to get my info from somewhere else maybe.

"So who's your OB?"

"Dr. Belton."

"Oh, yes. I think that's who my sister sees." Total lie.

"She's wonderful."

"Yep. That's what I hear." Now to figure out what I was going to do with this information.

* * * *

"Hello, and thank you for calling the office of Dr. Belton. For appointments, press one. For billing, press two--"

Beep

I pressed one before the automated system went any further. This idea was crazy, but I had to do it.

"Hello, how can I help you today?"

"Well, I'm looking for a new OBGYN and I was hoping to see Dr. Belton."

"Let me see now." The tapping of a computer keyboard echoed in the receiver. "I can get you in to see her on September the first. Does that work for you?"

"No! I mean, can't I get in sooner? I…um…" This was not working how I'd hoped. "I think I have a yeast infection and I'd really like to see her soon as I can."

"Oh, those are horrible, aren't they?"

"Yeah, they are. And this one's a doozie." Did I seriously use the word *doozie*?

More tapping on the keyboard. "Okay…though we don't normally do this for new patients, she does have an opening tomorrow morning. Can you be here at nine?"

"Yes. Thank you so much."

* * * *

After getting Preston into bed, Marcus, Kevin, Rich and I sat to tackle some much needed wedding planning.

"We need to start discussing the menu." Kevin laid out several papers with food choices on them. "I highlighted the menu selections I like most. But I need your input too."

I scanned the yellowed items: coconut shrimp with apricot mustard sauce, pan-seared scallops wrapped in pancetta, peppered beef tenderloin with sun-dried cherry and pinot noir sauce, crab cakes with smoked tomato remoulade, grilled salmon paillard with basil aioli. I had to stop reading or I might have drooled on the paper.

"I'm no help. Everything sounds delicious."

"Oh, I know," Kevin squealed. "So let's start with an easier question, sit down or buffet?"

At the same time Marcus said "sit down", Rich said "buffet."

"I think it's better to let everyone take what they want, and as much as they want," Rich said.

And Marcus immediately replied, "But this is an elegant event and I'm sure women in long fancy gowns will not want to traipse up to a food line and carry a plate to their seat."

I could almost smell the testosterone in the air.

"Now, boys," Kevin said, an attempt at breaking the tension. "I get what Rich is saying, but sorry, I do have to agree with Marcus. I'll be in white and I don't need the added stress of worrying that I'll spill my dinner down the front of my tux as I make my way back to the head table." He turned to me. "Lex, what do you think? Since you'll be donning white, too."

Rich spoke before I had a chance. "I know you Lexi, and you always complain about the portion sizes at sit-down catered parties. We were at that library fundraiser a few weeks ago and you said you wished you could have traded your asparagus and potatoes for more filet."

He had me there. It was no secret; I liked to eat.

"Yeah, but that wasn't our wedding. I think I agree with Marcus. I'll have enough to worry about with a white dress. I can't imagine walking in it in four-inch heels, while balancing a plate of food."

"But what if..." he started then trailed off. "Nevermind."

"No, what did you want to say?"

"It doesn't matter." He stood and walked toward the fridge, mumbling something under his breath that I didn't quite catch.

"O...kay, now that that's settled," Kevin continued. "We really need to get this wedding party under control."

"I agree," Marcus said and took a yellow legal pad and drew a line down the middle. In one column he wrote *Bridesmaids* and the other *Groomsmen*. "Let's start with the ladies."

"Abby is my Maid of Honor."

"Matron," Kevin corrected.

"Yeah, whatever. And I've already asked Amanda and Sheila to be bridesmaids."

"Sheila?" Marcus asked.

"Yeah, we've...bonded. Anyway, who else? I figured Jeanette, right?"

"Of course, she's totally my Matron of Honor," Kevin squealed and Marcus added her name to the list. "Is that it for women?"

Rich spoke after a long swig of his beer. "I'd like to ask my sister, Stacey."

"Oh. Of course." I knew he was close with her, his only sibling who'd made it out of the trailer park like he had. Since she'd moved to New York, we'd gotten together a few times, but her hectic model's lifestyle kept her pretty busy.

"Okay. I guess that's it. Now let's talk groomsmen."

Marcus put his pen back to the paper and began writing. "Jeanette's husband Jeff, and Andy, of course. Rich, who do you want?"

"Um, two guys from the band. Gryz, I mean, Keith...Gryzanksi. He'll be my best man, and then Mike, a groomsman."

"Okay, that takes us to five bridesmaids and four groomsmen."

"Oh, that's so not enough. We need at least a couple ushers," Kevin said. "No way will four guys be able to seat four hundred people."

"I'm sure Daniel would do usher duty." Then it dawned on me. "Wait, Marcus didn't add his best man."

"I've been meaning to talk to you about that. I don't have any siblings, like you all do. So I'm kinda left without an automatic honor attendant. And since Preston's too young to sign the marriage license, I wanted to ask the only person, beside my parents, who has known me my entire life."

"Really?"

"Yeah. You can be my Best Woman."

"Can we *do* that? Since I'm one of the brides and all?"

"It's our wedding. We can do whatever the hell we want."

Chapter 13

"You're not usually up so early," Rich said as I stepped into the shower with him.

"Yeah, I know. I have a doctor's appointment at nine and I thought we'd squeeze in a quickie first."

"Sounds fantastic to me."

He kissed my neck and moved lower, sweet nibbles on my breasts sending sparks of lust throughout my body. He turned me around, my back to his chest, and entered me from behind. I placed a foot on the side of the tub and grabbed the towel bar for support. God, shower sex was so steamy.

He reached his hand around to fondle my clit. It wasn't going to take much. Within a few seconds he had me writhing in his hand.

"That was awesome, as always." I placed my lips on his once again.

After only a second, he pulled away. "Since we used some of our shower time on more fun things, I gotta wash real quick and get out." He reached for the shampoo and worked some into his hair. "What doctor's appointment do you have?"

A wave of terror surged through my body. "I didn't say it was a doctor's appointment."

"Uh, yes you did."

"Oh." The plan was to keep this all quiet. "It's just an OB appointment."

He stopped mid-rinse. "Is everything okay?"

"Yes. It's nothing. Don't worry." Dammit, why did I open my big mouth?

"I do worry about you. What's going on?"

"Nothing. I might have a yeast infection. No big deal."

"You're lying. We don't have sex if you have a yeast infection. Tell me what's going on."

Shit. How was I going to get out of this one? "No, not usually. But this one feels different, so it might not be a yeast infection at all. And I was horny this morning. No yeast infection was gonna stop me from getting off and pleasuring my man." He wasn't convinced, so I kissed him again and pushed my tongue past his hesitant lips--started stroking him, too, for added distraction.

His kissed me back and after a few more seconds, pulled away smiling. "See what you did now?" His rock hard cock stared up at me. "And there's no time to fix it."

He reached behind him and next thing I knew, ice cold water sprayed down on us. I screamed and jumped out, grabbed a towel, and draped it around my body.

"Quickest way I know to get rid of a hard-on." He shivered, and soaped his body.

* * * *

"Ms. Marshall? The doctor will see you now." I set down the waiting room copy of *Vogue* and followed the nurse to the exam room. She did the usual stuff first: height, weight, blood pressure. Then handed me a paper gown.

"Open in the front please," she said, a little too chipper for so early in the morning. "Dr. Belton will be in shortly."

I changed and hopped onto the exam table, the crinkling of the paper sheet combined with my paper gown was so loud they could probably hear it in Canada.

A minute later, an apple-shaped woman came into the room wearing a white doctor's coat. "Hello, I'm Dr. Belton."

Wow. She was quite punctual. Maybe I would switch OBs after all.

"I see you're a new patient. You've been experiencing some symptoms of a yeast infection?"

"Oh, yes. The usual burning and itching."

Okay, here was my five minutes with Zak's wife's OBGYN. How was I going to use this situation to my benefit?

Dr. Belton sat on her wheeled stool and asked me to lay back and put my heels in the stirrups.

After scooting down, I felt the cool metal of the speculum. "A friend of mine referred me to you, Megan Young. She said you were the best and so far, I have to agree. It really is amazing how she got pregnant, isn't it?"

All I got was an "Mmm-hmm."

"Even with her husband having had a vasectomy a few years ago, they still got pregnant so easily. How do you think that happened?"

She peeked around my leg. "Ms. Marshall, I'm sure you know I am not at liberty to discuss other patients with you."

"Oh, we're good friends. I know she won't mind."

"Then you can ask her yourself." She smiled and pushed back on her stool. After pulling off her rubber gloves, she threw them in the trash and reached for my chart. "You appear to be chafed, but I don't see anything to suggest a yeast infection."

"Oh, okay. Good."

"All I can suggest is a nice warm bath and no sex for a few days. Call if it gets worse."

She started toward the door, but I hadn't gotten what I needed. I threw out a last ditch effort. "If my fiance ever has a vasectomy and changes his mind afterward, can you help us get pregnant?"

"Goodbye, Ms. Marshall."

Damn. This had been a waste.

I redressed and gathered my things, wracking my brain as I left the exam room. How the hell was I going to figure this out? Walking toward reception, I passed a room filled with file folders--patients' file folders. The hall was empty, so I peeked inside. It was empty too.

Okay. I could do this. I could be in and out in a few seconds. Surely it was alphabetized. I scanned the wall and found the Y section at the bottom. I squat down for a better view. Yancy, Yearling, Ying, Yip, Yorke, Young. Found it!

I pulled the manila folder labeled *Young, Megan*.

"Excuse me. What are you doing?"

I stood and pulled the file folder to my chest, a lame attempt to hide it. "Um, uh, nothing. I'll just be going."

"Oh, no you don't." The woman grabbed me by the arm and pulled the folder from my hands. She yanked me down the hallway as Dr. Belton stepped out of an exam room.

"Dr. Belton, we have a problem here." She held up the folder. "I found this woman in the file room."

The doctor eyed the folder, and then me. "Let me guess...Megan Young's file?"

The office woman glanced at the file. "Yes, it is."

"Ms. Marshall, come with me." She led me to her office and closed the door behind us. "Have you ever heard of a thing called Doctor-Patient Confidentiality?"

I stared at her. "Well, of course, but..." This was pointless. "Please Dr. Belton, cut me some slack here. Megan Young's husband is my ex and he supposedly had a vasectomy before he met me. Now I find out she's pregnant, and what if the vasectomy reversed itself? Who I thought was my son's father might not be after all. I was involved with Zak Young when I got pregnant, but we'd broken up, and I went and had a one night stand. I thought there was no way he could be the dad--the vasectomy and all."

I was a rambling mess, but continued anyway.

"Now there is a possibility he might be my baby's father and I was trying to find out if that was true or not. I don't want to tell the man who I hope is my baby's father--it would crush him to think for even a moment that our baby is not his. And I thought maybe if I came in here, since I know you're her doctor, you could help me. Please. I'm desperate here."

She blinked a few times. "Obviously."

"So, in your professional medical opinion, is it possible the vasectomy reversed itself?"

She gave me an are-you-fucking-kidding-me look.

"Okay, can we forget this ever happened?"

She sighed, walked around her desk, and sat on the edge of it. "I don't ever want to see you in this office again."

"No, never. I promise."

"You can go now."

"Thank you!" I knew she could have made this into quite a scene if she'd wanted to.

"Don't thank me. Just leave."

"I will. Thank you."

"A word of advice," she said as I turned toward the door. "Tell your baby's father the truth instead of sneaking around and trying to find out on your own."

Yeah, right. No way was I going to do that. I was worried enough about the whole thing. No need to make Marcus worry too.

* * * *

"How was the doctor's appointment today?" Rich asked when we were in bed.

"Oh, fine. Turns out it wasn't a yeast infection." And a complete waste of time and money. "But while I was there, my mom called and left me a message. She says you never emailed her the addresses for your family like you were supposed to."

"Yeah, I know."

"Don't you want to invite them?"

"Not really."

"I've never even met them. Why don't you want them to come?"

"Lex, they are complete trash. No one will want them there. I'm not sure *I* even want them there."

I didn't have the greatest parents and siblings either, so I could definitely understand. "Are you sure? This is your wedding. Maybe it's time to, I don't know, get past the crap. Don't you think your mom and sisters will want to come and celebrate your life and how far you've come?"

"Oh, sure they would--free food and alcohol--they'd be there in a heartbeat. But not to *celebrate me*."

"Well, I think you should invite them."

"Why do you care?"

"I love you and I've never seen who you came from or where you grew up."

"Trust me, I'd much rather forget."

I wasn't going to push him on this. "Okay, give it some thought."

* * * *

A week had gone by and I was no closer to finding an answer to my baby daddy question. I was out of ideas on where to get the information. And on top of that stress, pile on my first round of copy edits for *Which Way to Broadway*, and my mother nagging me every other hour with a different wedding-related question.

"Alexandra, have you talked with Richard about his family yet?"

"Has the dress shop started alterations on your dress?"

"Have you and Richard planned the rehearsal dinner?"

"We need to get together for a final bridal shower planning meeting. When are your friends available?"

"Did Richard and Preston get measured for their tuxedos yet?"

By the tenth call in two day's time, I turned my phone off and sat on the couch with my laptop, in silence, and worked on my manuscript.

At noonish, the door opened and Rich practically skipped in. "Go ahead. Ask me why I'm home early."

By the wide smile and jig he was doing around the room, something good had to have happened. "Tell me already!"

"I got a promotion. I'm the new Marketing Director." He picked me up and swung me around, covering my face with kisses.

"What does this mean?" I asked when I finally tore away from his hungry lips.

"A shitload of money!"

Before I could utter another word, my shirt had been ripped from my body and my bra tossed across the room. We did it right there on the floor in between the coffee table and the stand holding our DVD player and other TV accessories. Good thing the babysitter had planned on being gone the entire day.

Two orgasms later, we peeled our sweat-covered bodies apart. "I guess you're pretty happy about this?"

"Lexi, this is so huge for us. We will finally have some money of our own. I can support you, for once."

"You know you never needed to do that. I have my own money."

"I know, but I felt like such a loser before."

"Rich, you're twenty-five. No one your age is rolling in dough."

"We will be now." He pulled me on top of him again and took a still erect nipple into his mouth.

"No more," I said and pulled away from the inferno that was his body. Though I really didn't want to. "Preston and Nicole could be back any minute."

"Okay." No hesitation on his part. "We have some things to talk about anyway."

"Yeah?"

We both got up and gathered our discarded clothing.

"I'm in such a good friggin' mood," he said as he pulled his jeans on. "That I decided to invite my family to the wedding. I'm proud and I want to show off everything I have."

After we'd both redressed, we sat on the couch. "If that's what you want, I'm happy."

"I do. As white trash as they are, I still love my sisters and all their kids. It's my mom who's the asshole, but I figured I'd invite her anyway."

"Good for you."

"There's more." He pulled me in and laid a kiss on me, sending a tingle straight to my toes. "Now that we can afford it, I want to get our own place."

His smile was wide, his eyes bright. Every inch of his skin buzzed with excitement.

"Wow," was all I could form with my lips. He'd mentioned it before, but this time it seemed more serious.

"Lexi, this is gonna be great. We'll start our married life in a home that's all ours."

He pulled me to him again. I hadn't the heart to voice any of the concerns swirling through my brain. I loved Rich with my entire heart and soul, but our new age family worked perfectly. Maybe he didn't think so.

Chapter 14

To celebrate Rich's promotion, he wanted a day with me and Preston all to himself. Marcus and Kevin didn't complain. Kevin insisted on dragging Marcus to a few wedding-related errands including, but not limited to, a florist appointment, shopping for attendants' gifts, and a stop by the travel agency to book their Venetian honeymoon.

"Where should we go on our honeymoon?" Rich asked after we'd spread a blanket on the grass near the playground.

"I thought we weren't taking one--money and all."

"Well, that's changed." His smile gleamed at me. It hadn't dimmed once in the three days since he'd received his promotion.

"I don't know. Wherever you want to go. You should pick, since you're footing the bill."

I set the picnic basket on the blanket and pulled out the wine and glasses.

Preston stood there whining and pointing at the swings.

"Here, buddy. Have some lunch first." Rich enticed him with a PB and J sandwich, his weakness.

He plopped onto the blanket and chowed down.

"So, back to the honeymoon."

I handed Rich a glass of wine and poured one for myself.

He took a sip, eyes gleaming over the rim of his glass. "I'm thinking somewhere tropical, maybe a nude beach. You'd look pretty sexy walking in the sand, naked, with ocean waves crashing at your feet."

"Ha ha. And my stretch marks would shimmer fabulously in the bright sun."

"Who cares? I think you're smokin' hot."

"Your love has blinded you to the faults of my body."

"You know you're gorgeous." He winked and pulled the sliced havarti and our wedge of brie from the basket.

Before I could finish my glass of wine or down much cheese and crackers, Preston had gobbled his sandwich and was pointing at the swings again.

"Okay, okay! Let's go." I scooped him up and ran over, then plopped his little butt in one of the rubber infant swings. I gave him a big push and watched his face illuminate, giggles shaking his little body.

After a few minutes of back-and-forth on the swings, Preston's eyes focused on something else--a big, huge sandbox.

"You wanna go play over there now?"

He laughed and I took it as a "yes."

I held his hand and we walked over. He wasn't too great at the whole walking thing, but he was getting it. I set him inside the sandbox, taking a seat myself on the edge of the wooden box.

Two moms sitting nearby gave me polite smiles and quiet *hellos*.

"So, as I was saying," one said to the other, "I took Addyson for her interview at Wallington and was told they'd 'let me know.'"

She even used air quotes.

"Can you believe that? Maddox is already a student. How can they not automatically accept his little sister?"

"That is sooo ridiculous," the other mom commiserated. "You can't send your daughter to a different preschool than your son. Hopefully you'll know soon. They sent me Brynlee's acceptance letter within a month. And thank God they did--she was already six months old."

I snickered. Picking a preschool at six months?

"Is something funny?" the brunette asked with a flip of her blown-out hair.

"Nope." I turned my attention back to Preston, who scooped some sand and poured it onto his leg.

"You laughed. And I'm pretty sure it was at what we said."

I looked at her again. "I can't believe you're stressing over preschool for a baby who's barely a couple months old."

"Well, obviously you don't have a clue. Only the most brilliant children get into The Wallington Academy--it's the best. And you need to apply early."

"How can they possibly tell if a baby that young is smart?"

"Oh, they can tell." Her lips curled into a smirk. "Your son is eating sand."

They laughed while I dusted off his tongue with my hand. I picked him up and stalked back to the picnic blanket and Rich.

"Bitches."

"Excuse me?"

"Those snobby women over there." I took a napkin, wet it with some bottled water, and went back to wiping Preston's mouth, brown drool leaking from his lips. "Do you think Preston is smart?"

"Of course."

"You're not just saying that? You really think so?"

"Yes. What'd they say to rattle you?"

"Oh, it's just their pretentiously named children and their Ivy League Preschool. Forget I said anything. Let's talk about something else."

"Okay, back to wedding talk. We should figure out the rehearsal dinner."

"I thought we'd already figured it out. The inn said they could do a picnic-y barbecue for us--ribs and chicken and corn on the cob."

"That was weeks ago. Things are different now."

He refreshed my wine glass and handed me a bunch of green seedless grapes.

"Yeah, but we liked that idea because it was simple."

"And cheap."

"It had nothing to do with money. The wedding reception will be all formal and stuffy. I want something more relaxed for the rehearsal."

"Lexi, listen. I'm gonna have money now. The rehearsal dinner is the only part of the wedding I've been allowed to pay for, so I'm sure as hell gonna make sure it's spectacular."

"I like barbecue. It would have been spectacular enough for me."

He pulled me to him and kissed me, the creaminess of the brie lingering on his tongue. "No one else would have thought it spectacular. Can you honestly see your mom with a half-rack on her plate?"

"You most certainly know by now, I don't give a rat's ass what my mother thinks."

"I do. I guess we can still do barbecue, if you want. I'll have to think of something else to make it special."

"Yeah? Like what?"

"Oh, I don't know. Maybe I'll surprise you."

* * * *

"What do you think?" Amanda asked as she twirled in front of a full-length mirror at Trendy Threads, one of our favorite boutiques.

"I like it." The one-armed tank cocktail dress suited her frame well.

"What is everyone else wearing? I don't want to pick something too similar."

"Sheila bought the first three-quarter sleeve wrap dress she tried on. I don't think she's a big fan of shopping. And Jeanette went with a flowy, ruffled number."

Amanda took one more glance at her ass, then went back to the dressing room.

"What about Abby?" she yelled from behind the closed door.

"Oh, she pisses me off. I decided on black cocktail dresses to keep it simple, and you know what she did? She ordered a satin, floor-length bridesmaid's gown. Beaded bodice and all. But because it's black, she figured it qualified."

"Wow. Nervy of her."

Amanda strode out again, this time in a strapless with a super short bubble skirt.

"Sexy, huh? I think Andy will like this one."

"Any guy would drool over you in that dress. Well, maybe not Marcus, but Kevin would adore it--his slavery to fashion and all."

She laughed. "I bet Andy would enjoy taking me out of it."

"Yeah, probably."

"The other night--holy shit. He got me off twice before there was even any penetration."

"TMI."

"You can't be serious. We've always discussed our sex lives in explicit detail. I know so much about Rich's cock, I could probably pick it out of a line-up."

Perhaps I'd bragged a little too much about my man's genitalia.

"It was all fine and dandy when we weren't discussing my brother's... parts."

"Okay, okay. No more talking about my amazing sex life with your twin, even if his dick does taste delicious."

"Amanda!"

"Fine. What do you think?" She twirled. "Should I get this one?"

"It's cute...and very short. My mother would have a coronary on the spot." My eyes met hers, my lips curling. "You should totally get it."

Her smile faded. "Oh, well...I don't want to anger Maryanne."

"You did not just say that. And when did you start calling my mother 'Maryanne'?"

"When she told me to, at lunch a couple weeks ago."

"Oh, you're doing lunch now?"

"It's not like we planned it or anything. She came into the restaurant to see the new decor and since I'm working there this summer, I was there, so I took my lunch break and ate with her."

"How chummy."

She narrowed her eyes with a sly smile. "Oh, Lexi, you're not jealous, are you?"

"That's laughable."

"I'm going to try on the last dress." Amanda stepped away from the mirror and disappeared into the dressing room, reappearing a minute later in a v-neck halter sheath. "You like?"

"Perfect. Right amount of sexy without too much leg."

"Maryanne will approve?"

I just stared at her.

"Sorry. I don't want my future mother-in-law to think I'm a big ole slut."

Now my jaw fell to the floor.

"There's nothing official, if that's what you're wondering, but we've been talking...a lot."

"You're not even old enough to drink."

"I will be next month."

"Still. How can you be thinking of marriage? Do you know what I was doing at your age?"

She stifled her laughter. I sounded like such a wrinkled old douchebag.

"You have so much life to live, so many things you need to do--men you need to fuck."

"First of all, I'm pretty happy with the fucking I already have going on in my life. Second, how old is your fiance?"

She had me...again. I always seemed to forget his age. "But the point is--"

"The point is," she interrupted. "That we love each other and I never want to be without him. You know, all too well, that I know what a toxic relationship looks like."

The vision of Amanda at that party more than a year ago--bruised and only half-clothed--had been burned onto my brain. I nodded.

"And Glen was great. He really helped me heal after a disaster of a semester. He was patient and sweet, and well, he got to be kinda boring after a while. I know it's hard for you to believe, but your brother has such an adventurous side to him--a side he doesn't show many people. And I'm one of those lucky people."

"Oh, I know he's *adventurous*. His marijuana clients know that side of him too."

She sighed. "He doesn't do that anymore."

"Oh, so you do know about it?"

"Of course I do. I know everything. He told me about his former... *business*. But he stopped dealing a while ago."

"How do you know for sure?"

"I just do, okay. You may not believe it, but he doesn't even smoke it himself anymore. He stopped way before he even started dating me. And he especially won't now. He knows what I went through and he doesn't want me to ever feel scared again. He has too much going for him to screw it up with drugs."

"Oh." I guessed my brother had matured. Maybe he was capable of real feelings--even love.

I pulled Amanda to me. "I'm happy for you. Both of you."

When we parted, she wiped tears from her eyes. "Can you believe it? Someday soon we'll be sisters!"

Chapter 15

"I called a realtor today and he emailed me a ton of listings."

Rich's statement caught me by surprise. "I didn't think this was decided yet."

"I don't see why not."

"It's a big step. What if we go through with it and realize we can't afford it?"

He gave me his are-you-kidding-me look. "My new salary is enough, trust me."

"I do. I just want to be sure."

"Why are you being like this? I thought you'd love the idea. No more sharing the TV. Blaring music as loud as we want. Sex wherever we want. Privacy...remember what that felt like?" He laughed.

"Yeah, it would be great. But, I don't know."

"It's 'cause of Marcus, isn't it?"

Sometimes his mind-reading capabilities kind of sucked. "He's my best friend."

"But I'm your fiance, your soon-to-be husband."

"This isn't a him or you thing. And even if it was, you know who would win."

"Do I?"

I couldn't tell if he was serious or not. "Don't be like that. You know it would be you."

"Then what's the big deal?"

I walked to the end table and picked up a five-by-seven picture of Preston in a silver frame--his adorable cheesy smile staring at me.

"*He* is the big deal. How can I take Preston away from Marcus?"

"Lex, that's not what we'd be doing."

"Explain that to Marcus. He's been a major part of his son's life--" My brain interrupted my speech. Preston might not be Marcus's son after all. "Since his birth. How can I reduce that to every other weekend and alternate holidays?"

"We would never instill one of those stupid custody agreements."

"What other choice would we have?"

"I don't know. We'll figure it out." Rich took the picture and set it back on the table, then pulled me to him. "It's time for me to be a man and have my own place and provide for my family. I can't continue to live under another's man's roof. You have to understand that."

Rich rarely showed his macho side, but I got it. And I wanted my husband to be happy.

"Okay, we'll do it. But can we keep it quiet, at least a little while? I need to find the right way to tell Marcus."

* * * *

On a rare afternoon alone, Marcus and I took Preston to lunch at one of our old favs. The warm day was cooler than the scorchers we'd been accustomed to and the patio table we'd been seated at was perfect. A casual breeze rustled Preston's baby-fine hair as he played with his little car.

"Do you have any thoughts on preschool?" The comments from the park bitches the week before still pecked at my brain.

"A few. I've already been schooled on the dos and don'ts by one of my partners at the firm."

"Yeah, I've been *schooled* too, but by some stuck-up snob moms." After the waitress took our orders, I continued. "You don't think we should, like, apply, do you?"

"I was thinking of it. It's too late to apply at some. They're so inundated with applications and the cut-off age is twelve months."

"Is there even a point to sending him to preschool at all? I mean, we started with kindergarten and we're perfectly fine."

"School was much easier when we were kids. If he doesn't go, he'll be behind all the other kids. I think he should have the best start possible."

"Well, it all seems like a popularity contest to me. And I can teach him ABCs and 123s."

Marcus snorted a laugh before taking a sip of his water.

"What? You don't think I can teach him a few simple lessons?" He was starting to piss me off.

"You're not exactly the most patient person on the planet. Teachers know what they're doing."

"I know what I'm doing, Marcus. I *have* been his mother for over a year now."

"I know. Relax. But I think we should check into it."

"Whatever."

We sat in silence, broken only by the delivery of our lunches

"Oh, I wanted to tell you." Marcus swallowed a bite of his sandwich. "I'm taking Preston to my parents' house next weekend."

"Are you fucking kidding me?"

"Lexi, they *are* his grandparents."

"Who've made no attempt since his birth to meet him."

"Well, they have now."

I fought to extinguish the rage inside me. I'd never had any issues with Marcus's mother--until Preston was born. She'd always adored me, and even when she'd found out I was pregnant and Marcus the father, she'd wanted us to get married. She'd refused to accept Marcus was gay and happy and ecstatic with his new life. Not once had she tried to get to know her grandson or even called to ask how he was.

"Just like that. She acts like an asshole all this time, and with one phone call, you come running, Preston in tow."

"I'm not going to argue with you. They're my parents and I'm going to introduce my son to them."

He might not even be *his* son.

If Marcus's goal had been to piss me off, he'd achieved it. So badly I wanted to piss him off in return. How easy would it be right now to drop the bomb about me and Rich moving out and taking Preston with us? How would he like that little morsel? I needed to know Preston's paternity, and soon. If Marcus wasn't his father, he'd have no say. Only I would decide who was allowed in his life.

I didn't speak a word as we walked home. And I didn't wait while he retrieved our mail. I wheeled Preston to the elevator and waited, hoping it would get there before Marcus had finished. No such luck.

He flipped through the pile of mail. With four adults, there was always a pretty huge stack.

"This one's addressed to all of us." He handed it over and we walked into the elevator. The return address was a sticker printed with Andy's name and address, American flag on the left hand side. Probably one of those labels that come free in the mail--the ones asking for a donation to some charity.

"Strange." I ran my finger under the lip of the small white envelope. The elevator dinged at our floor.

Marcus tossed the stack of mail into the basket of Preston's stroller and wheeled it out.

I continued with the envelope, desperate to see what my brother had mailed us.

You're invited! the multi-colored invitation's front told me. Inside were details for Amanda's twenty-first birthday celebration, a surprise party.

Never saw that coming. Andy rarely even attended parties. I couldn't imagine him hosting one.

* * * *

Phase One of Find the Daddy had been a bust. Meg hadn't given me any info. And Phase Two--the trip to her OB--had been a disaster. What could I do next? What would give me the answers I needed? Nothing short of Zak's full medical history was going to help. Or someone who knew everything about his entire life. Aside from his wife, anyway.

Ruth, his secretary.

As guard dog to his office, she was more of a personal assistant than the administrative title that had been thrust upon her. She did his shopping, fetched his dry cleaning. She was the one who made and broke all of his appointments, business and personal. She knew everything.

Ruth was the key to unlocking Zak's life. Hard part was getting her to open it for me.

Think. Think. Think. If I wanted to butter her up and loosen her lips, what would I do?

Chocolate. Every holiday Zak bought her a box of Godivas.

I had no choice but to drop some more cash, only this time, it would work. An hour later, I was on my way to Zak's office, gold box in hand, but my time was limited. He left every day at exactly one on the dot for lunch, and he took only hour, never more than an hour and a half.

I strolled over to Ruth's desk and flashed my toothiest grin. "Hello, Ruth. It's been ages. How are you?"

Her eyes widened, then relaxed, and a small smile spread. "Hello, Ms. Marshall."

"Please, call me Lexi."

"Oh, um, Lexi. I'm well. And you?"

"Great!"

"Are you here to see Mr. Young? He just left for lunch."

I knew this, of course. "Oh, darn. Well, I guess you and I will have to eat these ourselves."

I placed the box on her desk.

"I couldn't. I'm on a new diet."

The plump woman had been on a diet for as long as I'd known her.

"But it's a proven fact that if you eat good eighty percent of the time, the other twenty you can be bad."

I opened the box and she stared down at the chocolate-covered dreams, licking her lips.

"I guess one or two won't hurt. I've had salads for lunch this whole week."

"Atta girl."

We took turns choosing a confection and sunk our teeth in.

"Mmm…these are good." Her eyes rolled back like she was going to orgasm.

"So, Ruth, how have things been around here? Since Zak met Meg and all?"

"Very good." She wiped her mouth with a napkin from her desk drawer. "He's been very different since meeting her. Happy all the time."

"Good. That's nice to hear." Okay, enough chit-chat. "So they're having a baby?"

"Yes. She was born a couple weeks ago. Sophia Aileen."

"They used his mother's name for the middle name?"

"And Megan's mother's for the first. So excited they are. You should see Mr. Young. Can't wait to go home to his two ladies each night. And he's late almost every single day, too."

Zak, late to work? And out of the office on time? Parenthood did suit him.

Back to business. "It's bizarre though, don't you think? He had a vasectomy years ago, remember?" Surely she did.

Ruth nodded. "He still came to work though, even in all that pain."

"So, did he, you know, have a reversal done?"

She sucked in a breath and her eyes opened wide. "Oh, I can't discuss that."

"Come on, Ruth. We're old pals. I'm dying to know." Would the I'm-your-buddy-so-let's-gossip thing work?

"You know how private Mr. Young is."

"I also know what he looks like naked." A sight she'd probably imagined a time or two. Her eyes went buggy and I needed to reel myself back in. "What I mean is, we were very close and I know he wouldn't mind if you told me."

"I can't. I'm sorry." She popped another chocolate in her mouth and gave her attention back to her computer screen. After tapping at the keyboard, she turned back to me. "Is there something else I can do for you?"

"No, that's all." I smiled and walked away, but I'd be back. There was proof in that office--somewhere. I just needed to find it.

Chapter 16

After grabbing my purse, I walked through the kitchen. "I'm taking off. I have a meeting with Sheila."

Marcus checked his watch. "It's almost eight."

"I know. She couldn't get together any other time." I felt only a tad bit bad for lying about where I was going.

Without further questioning, he gave a nonchalant, "Okay. See ya later."

The sun was still bright, as if it were midday, but the humidity had let up somewhat. Sidewalks were crowded with people--tourists mostly. I weaved in and around groups and families, making it to Zak's office building in no time.

Even though many of the companies in the forty-two story building closed at five or six, there were many that didn't. No one would think twice about me walking in and taking the elevator up. And with the info I'd scored from Ruth earlier, I knew Zak's office would be empty.

I stepped off the elevator on the tenth floor. The wide space, filled with bathroom stall-sized cubicles, sat dark with the setting mid-August sun as the main source of illumination. I started toward Zak's office, trying to stay as quiet and invisible as possible. Should have worn a black cat suit or something.

I slinked toward Zak's door. Almost there.

"Want anything, Bob?" A voice burst through the silence. "I'm gonna grab a Coke."

Shit! I ducked into a cubicle. The footsteps echoed, getting louder as the unknown man came toward me. I crawled underneath the desk and pulled the wheeled chair in front. Was I seriously this desperate?

Um, apparently.

The guy got what he needed from the vending machine and walked past. Once he was safely in his office and the door closed, I climbed out

Stephanie Haefner

of my hiding spot. Before taking another step, I removed my shoes. Last thing I needed was an accidental clack of my heel.

Ruth's desk sat in a darkened corner of the building. I wrapped my hand around the doorknob to Zak's office, and eased it to the right. It popped open. Sweet.

I shut the door behind me and pulled out the flashlight I'd shoved into my purse before I left the apartment. Where to search first? I set my shoes and purse on the leather chair in front of the desk and shined my flashlight over the massive piece of mahogany furniture. There was a date book. I grabbed it and thumbed through. It definitely looked like a personal date book, not business. But written inside were recent things--pediatrician and OB appointments. I flipped to the beginning. Damn. It was only for this year. I needed last year's appointments, specifically the months right before Meg got pregnant.

Where the hell could I find Zak's schedule from last year? Ruth probably had all the data in her computer. Maybe if I grew a big enough set of balls by the time I finished scouring the office, I'd turn her computer on.

I opened the file drawer in the desk. Zak kept his more personal stuff there. The business files were in cabinets on the wall and next to Ruth's desk. If he'd kept any paperwork pertaining to a vasectomy reversal or the freak chance it had reversed itself naturally, this was where it'd be.

There were several file folders, all labeled: *Property, Vehicle Information, Insurance, Marriage-Prenup.*

Whoa. Quite interesting. I almost yanked that baby and had a look-see, but I was not there to snoop. Well, at least not for that.

Tax Forms, Medical Forms

Bingo!

Finally, I was going to get the answers I needed. I pulled the folder from the drawer and opened it on my lap. My heart jack hammered against my ribcage. This was it. The moment I found out if my son had Daddy A or Daddy B.

I flipped through some allergy sheets, a HIPAA form, prescription for Propecia. Anti-hair loss medication? Poor Zak. What a nice head of hair he has, er, had.

But I didn't find anything from a vasectomy doctor. This was not working the way I needed it to.

All right, time to fire up Miss Ruth's computer. I put everything back the way I'd found it and crept out. The place seemed deader than when I'd arrived, the sun having completely set. Bob and whoever else had been there seemed to be gone.

I sat on Ruth's ergonomic leather chair and turned her computer on, dimming the monitor. The corner was almost pitch black and even the tiniest bit of light shone like a million-candle spotlight.

The computer booted up in seconds--only top of the line equipment for Zak's secretary. The kitty cat wallpaper almost made me chuckle out loud, but I held it in. Scanning the desktop icons, I found one labeled *Mr. Young's Schedule*. It couldn't have been any easier.

I clicked on it and right away the week opened. On the left-hand side were options to click on other weeks, months, years. I clicked on last year and when it opened, I swore I heard the angels sing a jubilant "Hallelujah."

Okay, when did Zak and Meg meet again? August?--and married a few weeks later. I clicked on September to check for any doctor's appointments. Listed right there in bold black type on September 8th: *2:30 with Dr. Radcliffe at RFD Urology.*

I suppressed a squeal for joy, but my insides did quite a jig.

The cursor hovered over the *Expand* button.

"What are you doing?"

Fuck! I jumped and rammed my knee into the desk, shaking it and knocking a cup of pens and pencils to the floor. The sound shattered through the entire office space. And all I could see was a looming black figure.

"Get over here!"

I stepped from behind the desk. My first instinct was to run, but he was quick. In two seconds he had me by the arm, a blunt object in his hand.

"Please don't hurt me."

He pulled me away from the desk, my heart beating a zillion times per minute. Was this how I'd die? Bludgeoned to death by some massive he-man? My baby boy. Would Preston know how much I loved him? That my last minutes on Earth were spent doing what I had to do for him?

"Please, I have a child at home. Don't kill me."

"Kill you?" He flipped on a light. "Hell, no. But I am gonna call the police."

I stared into his dark eyes, noticing the gray hair on his head and his janitor's uniform with *Frank* embroidered in red. In his free hand was the weapon to bludgeon me with--a toilet brush.

"Oh, no, that's not necessary, is it?"

"Yes ma'am, I believe it is."

Ma'am? Did I seriously look like a *ma'am*?

"Come on. I'm a friend of Zak Young."

"I don't care if you're a friend of the Pope. You don't belong here and I'm sure what you were doing was not exactly legal."

He grabbed the receiver off the wall and dialed. "Hey, Jerome, it's Frank up on ten. I have a trespasser." Pause. "Yep, I'll keep her 'til the cops get here."

Frank sat me on a chair in the reception area and sat across from me. I could've made a run for it, but no way I'd make it past. He was spry for a man his age.

It didn't take long for the police to get there. Apparently NYPD didn't have many other pressing affairs to tend to. They asked Frank what had happened and while one officer stayed with me, he took the other to the "scene of the crime." The officer came back carrying my purse.

"It doesn't look like she's taken anything."

"Let's read her her rights and get her in the squad car."

The babysitting officer grabbed my arm and yanked me up, then took the other and put my hands behind my back.

"No, wait. You can't be serious. He said I didn't take anything."

"Alexandra Marshall, you have the right to remain silent."

The cold steel of the cuffs clamped around my wrists. *Click. Click. Click.* That fucking hurt. Oh. My. God. This was actually happening.

"Anything you say can and will be used against you in a court of law."

"But…" Tears formed in my eyes. "I didn't do anything bad."

He led me to the elevator. "You have the right to speak an attorney. If you cannot afford an attorney, one will be provided for you."

The door opened in front of us. "Wait, my Jimmy Choos are in the office."

They turned to each other in confusion.

"My shoes."

The other officer rolled his eyes, then trotted back to fetch them.

"Do you understand these rights as they have been read to you?"

I turned to meet the officer's eyes and nodded my head.

Chapter 17

A light rain fell over the city as we walked to the waiting police cruiser, neon lights reflecting in every single drop. After ducking my head and sitting into the back seat, I turned toward the officer as he shut the door. A woman stood behind him. The raindrops on my window distorted the image, but I knew who she was.

Karma.

She stared at me, arms crossed over her busty chest, shaking her head in disgust.

"Yeah, yeah. I know," I muttered under my breath and tossed my head back. I closed my eyes, an attempt at sealing off my tears. No such luck.

* * * *

Never were puffy eyes and a tear-streaked face a good look on me. Even worse were those attributes behind a mug shot camera. After posing for pictures, they took my fingerprints and I was given the obligatory single phone call.

But who to call? Of everyone I knew, who would judge me the least and keep the whole thing quiet?

Amanda would have been my first choice, but I couldn't expect a twenty-year-old college student to bail me out of jail. And she'd be with Andy anyway.

I'd told Marcus I was going out with Sheila. Maybe I could call her. I dialed the seven digits for her apartment. Surely that's where she'd be at ten o'clock at night. One ring, two rings…after five rings her answering machine picked up. Where the hell was she?

I hung up. Fuck. What now?

I turned to the officer who was guarding me and observing my call-making. "Um, I know I'm only supposed to get one call, but no one answered."

"One more," she answered through a yawn.

Think. Who else would bail my ass out if jail? Three men popped into my head. But only one of them would keep it on the down low.

"Hello?" Rich answered his cell after a few rings, hesitant about the unfamiliar caller ID.

"Hey, it's me."

"Oh, hi. Where are you calling from?"

"Um, well, that's just it. I'm, um, in jail."

"What?"

"Please don't alarm Marcus or Kevin. I don't want them to know."

"They're in the nursery with Preston. Lexi, what the hell did you do?"

"I'll explain when you get here."

With the click of the line, he was gone. But I didn't want to hang up. Could I pretend to keep talking? I didn't want to go where I was going next. I turned and saw impatience in the officer's eyes.

"Um, okay. I'll see you in a bit," I said to no one. "I love you. Bye." Reluctantly, I placed the receiver back in its spot.

"Anyone else you need to call for a chat?" She took me by the arm and led me down a hall to a row of cells. Luck, or maybe Karma, was on my side and there was an empty one. I stepped in and before I'd even made it two steps, the steel gate slammed shut behind me and I jumped.

A low grumbling snicker erupted in the cell across the way. "First timer, huh?"

I didn't bother answering as I took in my *accommodations*. My feet stuck to the floor as I stepped toward a cot. Its inch-thick mattress was stained in several spots--blood maybe? Or something else. I didn't care to know. My other seating option was a metal toilet that had probably only been clean the day it was installed. Maybe I'd just stand.

"What a pretty little thing you are."

I leaned against the side wall and kept my gaze forward, the cracks in the plaster giving me plenty to focus on.

"I gave you a compliment, bitch. Look at me."

The tears came back and trickled down my cheeks. How did I get here? Yes, I'd broken into Zak's office and searched through his secretary's computer. I knew why I had gotten arrested. But why had I let it go this far? I didn't want Zak to be Preston's father, so why did I need to know? I made a vow, right then and there, to stop my quest. Zak would never know. Marcus would never know. We would all go on with our lives the way we were supposed to.

"Turn so I can see your ass. No, let me get a better look at those titties."

I tried to ignore him, instead envisioning my baby's face. Soon this would all be a distant memory.

"Guess I'll have to let my imagination wander."

A low moan. And then another. I turned my head, just enough to see the cell across from me out of the corner of my eye. My nightmare had been confirmed. The guy was staring at me and whacking off.

Could this get any worse?

Wait. The last time I'd asked that, a ton of misery poured down on me. *Oh Karma, please don't.*

"Baby, come on. Talk to me."

Anger, frustration, misery and despair, all those emotions flowed through my veins, willing Rich to get there fast.

"Wish you'd wrap those sexy legs around me."

Oh, God. I could hear him stroking himself. Why did I wear such a short dress? Next time I did something that could potentially get me arrested, I'd remember to wear less provocative clothing.

"You got someone at home who gets to taste that fine pussy?"

"Fuck you."

"Gladly." His moans bellowed throughout the cellblock and I tried my best not to think about the crack-head getting off to the mental imagine of me naked.

He panted as he spoke. "Was it as good for you as it was for me?"

Heavy footsteps interrupted his labored breaths.

"Murphy, put your dick away," an officer demanded, my knight in blue armor.

"Mmm-mmn. With such a hot piece of ass right in front of me, I'll be jerking off all night long."

My door opened. "Take a mental picture, 'cause she's leaving."

I stepped into the hallway--the guy across only a couple feet away. He stared me up and down, like he was absorbing as much of me as he could. Eww.

The officer took me by the arm and as soon as we turned into the main area of the police station, I saw Rich and ran to him. He folded me into his arms and held me tight. I burst into tears on his shoulder--an eruption of emotion.

"Are you okay? Are you hurt? They wouldn't tell me anything."

"I'm fine, now."

I pulled away, and behind him stood Zak. I hadn't even noticed him. We locked eyes and I couldn't tell what he was thinking.

"This is your fiance?"

"Um, yes."

Rich turned to face the voice. "Do you know each other?"

"Yes, I'm the one whose office she broke into." He held his hand out to Rich. "Zak Young."

"Rich Taylor."

Rich knew who Zak was. And probably had a million questions as to why I'd broken into his office.

"Okay, now that everybody is acquainted…" The officer turned to Zak. "Are you pressing charges?"

"Can we have a minute?"

"Sure. Take all the time you need."

Was sarcasm a prerequisite to becoming a New York City police officer? When he stepped away to his desk, I sat on a wooden bench with Zak and Rich standing above me.

"Lexi, why were you in my office? I know you were there this afternoon, talking to Ruth. Why did you come back?"

"I'm interested in the answer, too," Rich added.

I felt like a little girl being reprimanded for having a hand in the cookie jar. "It wasn't what it looked like. I was just, um, searching for something."

"What could you possibly have needed from my office?"

"I, uh, I…" Think fast, Lexi. "Remember that picture of me you had in your office? I wanted it."

"First of all, why would you think it was still there? And second, why didn't you ask me?"

"I thought it would be weird."

He shifted his weight and sighed. "I know that's not even close to the truth, but I have a wife and a newborn I need to get home to." He turned away.

I stood and caught him by the arm. "Zak, I'm sorry. Please believe that."

"It's fine. After everything I put you through last year, I think we're finally even." He turned and walked away, stopping at the officer's desk on his way out.

Rich and I sat back on the bench in silence. After a few minutes, the officer came to us. "You're in luck. All charges were dropped."

"Oh, thank God." I jumped and clapped my hands together. I turned to Rich, expecting to see a smile, but there wasn't even the hint of one.

He gave the officer a polite "thank you" and after we'd retrieved my belongings, we headed out of the precinct. We were three blocks down before he uttered a single word to me.

"I know you were lying to Zak." He stopped and turned to me, a storefront's light illuminating his face. "But you sure as hell will tell me the truth--all of it."

Rich had never been so stern, so forceful. Was it wrong that his intensity totally turned me on?

Chapter 18

Marcus and Kevin were already in bed when Rich and I got home. My thanks to Karma for helping on that one. Rich hadn't told them where he was going when he left. This whole debacle could be forgotten.

Rich followed me to the bedroom and I shed my clothes like I was getting an afternoon quickie.

"Yuck!" I would have thrown them in the trash, but the dress was new. I turned to Rich, my full nakedness on display. "I'm taking a shower. Wanna join me?"

"Nope."

Geez. Was he back to withholding sex again?

"I'm not gonna let you distract me or make me forget the conversation we need to have. I'll be right here when you finish."

A shiver radiated through my body. "Okay."

I started the water and stepped into its warmth. Might be the only warmth I got all night. Rich's tone had been quite frigid. Downright pissed, actually. I should be pissed that he was pissed, but his anger was justified. A thirty-three-year-old, soon-to-be married mother had no reason to get herself arrested. I shouldn't have let it go so far. I just wanted to forget. Pretend it had never happened.

Too little, too late.

Thinking of what was about to go down, my body filled with dread. I toweled off, slipped on a terry bathrobe, and stepped to the sink to floss and brush my teeth. After some close inspection in the mirror, I took out my tweezers and plucked a few stray eyebrow hairs. I applied my nighttime moisturizer and eye cream, then pulled out my favorite Passion Fruit Lime Body Butter and lubed myself head to toe. Hmm. Chipped toenail polish… Even though I desperately needed a paint job, I had dilly-dallied enough. No more stalling.

I walked back to the room and faked a yawn. "I'm exhausted."

"You're not getting out of this." Rich looked up from his issue of *Rolling Stone* and set it aside. "Start talking."

I disrobed, opting out of pajamas. Maybe my bare nipples would act as a distraction.

Using my sweetest voice I said, "What do you want me to say?"

He released an exasperated sigh and tossed his head back. "Lexi, come on. Don't fuck around with me. Tell me what happened tonight. All of it."

"Well, I was at dinner with Sheila and we got to talking about old times and all that. I described this hot picture Zak had of me. After a few drinks, I got this crazy idea to go and get it."

He just stared at me. "Try again."

"What?"

"That's the lie you told Zak. I want the real story."

"It is the real story." I hated lying to him, really, I did. This whole thing was almost over and done with. Why couldn't he let it go? I moved closer and pressed my body to his.

"Lexi, I love you. Nothing is gonna change that. Whatever this is, it must be pretty bad, or you wouldn't be trying so hard to keep it quiet. Come on. Let me help you."

I didn't want to, but I had to tell him. He'd understand, right? And he'd help me keep it a secret forever.

"Okay, I give up." I flopped back on my pillow. Where to start? I sucked in a breath, held it, then let it out. "I think Zak might be Preston's father."

"Huh?"

"You know the whole story of how I got pregnant--no need to rehash it. Well, I ran into Zak a while ago. He was with his new wife--a very pregnant wife."

"And? What's weird about that?"

"Zak had a vasectomy, remember?"

"Oh, yeah. He could have had a reversal done."

"Possibly. But the timeline doesn't jive. If the procedure had even worked, and it's not even all that successful, it's months before he's shooting baby-making semen."

"Sounds like you've done your research."

"I have. The only explanation is the vasectomy reversed itself naturally."

"You're joking."

"I read about it. There's a percentage of vasectomies that grow back together all on their own. And if that happened, Zak could be Preston's dad. I never had a DNA test done."

Rich shook his head. "Lexi, this is a lot of speculation. Maybe it's your writer's imagination working overtime."

"I'd love for that to be the case, trust me. But don't you remember? Preston was born almost a whole month before my due date. I could've gotten pregnant a month before the one-night-stand with Marcus. And I've started noticing things. Preston doesn't look anything like Marcus. His laugh the other day sounded just like Zak's. And sometimes, he tilts his head like Zak does when he's concentrating on something."

"A head tilt. Seriously? Those are hardly reasons to question a kid's paternity."

"No, but you're right about the questioning part. I'm done with it. All of it."

"What do you mean?"

"Tonight was a wake-up call. I'm done playing detective. I've decided to let it all go."

"You're not going to tell Marcus or Zak?"

"Nope. I want to go on with my life like none of this happened."

"But what if you're right?"

"So what if I am?"

"Lexi, you can't deny a man his own child. Or keep on pretending someone else is the father."

"Why not? I don't want Zak to be Preston's father. I want Marcus. And it's in my power to make that stay the truth. No one ever has to know."

"I know."

"Only 'cause you forced me to tell you. See, if you woulda just let it go, everything would have been solved."

"No it wouldn't." He ran his hands through his hair. "You know what you need to do, don't you?"

"Yep." I crawled on top of him and began circling one of his metal-clad nipples with my tongue.

"No." He pulled my face upward, making me meet his eyes. "You're gonna tell Marcus."

I sat up, straddling him, and shook my head so hard my brain hurt. A familiar sting pierced my eyes. "I can't."

"Yes, you can."

"It would crush him. That's why I never said anything before. I wanted to handle the problem on my own. And I have."

"Lexi, you didn't *handle* anything. You made it worse."

Yanking Zak from his family to go to the police station was not part of the plan. And neither was this conversation. "No, it's fine. Everything is how it should be."

Rich eyes softened. "You have to tell him."

"No, I won't do it."

His face was still, his voice calm. "Then I will."

"Don't be an asshole," I begged.

"I'm not. You know it needs to be done."

I covered my face with my hands and surrendered the battle with my tear ducts.

Rich pulled me to him and rubbed my back.

"How can I take his son away from him?" I sobbed on his chest.

"It might not even come to that."

"But the sadness in Marcus's eyes when I tell him he might not be Preston's father. That's what's kept me motivated to figure it all out on my own."

He squeezed me tight again. "We'll do this together, okay? I won't let you go it alone anymore."

Rich wiped my tears and captured my lips with his. And together we made love, slowly, sensually. He reminded me why I never needed to feel like I had to do anything alone again.

* * * *

Before falling asleep, I'd promised Rich we'd sit down with Marcus the next night after dinner. As he drifted off to dreamland, I was stuck tossing and turning all night, wondering what to say. How could I tell Marcus the boy he'd loved for over a year might not be his son after all?

My miserable night turned into a miserable day. I tried to start a new story, but felt zero creative inspiration. No point in staring at a blank screen. Amanda's surprise party was in a few weeks and shopping always helped cure my bad mood, even shopping for someone else. Well, there was no rule saying I couldn't shop for my friend and myself at the same time.

After a much needed caffeine fix, I browsed a few boutiques. Nothing jumped out and said *Buy Me!* This was a pretty special event. I recalled my twenty-first birthday. No surprise parties, but the night had still included some unexpected things. Marcus had already turned twenty-one, a few weeks before, and had taken me to an outrageously expensive restaurant in Manhattan. He'd still been in law school, but somehow managed it. We drank three bottles of champagne and had been politely asked to leave.

He'd left a real nice tip, then taken me to a few clubs. I danced with him, high on life, and maybe some other things, too. One slow song had us dancing so close I could feel his warm, peppermint-scented breath on my forehead. I'd looked at him, the hunger in his eyes like he'd wanted to devour me. That was the moment I'd known his feelings for me. And so badly I'd wanted to have them back. He was the perfect guy.

Still was, and ready to start his happily ever after with the man of his dreams. Here's hoping I didn't crush his soul.

Shaking off the looming doom, I walked on thinking of something to get Amanda, and passed a new lingerie shop. Might as well check it out. And maybe I'd find an outfit for my wedding night.

The tiny storefront was deceiving. Quite the selection they had. And all divided by fetish. A sweet section, a crotchless section, an edible section, and a whips and chains leather section. I passed them all and headed toward a gleaming white section. There were all kinds of bridal getups, from fully-covering satin negligees to see-through lacy bras with heart-shaped nipple cut-outs. What would Rich want to see me in on our wedding night? We'd had some kinky nights and also more simplistic and sensual encounters. But what about the most special sex night of our life?

As I pondered that thought, I spotted bride and groom thongs on the other side of the room. Upon closer inspection, I realized the bride thong had quite a pocket on it. His and his thongs. How cute. The entire wall was dedicated to gay couples, with all kinds of fun items. And I just had to get the bride and groom thongs for Marcus and Kevin.

I headed toward the register and on the way bumped the arm of someone in the red lace section. "Oh, I'm sorry." I turned as I gave my apology, immediately recognizing the woman holding a very racy red teddy.

"What are you doing here?" Sheila growled at me.

I contained my laughter. "I think I should be asking you that question."

Her gaze fell to the tiny outfit in her hands and she hugged it to her chest, trying to cover it with her arms. "Nothing. It's nothing." If there had been a giant hole nearby, she probably would have dove in head first.

"Yeah, that pretty much describes the nightie you're holding. There's isn't much there."

Her eyes narrowed at me and her mouth opened.

"Can I help you ladies with anything?" a chipper saleswoman asked.

"No," Sheila barked, not turning her attention from me.

"Oh, um, would you like me to hold that at the register for you?"

Sheila looked to the girl, then to the crumpled red lace in her hands, then to me. She handed the outfit to the girl. "Yes."

I waited until the girl was out of earshot before making a peep.

"So..."

"Shut it!"

My eyes teared as I pressed my lips tight to hold in my laughter and nodded. "Mmm-hmm."

"I met someone, okay? We've been dating for a month and tonight we're going to have sex. Happy now?"

"Yes." I held my hand to my mouth, giggles almost escaping.

"It's been a while. I'm nervous as hell and you laughing at me isn't helping."

I swallowed my laughter, pitying the poor middle-aged woman in the midst of a nervous break-down. "Is there something I can do?"

"Unless you can give me blow job pointers, no." Her eyes met mine. "What am I saying? Of course you can give me blow job pointers. You fuck so much your twat is probably in a constant state of raw. God, look at me. I'm shaking!"

"Okay. Let's get out of here. You need some wine or something."

"Double vodka."

"Or that."

Sheila and I paid for our purchases and grabbed a late lunch. Never in my wildest dreams would I have predicted we'd be discussing sexual positions and how to avoid gagging on cock.

Chapter 19

I'd needed the lunch with Sheila almost as much as she had. It relaxed me and took away the migraine I'd had since waking. It would be nice if the feeling lasted and helped me though the rest of my day and evening.

We ordered dinner in, but I couldn't enjoy the Pad Thai. My stomach churned with what I was going to do when we were done eating. After pushing food around my plate, I picked up a tiny piece of shrimp and stuck it in my mouth. Everyone else had already finished their food.

"You gonna eat that or play with it all night?" Marcus asked, a lame attempt at comedy. His goofy smile was going to make this all so hard.

"Oh, yeah, I guess I'm done."

"You hardly ate anything. It's your favorite--are you okay?"

Rich's frown reminded me I wasn't alone and he felt my pain.

I turned back to Marcus. "Yeah, I guess my stomach has been bothering me a bit today."

Marcus took my plate, scraped its contents into a plastic bowl, and pressed the lid in place. After stacking the leftovers in the fridge, he washed his hands and started toward the living room, where Kevin had taken Preston to play. These days, his table time was very limited. He ate, or didn't, and then began throwing his food across the table. We'd found it best to remove him after the first handful was tossed.

"Um, wait," I said after Rich's urging. "Can we talk?"

"Sure."

He crossed back to the table and my heart began beating so fast under my skin I thought for sure it would bust through my ribcage and splat on the table in front of me. Oh God. This was it.

"Um, well, I have something I need to tell you." I looked at Rich, but my vision had already blurred.

His nod told me to go on. He'd be there to help pick up all the pieces.

Marcus stood behind the dining room chair with his hands rested on top. "What? Some other wedding disaster? It's okay. Whatever it is, we'll deal with it."

He was smiling. Fuck. How could I deliberately rip that smile off?

A single tear rolled down my cheek and his expression changed. "Oh. This is something serious. Lex, what is it. Is everyone okay?" He sat down and scooted his chair close to me.

"I…Oh my God." I turned back to Rich again as tears streamed from my eye sockets. This was so much harder than I'd ever imagined. "I can't do this. Please. Don't make me do this."

"What's going on? Tell me now. Someone…"

"We've discovered something," Rich said, rescuing me from my hysterical outburst. I sat there dabbing my water-logged eyes and runny nose as Rich explained what I'd found out.

Marcus stared as Rich relayed the entire story. His eyes stayed straight, his lips a solemn line. Had he blinked the entire ten minutes Rich talked? When it was all through, he sat quiet. And that terrified me the most.

Instead of turning into lawyer Marcus who asked a million and one questions, he simply stood and walked out. He strode past Kevin and Preston on the living room floor, amid dozens of block towers, and out the front door.

"You have to go after him," I said to Rich.

"No. He needs time to process it all."

* * * *

Hours passed before Marcus came home. I'd wanted to wait up, but Kevin had insisted Rich and I go to bed. At first I'd refused. I had to be there when Marcus came in--the questions he'd have, the anger and hurt to express. And I was the one who deserved his rage.

But Kevin had made one convincing argument--apparently Marcus's lawyer-ness had worn off on him. Marcus needed a rock, someone he could cry on and melt into. If I waited and was the one here when he walked though the door, whenever it may be, he'd feel the need to be strong and be my rock--as he'd always been our entire lives. How could Marcus fall apart if the person who was supposed to catch him was already in pieces?

Rich and I went to bed, and like the night before, I lay there wide awake. My mind wandered and worried and kept my eyes open.

Sometime around two, the front door opened and I heard muffled voices and what sounded like sobs. And I couldn't hold my own in. Kevin had been right. No way could I have held it together, and I hated that.

The one moment in our lives Marcus needed support, my own emotions wouldn't suppress themselves long enough to give it.

* * * *

It had been after four by the time my brain allowed my body to sleep. I'd woken when Rich's alarm went off, but stayed in bed. Complete exhaustion rendered me unable to get up and start my day. Seemed like the perfect opportunity to stay in bed and veg the day away.

When I did wake up, and had enough energy to get out of bed, I found Preston and Nicole, the babysitter, in the kitchen having lunch. I kissed my boy on the head and poured a glass of juice.

"How's he doing today?"

"Good. We played some games and he's eaten most of his lunch. Mr. Wells wants to take him to the park when he's done."

"Is Marcus coming home early?"

"No, he's here--took the day off. He's in his bedroom."

"Oh. Thanks." My heartbeat quickened as I walked toward Marcus and Kevin's bedroom. I demanded my eyes stay dry and my voice even and calm. The door was closed all but a crack, so I knocked gently.

"Come in."

Marcus sat at the corner desk on his computer when I walked up behind him and wrapped my arms around him tight. He stopped typing and moved his strong hands to my arms.

After a deep breath and exhaling, he asked, "Why didn't you come to me the second you got the idea?"

"I was scared out of my mind. And I thought I could find the answers I needed without involving you. Why upset you if I didn't have to?"

He nodded his head. "I did a lot of thinking last night. None of it makes any sense and there are dozens of explanations. But I don't care about any of them. Preston is my son--I know it. I don't need a test to tell me that."

This was not the reaction I had expected. "You don't want to have a DNA test done?"

"No." He turned to me in his compact swivel chair. "He's my son. End of discussion."

Wow. Marcus wanted to do exactly what I'd decided in that grimy holding cell--forget it and go on with our lives. This was working so much better than I'd thought.

"Let me finish this email and we can take our son to the park." Marcus smiled, though his eyes didn't sparkle like they usually did.

* * * *

The next week and a half were a tsunami of wedding preparations, whether I wanted to participate or not. They'd dragged me to dress fittings that weren't even for me, shower outfit shopping, and even a day of arts and crafts. We couldn't order special soaps--oh no. Mom insisted on making cinnamon, pumpkin, and apple-scented soaps for the bridal shower favors. My job, one requiring the least amount of crafting talent, was placing the soaps in organza bags and attaching the preprinted *Thank You* tags.

But there was one wedding planning event I didn't mind too much. Mom had insisted on a cake tasting with both brides and grooms present. Apparently we had to decide which flavor of cake we wanted smashed on our faces.

And since we were all together, she dragged us to the rental shop to choose linens, chair covers, and other miscellaneous items we just *had* to have.

"Is this really necessary?" I asked, interrupting a debate between Mom, Kevin, and his mom about satin, damask, lamour, imperial stripe, and classic finish napkins. Their blank stares told me it was very necessary. They all looked like plain old napkins to me, but whatever.

After the tough decision had been made, we were on our way to sustenance. Amazing how hungry these life or death decisions made me.

"I still don't see why we have to eat here today," I said as we walked into Marco's Ristorante, where the bridal shower would be held in a few weeks.

Mom, Kevin, and Kevin's mom shared another of several giggles for the day. "Alexandra, we'll be feeding almost one-hundred and fifty guests at the shower. We need to make sure the lunch selections are satisfactory."

"So, we'll be eating the same food today that we'll be eating at the shower?"

"Yes."

"Wouldn't it be nice to be surprised?"

Another shared giggle between the The Three Wedding Musketeers. "Don't be silly."

I looked at Marcus and Rich, and the three of us shrugged.

After the wine punch samples had been poured, my mother opened her folder and handed out sheets of paper to each person at the table.

"Kevin and I have been hard at work on these itineraries, but we need your input as well. Please read them over and email us as soon as you can. We need to make sure they are correct."

I scanned mine.

Three weeks before wedding: Final dress fitting. Write and mail shower thank you cards. Purchase and size wedding rings, if haven't done so already. Purchase bridesmaids' gifts.

Two weeks before wedding: Pick up travel documents. Makeup and hair trial. Start breaking in wedding shoes. Turn in your list of reception song requests. Meet with photographer and make a list of must-have photos.

One week before wedding: Finalize honeymoon plans. Pack for honeymoon. Pack a separate bag for the wedding weekend. Pack Preston's bags for his stay at Grandma and Grandpa's house. Take Preston for his final tuxedo fitting. Check over seating arrangements.

Five days before wedding: Purchase toiletries for honeymoon and wedding weekend. Confirm rehearsal dinner plans. Confirm transportation to the inn. Confirm transportation to the airport for honeymoon departure. Confirm bridesmaids' and groomsmen's travel plans.

Three days before wedding: Pick up wedding dress. Get a facial. Purchase traveler's checks.

Two days before wedding: Arrive at The Inn at Harbor Hill by three o'clock. Settle into rooms. Welcome dinner at six o'clock.

> *Day before wedding:*
> *Nine AM: Breakfast*
> *Eleven AM: Massage*
> *One PM: Lunch with bridesmaids*
> *Three PM: Manicure and pedicure*
> *Six PM: Rehearsal*
> *Seven PM: Rehearsal dinner*
> *Wedding day:*
> *Nine AM: Breakfast*
> *Ten AM: Hair appointment*
> *Eleven AM: Makeup application*
> *Twelve PM: Get dressed*
> *One PM: Pre-wedding photos with bridesmaids*
> *Two PM: Begin procession.*

I blinked a few times. Geez. Only planned down to the hour on the day of the wedding? They weren't listed, but I assumed pee breaks were already figured in. I took Rich's list and saw a brief moment of shock in my mother's eyes when I folded ours together and casually shoved them into my purse.

"Well, then." She reached back into her folder. "We'll be mailing the invitations in a few days. Here is one, if anyone is interested in seeing it."

Mr. and Mrs. Robert Marshall
and
Mr. and Mrs. Jonathan Jacobs
invite you to share in the joy
as their children are joined in matrimony
Alexandra Elyce Marshall
to
Richard Michael Taylor
and
Kevin Jonathan Jacobs
to
Marcus Langley Wells
Please join us for a double ceremony
on Saturday the seventh of October
two o'clock in the afternoon
The Inn at Harbor Hill
37125 Harbor Hill Road
New Paltz, New York

I read the cream-colored invitation, rubbing my fingers over its chocolate brown embossed lettering, and a tingle traveled from my chest to my toes. This was actually going to happen. I was marrying Rich. Our names were printed on this simple piece of five-by-seven card stock, and its significance hit me.

I'm gonna be a bride!

Admiring the faces around the table, I couldn't imagine sharing this grand event with anyone else in the world. It was going to be fabulous and memorable and the perfect start to our happily-ever-afters.

And a bonus in all the hooplah, it seemed as if Marcus and everyone involved had forgotten the baby daddy drama. I couldn't have been more excited. Sappy as it was, the wedding really would be the start of the rest of our lives.

Chapter 20

Marcus knocked on my bedroom door while I worked on the second round of copy edits Sheila had emailed me the week before. It was the first chance I'd gotten to work on them.

"Got a minute?"

"Sure." I saved my file and turned to him.

"My mom called the other day. I never took Preston to my parents', as you know. But she still wants to meet her grandson."

I'd hoped this subject was dead and buried. Apparently not. "If that's what you want, there's nothing I can say about it."

"She's coming to the shower, you know."

I noticed the momentary smile. He'd never gotten over his parents' abandonment when he'd come out of the closet. If she'd agreed to come to the shower, maybe they were finally accepting his new life.

"They'll be in the city for the weekend and asked if we could get together for dinner on Friday--all of us."

"Like me and Rich, too?"

He nodded.

"Uh, I don't think so. You can do whatever you want--have a relationship with them, let them meet Preston--but that does not mean I have to tolerate their ignorance."

"Lex, I think they're coming around. They want to be a part of Kevin's and my life. And you are part of that too."

"They've been awful to you for the last year and a half. I can't just forget that."

"I love that you've supported me, but they're my parents and if I am choosing to let the past be the past, then so should you."

He had a point.

"Okay, fine, but one snide remark and I'm gone."

Marcus left the room and I got back to work, but barely a minute later, my cellphone rang.

I didn't recognize the number. "Hello?"

"Lexi, it's me, Andy."

"Oh, um, hi." I could count on one finger the number of times my brother had called me on the phone. "What's up?"

"Well, Amanda's surprise party is tonight."

"Yeah. I know. We'll all be there."

"I know, but, um…"

Was Andy nervous?

"She's here…at the restaurant. I can't get rid if her. And we need to get the place ready for the party."

"What do you want me to do?"

"I don't know. Call her and make something up. Please? I really want it to be a surprise."

Aside from an isolated incident in the sixth grade when Andy desperately wanted Krissy Patterson's phone number, he'd never begged me for anything in his life.

"Okay. I'll think of something."

He gave a relieved "Thanks," and the phone clicked off. Wow, gratitude too?

I searched for Amanda's cell number in my contact list and pressed *Send*.

"Hey, Lexi," she answered in two rings.

"Hi, I um, I need your help. Like, now."

"For what?"

"I, well, I…" Shit. I was not the best at thinking quick. It might have been a good idea to think this through before dialing her number. "I need to go shopping for my, ya know, trousseau."

"Today?"

"Yeah. If I don't go today, who knows when I'll be able to do it." I was such a bad liar. She'd never fall for it.

"I have plans to help Andy at the restaurant later tonight, after the dinner rush. We're gonna paint the new banquet room."

"But as my bridesmaid, it's your duty to help me with any and all pre-wedding errands." That was good--playing the bridesmaid card. It had to work. "And I'll make sure you're back by a decent time."

She sighed. "Let me go find Andy. I'm at the restaurant with him now. I don't want to leave in case he needs me."

After explaining my made-up situation to him, she asked if he minded that she take off. He replied, "Of course not, baby. Go have fun." Then the smack of a peck kiss.

Aww. I never knew my brother could be so sweet.

Amanda turned her attention back to me. "Okay, I'll be at your place in like an hour."

So much for getting my work done. Since I was still in my pajamas, at one o'clock in the afternoon, I shut down my computer and hopped in the shower. I dressed and beautified and was all ready when Amanda knocked on the door.

Once we were on the sidewalk, the humidity so thick my hair instantly started to frizz, Amanda asked, "What exactly do you buy for a trousseau?"

"Um, I don't know. Like lingerie and stuff. Clothes to wear on my honeymoon."

She raised an eyebrow. She was so onto me.

But she just shrugged her shoulders. "Cool."

I did need to get some things for our trip, so it wasn't a complete lie. And seriously, who'd want to be seen in old clothes on their honeymoon? I'd need at least five or six new bathing suits too, since Rich and I would be spending an insane amount of time on the beach in Oahu.

First stop, a lingerie store. Within a half hour's time, I had an armload of see-through outfits to try on and Amanda had grabbed a few things, too. We headed toward the dressing room. I shimmied into the first item and checked my rear in the mirror. Unfortunately, I was still holding some pregnancy weight in my ass. I frowned and grabbed a nightie with a little more fabric in the back.

Knock. Knock. "Lexi?"

"Yeah?"

"Can I come in?"

"Um…sure," I said and let her in. I didn't care if Amanda saw me in lingerie, but the tiny room was awkward and the outfit I had on at that moment was nipple-less.

"What do you think of this?" She wore a black lace babydoll.

"It's cute."

"Do you think Andy will like it?"

"I don't know what gets my brother all horny. He's a man, anything will turn him on." I laughed, but when I caught her expression, she wasn't even smiling. In fact, she looked like she wanted to cry. "What's wrong?"

"I don't know. Andy's been weird lately. He's been getting a lot of calls on his cell and he tells me they're nothing. He's been, I don't know…

distracted, I guess. Do you think he's cheating on me?" Her eyes filled with tears.

"Oh, God. No." Forgetting we were both in skimpy outfits, I pulled her to me. Her scratchy lace brushed across my bare nipples and I caught our reflection in the mirror--we totally looked like a girl-on-girl porn flick.

I gave her a tissue from my purse.

"Everything was fine 'til a couple weeks ago. He just seems so...*off*. Like his body is there, but his mind's not. Could he be thinking of another girl?"

"I might not know my brother well, but I know what I see when he's with you. He loves you." I knew where his mind was, but I couldn't exactly tell Amanda. "Give it some time. He's real busy at work, right?"

"Yeah, I guess. He's trying to get the banquet room ready so they can start booking parties."

"See. That's all it is."

"You're probably right. Thanks, Lexi." She hugged me again.

"Okay, enough of this hugging. You're rubbing my nipples raw with that lace you're wearing."

She laughed and stepped back.

"You should definitely buy that. And wear it tonight."

"I will," she answered and went back to her own dressing room.

* * * *

Amanda and I were walking back toward my apartment building when my text message alert sounded.

> *need u to hold A off bring to restrant at 8text me wen yur almost here*

I could only assume my brother had sent this grammatical train wreck of a text.

Amanda pulled me into a hug when we reached my building. "I'll see ya later."

"Wait, don't you want to come up for a while? We can order in."

"I need to get back to the restaurant and help Andy. He told me the dinner rush should be done around eight."

I checked the time on my phone. "But it's only six."

"I know, but I'll go early and see if the wait staff needs any help."

"Amanda, I hardly ever see you. I miss us hanging out." A guilt trip was sure to work. "Come on, please?"

She pulled out her phone and checked it, and apparently she didn't have any messages. "Okay, but I only have like an hour."

"Great."

We went upstairs and I right away pulled Marcus and Rich into the bedroom and explained the situation. They were getting ready to leave for the party and had been wondering where the hell I was. After they ducked out, Amanda and I were alone.

"Wanna order something?" I asked.

"No. I'm not hungry."

"Glass of wine?"

"Thought you'd never offer." She smiled somewhat.

We took seats in the living room with our glasses. Amanda still looked upset, probably obsessing about Andy cheating on her. I knew he wasn't. He was busy with party preparations. In a few hours it would all be fixed. I just had to wait it out with her.

After five minutes of silence and with most of her wine gone, she spoke. "Do you know, my birthday's next week and Andy hasn't even mentioned doing anything. Not even once. And it's kind of a big birthday."

Oh, Andy. This was Surprise Party 101. He still needed to make plans for the actual birthday to throw the honoree off the scent of the surprise. Or in this case, to make sure she didn't think he was cheating on her.

"I'm sure he'll do something on the actual day."

"You're probably right." She downed the rest of her wine and held the glass out for more.

Amanda continued to check the time every other minute. If I didn't do something, she was going to leave.

"Oh, I have to show you the latest pictures of Preston." I grabbed my digital camera and began scrolling through his latest photo shoot-- amazing how fast a four gig memory card can fill up.

When we'd circled back to the first picture, she stood. "Okay, I gotta go."

"Already?" I looked at the clock. Only 6:42. "I still have pictures on my phone to show you."

"If I wanna get to the restaurant before eight, I have to leave now. Andy should be ready to paint when I get there. We'll do it another time, 'kay?"

"Um, okay."

She hugged me, gathered her things, and headed toward the door.

"Wait, I'm coming with you."

"What?"

I had to get to the party somehow. "Yeah. I want to see the place. Give me a minute to change."

She glanced at the time. "But--"

"I'll be quick. Promise."

"Okay." Her tone was hesitant, but she nodded anyway.

I took my sweet ole time fixing my makeup and applying the new eye shadow I'd bought. Had to hold her off ten more minutes to ensure we'd get to the restaurant after eight. Lucky for Amanda, I was having a good hair day, or she'd be real late to her party, or rather, her *painting date* with Andy.

After slipping into the outfit I'd pre-chosen for the party, I checked the time. 7:07. That should be good.

"Geez, took ya long enough." Amanda observed my pencil skirt and satin ruffled halter. "Why are you all dressed up?"

Shit. Explanation, fast.

"Oh, I, uh, got a call from Rich. He's picking me up at the restaurant and we're going out tonight."

Crap. She'd never believe me. I'd blown my cover and the whole thing was done. The surprise ruined.

"Okay. Can we go now?"

I followed her to where she'd parked Andy's car, and instead of finding the eighty-nine Chevy Beretta he'd been driving since high school, Amanda clicked a button and the lights of a sleek black SUV flashed. Hmmm. Things really were going good for my brother.

Amanda drove and was mostly silent. Her eyes were on the road, but I'm sure the visions on her mind were of infidelity. Remembering what it was like to be her age and insecure, I tried to keep the conversation going, and her mind occupied, but I wanted to scream, "He's not cheating on you. He's throwing you a party" just so I could wipe away her miserable expression.

She'd know soon enough and feel stupid for ever thinking such thoughts.

Amanda slowed the truck onto the off-ramp. Five minutes until arrival time. I sent Andy a quick text.

just pulled off the thruway

good wer ready

I sighed.

"Everything okay?" Amanda asked.

"Yes it is."

We pulled into the parking lot. A few cars, but none I recognized. The place really had changed since I'd last been there. The expansion had taken over the old parking lot next door and the new lot was behind the building, paved over what used to be an abandoned house. The ancient neon sign had been replaced with a new one: *Zuppo's Italian Restaurant and Catering.*

I followed Amanda to the banquet entrance--the windows along the outer wall were dark, as expected. Amanda didn't seem to notice. She opened the door and stepped into darkness. The only light in the room came from an illuminated *Exit* sign.

"Andy must still be busy in the restaurant." She fidgeted and finally found the light switch near the doorway.

"*Surprise!*"

Amanda jumped a few feet and clung to me, shaking. Cheers, clapping, and laughter erupted around us. She took in the pink and white balloons and *Happy 21st Birthday* banner, and her terrified expression changed to shock, and then softened to amusement.

Andy stepped forward and pulled her to him. Both their eyes brimmed. "Happy Birthday, baby," he said before kissing her.

"I can't believe you did this," she said, the standard surprisee's first words. "Even my parents are here."

Amanda turned to me. "Oh, you're good. I had no clue."

Once again surveying my party attire and remembering my prepping, she realized she was in skinny jeans and a ribbed tank. "Oh my God! I look horrible."

"No. No, you don't." Andy offered immediately. "But I figured you might feel that way. My mom has some stuff in the back for you."

After greeting throngs of guests, Amanda finally made it to the bathroom and emerged in a royal blue strapless sheath, makeup done, hair let down from her pony tail and fluffed. She glowed as she mingled around the room--her family, school friends, my family, all in attendance.

And when one of Andy's waiters wheeled in a three-tier pink and white confection with a glittering *21* on top, the entire room broke into song. Andy wrapped his arm around Amanda's waist and kissed her cheek.

"Make a wish," he said.

She closed her eyes tight and as she blew out the twenty-one blazing candles, Andy dropped to one knee. The crowd gasped before Amanda even knew what was going on. She turned and Andy was no longer beside her, but at her feet with a black velvet box.

The room silenced.

"I know we haven't been together long, but it's been long enough to know I love you and want to spend the rest of my life with you." His voice wavered as he continued. "Will you marry me?"

Tears tumbled down Amanda's cheeks, the corners of her lips heaven-bound.

"Yes," she screamed and bent to kiss him, throwing her arms around his neck.

They stood and parted only long enough for Andy to place the sparkly gem on her left ring finger. They were then surrounded by party guests, offering hugs and wishes of congratulations.

When it was my turn to hug the bride-to-be, Amanda said, "I know you don't approve--"

But I interrupted. "I am *so* happy for you. That smile erases every word I've ever said." And I truly meant it.

I turned to Andy. "So, you're getting hitched?"

"Yeah, just takes the right person to change your entire life."

I nodded, knowing exactly what he meant.

"Thanks for all your help today. I owe you. Party never would have turned out so well if you hadn't."

"No problem. As long as Amanda's happy, I'm happy." I lowered my voice while Amanda showed off her ring to Marcus and Kevin. "And if you ever hurt her, brother or not, I'll rip your balls off."

He smiled. "No chance of that. She's everything to me."

Chapter 21

"Have a seat."

Sheila had asked me to stop by her office when I had a chance. I obliged, curious as hell. She wouldn't ask me to come in for something insignificant.

"We're working on the book tour. Having some trouble with funding, but it will be fine." She shuffled some papers around on her desk.

"Is that all?"

"Should there be more?"

Geez, why so defensive? "I…guess not." I hated when she was in a mood. I stood to leave.

"Where are you going?"

"I figured we were done."

"No. I wouldn't ask you to come all the way over here just to tell you that."

"O…kay." I sat back down.

"So, I um…" Her eyes stayed focused on a paper on her desk. "Paul and I, ya know, did it."

Oooh. So she needed some girl talk.

"And?" I asked, eager for her response.

Her eyes met mine over the rim of her glasses and the corner of her lip curled upward. "It was good."

"Yay!" I actually clapped.

"Is this reason for a celebration?"

"Yes. Great sex should always be celebrated. Have you done it again?" I was so horny for details.

"The man is insatiable." Her voice stayed steady, almost annoyed. "There's not a square inch in his apartment that one of our bare asses hasn't touched."

"And this is a good thing, right?"

She fiddled with some more paperwork and answered, her semi-smile returning. "Yes. It is a very good thing."

"I'm happy for you."

"Don't get all sappy on me." She stood and searched through some files in the wall cabinet. "But I wanted to tell you I'll be bringing a date to the wedding."

"And will he be staying in your room with you the entire weekend of festivities?"

"Not that it's any of your business, but yes. We're even staying until Monday so we can enjoy ourselves after all the hoopla has ended."

Sheila put up a tough front, but she had a pretty pink sugary goo center.

"Sounds like a great plan."

* * * *

Eight-thirty in the evening, and Preston was racing around the coffee table as if he were a NASCAR driver on speed. He'd been walking only a short time, but man did he have the running thing down pat. He threw his head back and laughed. Marcus grabbed him and blew raspberries on his stomach, causing him to erupt in hysteria.

"All right, mini Carl Lewis, it's time for bed."

"He had a late nap," Rich said as he cleaned up some of the mess from the toy tsunami. "Might as well let him stay up a while longer."

"Yeah, well, if he stays up, he's going to be a bear to wake in the morning."

"If you put him in his crib now, he'll just scream for an hour. Why not let him stay out here instead and then go to bed peacefully?"

"I don't want to start this cycle. He needs to learn when bedtime is."

"But he's just a little kid."

I took Preston from Marcus. "I'll put him to bed."

Rich followed me to the nursery. "Come on, Lex. You know he's gonna be miserable if you stick him in the crib now."

"Yeah, but Marcus is right. If we let him stay up, he'll want to sleep in tomorrow morning."

"So, you're okay with listening to him scream and cry for the next hour? That won't bother you at all?"

"It will. But what else am I supposed to do?"

"Let him stay up."

I pulled Preston's t-shirt off and replaced it with a pajama shirt. "I can't."

"You're his mother. You can do whatever you want."

"Marcus has read all kinds of parenting books and if he thinks this is best, well, then I believe him."

"What about what I think? I'm Preston's father too."

Shit. I'd hoped we'd never have to have one of these conversations. I finished changing Preston's diaper and pulled up his pajama pants. "I know, but I think he's a little more educated about parenting than you are."

"Says who? Did you forget that I helped raise five babies when I lived at home?"

"Yeah, but that was different."

"How?"

I kissed Preston and placed him in his crib. He stood and stretched his arms to me, whining. I took a deep breath, turned toward the door, and flipped the light switch. The wailing began before I closed the door behind us.

Rich followed me to our bedroom, the screams piercing through six inches of wood and drywall. "Babies are babies and I think I've helped take care of a whole lot more than Marcus has. So what makes him so much more informed than me?"

"He just is."

"That's your answer?"

I sighed, not wanting to give the real answer. Yeah, Rich had helped take care of his sister's babies when he was a teenager, but that was different. Marcus had done his research. He'd asked parenting advice from some of the most well-to-do families in New York. He knew what he was talking about, even if he hadn't raised a bunch of babies in a trailer park.

And though I'd never admit it out loud, in the ranking order of Preston's three fathers, Marcus most definitely held the number one spot.

"I'm sorry," I said as I shuffled off to the bathroom and started the jets, relieved that it blocked out my little boy's cries. If I'd had to hear them one minute longer, I would have run in and taken him in my arms.

* * * *

We met at La Rue, one of Marcus's parents' favorite restaurants. It was super fancy and not what I would have suggested for a child, but it wasn't my call. We arrived before Mr. and Mrs. Wells, and were shown to our table, a quiet spot in the back of the restaurant.

Marcus had changed Preston's outfit at least a half dozen times before leaving the apartment, and had made Kevin change his shirt twice. He'd started with something about my dress, but I silenced him immediately. No way was I dressing to impress his mother.

At the restaurant, Marcus gave everyone their seating arrangement. He would be next to his mother, then Kevin, Preston, me, Rich and ending with Mr. Wells. The waiter came with a basket of sliced baguette and filled the water glasses. With a whimper, Preston reached his arm toward the bread. I took a slice from the basket and handed it to him.

"What are you doing?" Marcus asked. "He can't start eating before my parents get here."

"Marcus, he's one. And he's hungry. I'm gonna give him some food."

He said "okay" but continued to gnaw on his fingers, the way he always did when he was nervous.

Kevin put a hand to his back and rubbed. "It's going to be fine. Just relax."

The hostess appeared, followed by Mr. and Mrs. Wells. Marcus stood and Kevin followed.

"Mother, you look lovely," he said, and kissed her cheek.

He held out his hand. "Father."

I could almost see Marcus's heart thumping wildly in his chest. He pulled Kevin forward. "I'd like you to meet my fiance, Kevin."

"Such a pleasure to finally meet you," Kevin said and shook both their hands.

"Likewise," Mrs. Wells said, managing a small but pleasant smile. She glanced around the rest of the table and her grin widened. "There he is."

She started toward Preston and Marcus took him out of his high chair. He dusted the breadcrumbs from his lips and shirt.

"Well, hello, little one," she said and held her hand out to him. He put his tiny hand in hers, then pointed at her diamond tennis bracelet. "It's pretty, isn't it?"

Mrs. Wells looked from her grandson to her son. "He has your smile."

The waiter reappeared for drink orders and everyone took their seats.

"Lexi, I assume this is your fiance?"

Oops. In all the commotion when they'd arrived, I hadn't introduced Rich. "Yes, I'm sorry. This is Rich, um…Richard. Taylor."

He stood and shook their hands. "Nice to meet you."

All around the table, blank faces--the epitome of awkward. The silence held until the waiter reappeared with our drinks and took our meal orders.

"How are the wedding plans coming along?" Mrs. Wells asked.

"Quite well." Marcus answered. "Kevin has been doing most of the work. It's going to be beautiful."

"Oh." She turned her attention to Kevin. "Tell me about it."

Marcus's shoulders relaxed as the love of his life energetically chatted with his mother. He looked at me and smiled. Maybe this would work out better than expected.

Our appetizers arrived. I gave Preston a small plate and set a tomato slice and a piece of goat cheese from my salad on it. Before I had a chance to stop him, he picked up the tomato and threw it clear across the table, hitting Mrs. Wells in the shoulder. Everyone froze and watched the tomato flop into her lap, the vinaigrette dressing leaving a huge oil mark on her vintage Chanel suit. Chanel!

"Oh my God. I'm so sorry," I said to Mrs. Wells, then turned to Preston. "Bad boy. No throwing food."

Marcus right away called for a waiter. "Please get us some club soda and a towel."

Mrs. Wells stayed calm, not at all what I'd expected. She asked me, "Can I see him?"

"Um, of course."

I took Preston out of his seat and handed him to his grandmother. She smoothed his hair and rubbed a finger down his cheek, smiling. "If I'm going to be spending more time with you, I guess I better get used to flying food."

Preston giggled and reached for her diamond teardrop earring.

She laughed and gently removed his hand. "But I draw the line at jewelry."

Chapter 22

"Wake up, everyone!" Kevin's voice boomed through the apartment. "It's shower day."

I snuggled against Rich's warm back, ignoring Kevin's jubilance, until *Wagner's Wedding March* began playing throughout the apartment, gradually increasing in volume.

"Make it stop," I screamed at the nautical star tattooed between my fiance's shoulder blades.

"Lexi and Rich." A knock at the door. "Time to get up. We only have two hours to beautify."

"Oh my God. How does Marcus deal with all that pep?"

Rich laughed and rolled to face me. "I'm sure the pep comes in quite handy, if you know what I mean."

He lowered his head and took a playful bite of nipple, his hand already finding the sweet spot between my thighs.

"I can show you *pep*." I climbed on top of Rich, spearing myself with his eager morning wood. Wake-up sex was always the best. I ground my pelvis into his as classical music surrounded us, rocking in tempo with the violins and whatever else.

"Mmm," he murmured. "I think I'm starting to dig Vivaldi."

Another knock on the door. "Cover whatever you don't want seen. I'm coming in."

As Rich pulled my body down to his, and the comforter over our heads, Kevin burst in.

"Lex, I got your dress and here's Rich's suit, fresh from the dry cleaners." He hung them on the back of our door. "Carry on."

Once the door clicked shut, Rich threw the blanket off our heads. "That totally wrecked my hard-on."

"I'm sorry."

"We really need to find our own place. We can't live like this after the wedding."

He was right, but instead of talking, I climbed out of bed and yanked him toward the shower. "I know how to fix your hard-on."

* * * *

"You nervous?" I asked Rich during the cab ride to Marco's. His knee bounced like a jack hammer as he stared aimlessly out the window.

"A little." He turned to face me. "I've never been to a bridal shower before. Tell me again why I have to be there."

"If I have to endure this pain and aggravation to cash in on some domestic swag, so do you." My joke didn't faze him. "It's the new thing to do and since the other bride is a man, my mother thought the grooms should be there too."

He sighed and turned back to the window. "I know, but there's gonna be a lot of people I've never met before--your relatives and such. And my mom and sisters... Who knows what they're going to do to embarrass me."

"I'm sure it will be fine." I squeezed his hand.

"Just remember..." He looked at me and smiled. "It was your idea to invite them."

We pulled up to the restaurant and through the floor-to-ceiling windows I could see my mother and Mrs. Jacobs running to and fro, huge smiles on their faces. Rich and I walked in and were met with squeals.

"There's the other bride and groom."

Mom ran over and hugged us both. "So glad you're finally here. Come. We have to get your flowers."

She led us to a box filled with miniature orchid creations and took one, reaching toward me with a super sharp gleaming pin.

"Whoa. What are you doing with that?"

"Alexandra, it's a corsage. I have to pin it on you."

"I'm sorry, but this is Jean Paul Gaultier." I motioned to my dress. "There are no pins coming anywhere near this."

"But the bride has to wear a corsage."

Was she going to cry?

Rich rubbed his hand across my back and I caught his gaze with mine. He didn't need to say a word.

It's just a dress. It's just a dress. It's just a dress.

"Pin it quick before I change my mind."

A wave of nausea swept through my stomach as the pin punctured the fabric, though I managed to shake it off. Mom pinned on Rich's flower, then ran off to tend to some other shower thing.

"I'm proud of you," Rich said and leaned in to kiss my ear.

"Yeah, well, I guess my mother's happiness is worth the execution of a designer dress."

I found Amanda and Jeanette, busy placing favors at every place setting. We exchanged hugs and "You look fabulous" comments. I found Sheila in the corner making demands of a waiter. She gave me a quick wave and a nod.

Abby emerged from the bathroom. Holy crap. She saw me and rushed right over.

"Man, you've popped."

She semi-hugged me, her big, round belly hindering a proper hug.

"I know," she squealed and rubbed her stomach. "Isn't it adorable?"

I stared down at her mid section. When I was pregnant with Preston, the protrusion had been such an annoyance. I'd never appreciated what was going on inside my body. Standing there, the first time seeing Abby with physical proof of the life growing inside her, the ache of the baby I'd lost hit me. I hadn't thought of him or her in a while, being so busy and all. But like I often did in those times, I imagined my baby with a shiny gold halo, laughing and singing, smiling down on me. Especially on a day like this--a celebration of his mom and dad.

I looked at Abby, a small grin reaching my lips. "Yeah, it is. You are radiant."

Guests began arriving, toting packages wrapped in silver bell paper with bows and curling ribbon ringlets trailing down. Was it bad to enjoy cashing in on all the gifts I'd paid out over the years? I resisted the urge to give each one a little shake as our minions--I mean bridesmaids--placed them on the designated table.

Just when I thought I couldn't hug another person, my favorite aunt arrived. "Hi Aunt Matlilda." I reached for her.

"Yeah, hello, congratulations. Where's the toilet?"

I could sense Rich's need for a break and tucked Aunt Matilda's arm through his. "Rich will show you."

"Good." They walked off and I heard her continue. "And while I'm in there, fetch me a gin and tonic."

A drink sounded like a mighty fine idea. Amanda dashed past with gift bags hanging from both arms to her elbows. "Hey, can you grab me a glass of wine or something equally alcoholic?"

She winked. "Gotcha."

I turned and my mother walked toward me, faces on each side of hers. Crap. I'd told her not to invite them.

"Alexandra." Aunt Deborah leered through rimless glasses. "Congratulations on your upcoming marriage."

Was her face incapable of cracking a smile?

My cousin Wendy sneered at me. "We *never* thought we'd see this day come."

Her mother continued. "We have to meet this fiance of yours. Shame on you for not introducing us sooner."

There were reasons why Rich hadn't met them yet, namely because I would have to see them and I couldn't stand being around either of them. I certainly wasn't going to subject Rich to their snobby, better-than-thou venom.

"He's busy right now," I managed through clenched teeth.

"There he is," my mother exclaimed and waved her arm. "Richard, you hoo! Over here!"

Oh God. I gave him an apologetic smile as he stepped closer. Mom swooned as she introduced him to my aunt, her sister-in-law.

"Isn't he a hot piece of ass," Wendy hissed in my ear. "Musta had to pay him pretty well to marry *you*."

Was she seriously being a colossal bitch to me at my bridal shower? "You fucking--"

"Let me show you to your table." Sheila appeared at Wendy's side and grabbed her by the arm. She yanked her toward a table in the far corner of the room.

When Sheila turned over her shoulder, I mouthed "thank you" and she nodded in return. I knew there was a reason I'd chosen her as one of my closest friends.

Amanda handed me the glass of wine I could have used three minutes earlier. Before I could gulp it down, someone screeched behind me. Rachel had thrown her arms around Marcus's neck and was nearly cutting off his oxygen supply. She caught a glimpse of me and waved me over, pulling me and Brenda into a tight group hug.

"I can't believe it. Half of our little group is getting married." Tears had welled in her eyes. "I am so excited for you guys!"

Marcus's mother arrived and he rushed to greet her.

I felt a hand on my back, and when I turned, Rich looked pretty frazzled. "They're here."

I didn't have to ask who he was talking about. "Okay, let's go."

He took a deep breath and reached for my hand. It trembled in mine and I squeezed it. "It's gonna be fine."

When we walked toward the entrance, Rich's sister Stacey stood with three women and two preteens. I put on my biggest smile.

"Hi, Mom," Rich said.

"It's been two years. Don't ya at least have a hug fer yer mama?"

Rich hesitantly embraced the woman who was double his width with boobs bigger than his head. He moved on to the other women, more natural with his affection. He finished with the youngest girls and turned back to me.

"Mom, I want you to meet Lexi, my fiancee."

I extended my hand. "So nice to finally meet you."

"Oh, I think I need a hug from my soon-to-be daughter-in-law." Donna pulled me to her in a jovial bear hug, the heavy scent of Marlboro Menthols burning my nostrils. When she stepped away, a yellowed toothy smile stretched across her face. "You're so damn tiny! Don't you ever eat? I'm sure youz have money to buy food."

I forced a laugh at her joke.

Rich sighed and continued with his introductions. "And these are my sisters, Cara and Angela, and my nieces Ashley and Brittany."

"Hi." I gave a little wave to the rest of the women.

The sound of muffled taps echoed throughout the room. "Is this thing on?" My mom's voice blared through the speakers. "Oh, I guess it is! I'd like everyone to take their seats, please."

Rich's family shuffled off to a table while we headed toward the front of the room where a decorated head table waited for us.

"I can't believe they all wore jeans," he muttered. "This is like a five-star Manhattan restaurant and they friggin' chose jeans."

"It's fine. No one cares what they're wearing."

"My mom's shirt looks like it's gonna burst open. It's embarrassing."

We sat at the table and Kevin took control of the microphone.

"Welcome, everyone. I want to start by saying how much the four of us appreciate every one of you being here to share in this special day. I know some of you were surprised to see an invitation for a double wedding, but I'm sure you also know just how perfect it is. Lexi and Rich and Marcus and I have built something special over the last year and a half." He looked at us and took Marcus's hand as his eyes teared up. "We love each other and make the perfect family unit. I honestly can't imagine not sharing this special day like we are."

Marcus stood and hugged and kissed his fiance, amid a chorus of "awww."

They passed the microphone to me. I had not planned on making a speech.

"Oh, um, hello everyone. Gee, how do you follow that?" I got a few laughs. "Thank you for coming to our shower. We are so happy all of you could share this with us and we can't wait to see you at the wedding next month."

I put the microphone down and sat. My mother scooted up to the table.

"Alexandra, you haven't introduced the wedding party."

"Oh, well, okay." I stood again and brought the microphone to my mouth again. "Um, sorry. I forgot to introduce our wedding party. Uh, here at the end is my good friend and editor, Sheila Brown. And next to her, my other good friend and soon to be sister-in-law, Amanda. And this is Abby, my sister and Maid of Honor."

"Matron," Kevin whispered.

"Uh, yeah, make that Matron." I tried to smile.

Kevin stood and rescued me from further embarrassment. "And next we have my lovely and beautiful sister, Jeanette, who will be my honor attendant." He motioned as perfectly as Vanna White would have. "And the shimmering beauty next to her is Stacey Taylor, Rich's stunning little sister. If you haven't seen the latest Dior ad, you better Google it right now. She's spectacular."

The wait staff began circling the room with appetizer plates.

"Oh, it's time to eat. *Mangia,* everyone!" .

Kevin sat and pulled his napkin to his lap. "Thank you," I said over Marcus.

"No problem, honey."

The room quieted as servers delivered one course after another and kept glasses filled with wine. We laughed and talked as we ate, and I enjoyed the experience as one of the party's honored attendants. When our plates had been cleared, Mom came to the table with camera in hand. She snapped a couple pictures of the four of us.

"Richard, dear," she said. "I see your mother, sisters, and nieces are here. I didn't get the chance to meet them before lunch was served. I'd love it if you could make the introductions now."

He obliged, clearly hesitant. I rose and went along for moral support. We stood at Donna's back as she talked with Cara.

He cleared his throat. "Mom."

She laughed and snorted at some apparent joke her daughter had made, then let out a burp.

Rich sighed and closed his eyes for a second. "Mom," he said louder.

She turned to face him. "Geez! We're in a fancy restaurant. You don't need to be so damn loud." She laughed and snorted again.

His jaw tightened, as well as his hand in mine. It took everything inside him to stay put and do what he'd been asked by my mother. "I want you to meet Lexi's mother. This is Maryanne Marshall."

"Oh." She stood, her linen napkin falling to the floor. Bending to pick it up, she bumped the table, spilling wine on the pristine cloth. Mom held out her hand and Donna grabbed it, pumping vigorously. "Nice to meet ya."

"Likewise. Your Richard is such a wonderful boy."

Donna snorted again and laughed. "Yeah, a wonderful boy who deserted his mama." She laughed again.

The comment left my mother dumbfounded, but she recovered quickly. "Did you enjoy your meal?"

"She's fucking wasted," Rich whispered in my ear. "We have to get her out of here."

"We can't ask her to leave."

"Oh, yes we can."

I turned back to our mothers, mine still chatting away. "Donna, you'll have to come to the house for dinner one of these weekends, so we can get to know each other better."

For once, I appreciated her never-ending politeness.

I leaned to Rich. "I think it's fine. Let's just continue with the party."

My mother left to tend to someone else and Donna sat and dug into the Italian dessert sampler in front of her.

Rich and I took our places at the head table for present opening. The bridesmaids began setting multi-colored gifts in front of each couple and it was kind of fun. Rich relaxed while we opened gift after gift, all the things we would use in our new life together.

After an hour the gift table had been emptied, and as we prepared to give our final "Thank you for coming" speech, Amanda brought over a battered birthday gift bag.

"There's no card on this one."

I peeked inside, shrugging my shoulders.

Rich stood next to me and sighed. "I know who brought it."

The words had barely left his lips when we heard a commotion in the back of the room.

Stephanie Haefner

"Girls, that's ours! They're opening our present."

The entire room turned toward Rich's mother as she jumped from her chair and knocked it over behind her. She snorted and picked it up, then sat back down, almost missing the chair.

"Sorry we didn't bring a present for the queers. We didn't know what the hell to get."

Her laughter pierced the silent room.

"Let's get this over with so I can get her the hell out of here."

Rich reached into the bag and pulled out a wooden spoon, rooster print kitchen towel with matching pot holder, and a bottle of apple-scented body lotion. He then lifted a book of sorts, covered in rows of ivory lace. But after catching a whiff of its musty odor, I realized it had probably been white at one point in time, a few decades ago.

"Oh, God," Rich muttered.

"Um, what is it?"

"That was my wedding album," Donna yelled from the back of the room. "But when the asshole left me, I burned all the pictures." She cackled and continued. "Saved the album though. My mother-in-law made it--crafty bitch she was. Knew it'd get some use someday."

Rich set the book down and stepped away from the table.

Stacey caught his arm. "No, I've got it. Don't let her ruin this for you."

"Too late."

"I'll take care of them. They're staying at my place anyway."

Rich pulled his sister to him. "Thank you. Call me later, okay?"

She nodded and hurried to the back of the room.

Kevin had the microphone and had started giving his thanks for "all the fabulous gifts and unending love and support."

Chapter 23

After lugging our booty to the apartment and bringing most of our gifts into the bedroom, Rich called Stacey. He wasn't on the phone long, but when he came back to the room, his shoulders and eyelids sagged. I quickly moved some things from the bed and motioned him over. He slipped out of his suit jacket, shirt, and tie, and flopped down on the bed face-first.

"Are you okay?"

It took a few seconds for him to answer. "Yeah."

I rubbed his tense back. "Wanna talk about it?"

"Mom's passed out on Stacey's bed. She'll probably sleep 'til morning. That's what happens when she gets plastered."

"Oh." I didn't know what else to say. As much as I complained about my *Leave It To Beaver* childhood, I'd never had to deal with an alcoholic parent.

"Ang will drive them all home in the morning."

I stayed quiet and kept massaging, wishing there was something I could do to make it all better.

"I'm sorry she acted like that. And those gifts. Oh my God, they were awful."

"It's the thought that counts."

"Trust me, no thought went into any of it. And that album? What the hell was she thinking?"

"Well, I don't know. Maybe she thought you would want it 'cause it was hers and your dad's."

"What?" he asked, amusement in his voice, and turned toward me. "That album didn't have pictures of my dad in it. She was never married to him."

"Oh." I didn't know much about Rich's family. He never wanted to talk about them. Ever.

"She got pregnant with Cara when she was sixteen, and by the time she was eighteen she was pregnant again with Angela. She married their dad, but by the time Ang was a year old, he had already split. She pretty much became the trailer park whore after that."

I snuggled into the crook of his arm, rubbing my hand over his chest and heart.

"According to my mom, my dad was one of the trailer park owners. Went on for a couple years--he made her all kinds of promises. I guess when I was a baby, he visited a lot. But when his wife found out he was screwing one of the residents, he sold his share. Cara says it got bad after that, drinking all the time, different guys every night. We have no clue who Stacey's dad is."

I tried to think of something to say, but what *could* I say? I knew Rich's childhood had been pretty fucked up, but I had no idea it had been this bad.

"She had problems when Stacey was born...had to have a full hysterectomy. Probably the best thing for her. Could you imagine how many more bastards she'd have if that hadn't happened?"

"You're not a bastard."

"I am. And I have accepted that. But I won't let what she did to me affect who I am and the kind of parent I'll be."

It was the first time since the miscarriage he'd mentioned wanting to have kids. It had put quite a scar on his heart and I didn't know if he would ever be comfortable enough to move on.

He propped up on his elbow, our faces only inches apart, as the sun began its descent over the city. "I hope you know I will never be like her."

"I do."

He pulled me close. "How can a mother get so drunk she passes out, leaving her kids completely alone? Or throw a jar of peanut butter and some bread on the table before running off to get fucked? What kind of person does that shit?"

"I don't know."

"I promise you I'll never treat our kids like that."

A tear trailed down his cheek and I brushed it away. "You still want to have kids?"

"Of course I do."

"You were so scared after the miscarriage."

"I know, but I understand it better now. And I can get through anything as long as you're here to help me."

"I am and I always will be."

* * * *

The countdown to the wedding was on and my mom updated me almost daily with the head count. Currently we were at a hundred and eighty-three yeses of the four hundred and twelve people on the guest list. Only a handful of nos had come in. So glad I was not footing the bill on that one.

After lunch I checked my email, eyes darting instantly to one with a subject line of *Book Tour*.

I clicked on the email and scanned Sheila's message.

Tour is set. Sorry it's rather last minute. Up until today, I was told the whole thing might not even happen. Funding approval came in this morning. Here is your itinerary:

> *9-18: Talking Leaves Bookstore, Buffalo*
> *9-19: Chapters, Toronto*
> *9-20: Barnes and Noble, Syracuse*
> *9-21: Barnes and Noble, Pittsburgh*
> *9-22: Robin's Bookstore, Philadelphia*

Yay! My first book tour. It wouldn't be anything extravagant, but I was excited to do some promotional events in other cities. My eyes darted to the calendar; it was already the thirteenth. Only five days to prepare.

What was I going to wear?

And when I came back, there'd be just two weeks left before the wedding. Yikes.

When Rich came home, he walked into a clothing tsunami. I'd tried on a million different book tour outfits and discarded the nos all around the room.

"Oh, I have some exciting news!"

"Me too."

"You first," we both said in unison.

We laughed and Rich admitted he was way too excited to wait. "I have a ton of listings we can look at tomorrow. I took the day off."

I still had my doubts about moving to our own place, but couldn't bring myself to wipe away even a smidgen of his smile. "Great."

"Okay, what's your news?"

"I'm going on a book tour."

"Awesome. When?"

"Next week."

His eyes widened. "Oh."

"I know, it's last minute, and really close to the wedding, but I think it will be fine."

"Okay, if you say so. Glad I'm not the one who has to tell Kevin and your mom."

"Ugh. Don't remind me."

* * * *

When we sat for dinner--Kevin's famous Puttanesca--I dreaded telling him about the book tour. My mom had been a piece of cake. She simply said "Okay. I guess we can work around that." She didn't have the balls to say what was really on her mind. Kevin sometimes did, and I had to tell him face to face rather than on the phone like my mother.

I waited until he had a mouthful of meatball. "I leave next week for my book tour."

The room was quiet and I kept my gaze on my plate.

"That's exciting," Marcus said breaking the silence after what felt like hours. "Where are you going?"

"Um, Syracuse, Toronto, Philly, Pittsburgh. Buffalo too."

Kevin wiped his mouth on his napkin and I took a big swig of my wine.

"When did you find this out?" he asked, somewhat calm.

"This afternoon."

"So...out of the blue your publisher is sending you on a multi-city book tour and you knew nothing of it until today?"

"Well, I kinda knew it was gonna happen, just not when."

"And did you even think to tell them you have a wedding in the very near future?" His coolness was waning.

"Yes, but it's only a few days, and I'll be back with two weeks to spare."

He stood and set his half-full plate on the counter, dishes rattling.

"Kevin, I'm sorry. There's nothing I can do."

"What about your dress alterations? And the bridesmaids luncheon? And the bachelorette party? We still have to select songs for the reception and get the favors. Do you even have a single clue of how much is *still* left to do?"

"Yes, and I promise I'll get it all done, okay?"

He rolled his eyes, gave me a cold, "Whatever," and stormed off.

* * * *

"Uh, that was brutal," I sighed and plopped onto the bed that night. "I didn't think Kevin would be that mad."

"It will all be fine. Sometimes I think he takes the whole wedding thing a bit too seriously. Total diva, ya know?"

I laughed. It was so true. Kevin could be a diva from time to time.

"Marcus said he would talk to him. I'm sure it's all smoothed over by now." Rich stripped down and pulled the sheets back. I did the same and joined him, our bodies finding each other in the dark.

"Are you excited for tomorrow?" he asked, then kissed a trail from my earlobe to my breasts.

"Mmm, what's tomorrow again?"

"Apartment hunting."

"Oh, yeah." It was hard to comprehend anything with his teeth nibbling at sensitive parts and his hand between my thighs. "Very excited."

"I found some great places. They sound perfect."

Conversation during sex had always been a turn on for me, but this topic did nothing to increase my sexual desire. I scooted down and licked his cock, shaft to tip. "Are there lots of places for you to fuck me?"

"Oh yeah," he breathed out as I took him fully into my mouth. "One even has a fireplace. And a kitchen with a giant island with a built in stovetop and sink. You can put a few stools on the one side. Preston can eat his breakfast there."

Okay, one sure way to kill my mood was to mention my son's name while I was sucking dick. I released him from my mouth and crawled up to lay my head next to his.

"Hey, why'd you stop?"

"'Cause you're obviously excited about these apartments. So, go ahead and tell me about them."

"I'd much rather you finish what you were doing."

I wanted to, but he had too much swimming through his brain at the moment. "I will. When you're finished talking."

Rich and I cuddled in the moonlight and he went on and on about the places he'd seen online. The excitement was contagious, and by the time we actually did get back to what we'd started, it didn't take much for either if us to find euphoria.

Chapter 24

Rich and I went on with our morning as usual, failing to mention what we were really doing that day. Marcus and Kevin didn't need to know. We were free to take a day off together and do whatever we wanted. It wasn't any of their business.

Yeah, maybe I was being a coward.

As much as I understood Rich's reasons for needing our own place, I hadn't the heart to tell Marcus we were planning to move. Especially not after what had happened. Ever since the whole baby daddy drama, he'd become protective of Preston. He spent almost all his free time with him--playing, reading stories, going to the park--like he was soaking up every last drop of him.

Nicole arrived right on time and took Preston into the nursery to get him dressed and ready for the day. Rich and I gave him kisses goodbye and headed out the door. After grabbing coffees, we sat and waited for the realtor, who'd planned on meeting us at the coffee shop.

"Oh, I have to call Nicole. I forgot to tell her about Preston's boo boo. If she tries to take off that *Toy Story* Band-Aid, he's gonna flip." I rummaged through my Christian Louboutin tote. "I think I left my phone at home. Can I use yours?"

He handed it over without a word, scanning the listings the realtor had printed. I wasn't real familiar with how to operate his smarter-than-me smartphone and accidentally accessed his incoming call list.

"Um, who's Amy Simon?"

His hands froze mid page flip. "No one." He looked up.

"Then why's she on your call list?" I waved the phone around.

"Oh, um, I think she's one of the people from the realtor's office."

Her name was there a bunch of times, just over the last two days. "Okay."

I shook it off and called Nicole. By the time I'd hung up, the realtor had arrived.

"Lex, this is William Craig."

"Please, it's Bill."

I shook his hand.

"Ready to see some apartments?"

* * * *

I never knew how exhilarating and disappointing apartment hunting could be. For every fabulous place that was too expensive, was one in our price range that looked like it had been through a war, tornado, or hostage situation.

"It's only the first day," Bill consoled as we sat around the dining room table. "There are new places being listed every week. Every day, even."

"Yeah, I know." Rich kept his eyes on the listings on the table, then stood and tossed them all in the garbage. He ran his hands up his face and through his hair, like he always did when he was frustrated.

"Rich, I'll shoot you an email in a few days with anything and everything new on the market. We can expand our perimeters, too."

"Thanks, Bill." He stretched and they shook hands. "I'll be waiting for it."

Rich walked him to the door, then dropped onto the couch with an exasperated sigh. More face rubbing.

"It will be fine. We'll find something." I sat next to him and kissed his cheek. "It's not like we're in a hurry. We can stay here as long as we need."

He shook his head.

"You know Marcus loves that we're here."

"No, he loves that Preston's here." He turned to face me. "Lexi, I thought you understood."

"I do. But you know Marcus thinks of us as one big family. It's not a big deal if we don't find a place right away."

"It's a big deal to me. I've sponged off someone else for long enough."

He left the room and headed toward the bedroom. I knew better than to follow him and continue the conversation.

* * * *

"Hey." A few days later, I caught Rich before he left for his evening run. "I talked to my mom today."

"Yeah?"

"She got the response card from your mom and sisters. None of them are coming to the wedding."

Stephanie Haefner

He silently tied his sneakers. Was he relieved or hurt?

"How do you feel about that?"

"I don't know. How am I supposed to feel?"

"Does it bother you that they're not coming?"

He stood and stretched out his back. "I'd hoped my sisters would still come, but my mom...after that whole mess at the shower, I really don't care if I ever see her again."

"But she's your mother, your family."

"Not anymore." He stepped forward and wrapped his arms around me. "You're my family now."

* * * *

I was officially airborne, on my way to the first tour stop in Buffalo, and I already missed my little man and my big man. I'd never been away from Preston more than one night. And since Rich and I had gotten together, we'd never spent a night apart. How would I sleep in a big, cold, hotel room bed all by myself?

I'd lived in New York State my entire life and had never been to Buffalo before. We'd taken family vacations as kids, usually to places South--summer trips to Virginia and Myrtle Beach, winter trips to Florida. And this trip didn't leave much time for sight seeing. Not that there was anything to see. From what I'd heard, Buffalo was a bit on the backward side.

My flight was due to land at 3:10. I'd have enough time to grab a cab, check in to the fabulous Holiday Inn Smith & Roland Publishing had put me up in, beautify, and get to the book signing by seven.

In the meantime, I had an hour to sit and relax and hope the middle-aged businessman in the seat next to me kept quiet. To help insure that, I pulled out my newest toy: a digital book reader. With so many of my fans going digital, it was probably in my best interest to support this media alongside them. Rich had helped me figure it out and downloaded a bunch of the newest chick lit books. Had to keep on top of my genre.

After scrolling through the title list, I settled on the latest Emily Giffin. The handheld gadget opened the book and within seconds, I was already in love. Never again would I get a paper cut turning a book page or a cramp in my hand from holding a twenty-pound hardcover. I was so buying one for every person on my Christmas list.

Before I made it too far into Emily's newest drama, we had landed. I followed the herd of passengers toward baggage claim, passing a Buffalo wing joint on the way. Guess they thought people needed a fix right when they landed.

I grabbed a waiting cab and rode all of a half mile to the hotel. After checking in, and changing into my favorite black dress and Fendi giraffe sling backs, I asked the desk clerk where to grab a bite to eat.

"Uh, there's a Denny's next door."

No thanks. Last thing I needed was a grease-laden meal.

The clerk called a cab and I gave the address for the bookstore, Talking Leaves. Cute name.

We drove past the airport and onto a freeway, nothing spectacular. But once we'd exited, the cab drove though a trendy district, bustling with people and filled with boutiques, bars and restaurants. Suddenly I felt right at home. Maybe this city wasn't as backward as I'd been told.

"Where are we?" I asked the cabbie.

"This is the Elmwood Village."

We pulled up to the bookstore at six-fifteen. I paid, then climbed out, taking in my surroundings. The sun still shone bright, but a slight chill surrounded me as I walked down the sidewalk. Restaurant patrons dined on patios, the divine smells floating into the air and making my stomach growl. I stopped at a coffee shop and ordered an iced cap and a muffin to tide me over.

Walking back to the bookstore, I tried to pick a place to eat at later on. Impossible. I stopped to ogle the window display at a cute boutique, but luckily I checked the time before going inside: 6:46. Better get back.

Two hours later, I had greeted my last fan, signed her book, and sent her on her merry way. A sigh of relief. I loved these things, but man were they exhausting. After two readings and signing about a hundred autographs, I was ready for some food and relaxation.

"Great job," the owner, Jon, said as he walked up to me. "We had quite a successful night."

"A successful night for you means a fantastic royalty check for me."

He laughed. "Thanks for stopping by. We really enjoyed having you. Please make sure you call us when you tour for your next book. We'd love to have you back."

"Thanks. I will." I gathered my things, the hunger pangs returning. "Hey, Jon, I'm starving. Can you recommend someplace to eat? There's so many amazing looking places out there, I'd have a tough time narrowing them down myself."

"A bunch of us are heading to Allen Street Hardware. You're more than welcome to join us."

"And they serve food at this hardware store?"

He laughed. "Yes. Great food, actually. And it's open mic night."

"Sounds good." I was all for the food, hesitant on the open mic part. I'd never been to one. Was I in for a night of bad stand-up and weird performance art?

I walked to the exit with Jon and a few of the employees who had stuck around until the end of my signing. After he locked up, I asked if they wanted to share a cab.

They kinda smiled at me, like they shared an inside joke.

"We all have cars, so we'll just drive over."

"Oh." Yeah, I forgot. Most people outside New York City actually owned cars and drove themselves where they needed to go. "I'll meet you there."

"You can ride with us," one of the girls said. "We won't make you take a cab."

Normally I'd hesitate before accepting a ride from complete strangers, but…the people there were different. It wasn't *The City of Good Neighbors* for nothing.

"That would be great. Thanks."

After the daunting task of searching for a parking spot, we walked into the restaurant-slash-bar. The place was already packed--an acoustic guitar player stood in the corner of the room, jamming away. We found a table in the back, candles in the center and in wall sconces, abstract art decorating the place. It had a cool, SoHo vibe to it and I was told it actually used to be a hardware store.

I ordered a glass of wine and a Portobello panini, per the recommendation of Joleene, the young and bubbly bookstore employee who'd offered me the ride. I thoroughly enjoyed my meal and after paying the extremely tiny food bill--people were right when they said NYC is expensive--we took seats near the bar, closer to the entertainment.

As one ruggedly urban slam poet finished, an older woman took the spotlight. Her dramatic fusion of poetry and *a cappella* jazz blew my mind. I fought the urge to drop my jaw in complete awe of her.

Nothing amateur about this open mic night. Even as a multi-published, nationally known novelist, I felt quite inferior to the level of artistic ability being displayed.

"Lexi, you should totally sign up to read. I bet there are still slots available," Joleene said, exuberance shining through.

"Oh, no! That woman is amazing. I am not on the same level as these people."

"Come on," Aaron begged. "You were great today at the store. They'll love you here, too."

I gave it some thought, two and a half seconds worth, and shook my head. "I'm happy just sitting here and enjoying myself."

We watched a few more acts and Jon stood. "Okay ladies and gentlemen, I am going home." He turned to me. "Lexi, it was such a pleasure to meet you. Please come back soon." He shook my hand and waved to the rest of the group.

I checked my phone. "Wow, it's almost midnight. I should get back to the hotel."

"What? Why?"

"I have to catch a flight tomorrow to Toronto. Another book signing at seven. I should get to bed." This was responsible Lexi. But I wasn't remotely tired.

Joleene and Scott groaned in unison. "You can't leave yet. Come out with us tonight."

"Where?"

"Chippewa."

"Chippa-what?"

"It's our club district. Come on!"

It was hard to say "no" to four sets of pleading eyes. "Okay, I'll go."

Since Scott had already been determined the DD for the night, we piled into his car. It didn't take long to find this Chippewa Street, further proof that Buffalo was not a backwoods hickville. If I thought the Elmwood Village was lively, that was nothing. Clubs with neon signage lined the streets, with club hoppers and dance music spilling onto the sidewalks. Joleene pulled me into the line at our first stop of the night, and once inside, we shuffled up to the bar with the heavy beat of techno music thundering in my chest. She ordered a round of shots.

"Bottoms up," Aaron yelled above the dance tune.

Chapter 25

I woke the next morning, still in my little black dress; my shoes, who knew where. The other bed in my room was occupied, looked like two bodies. Had to be Joleene and Scott. Something moved next to me and I froze in sheer panic. Slowly I turned my head, thankful it was just Jaime. Was Aaron here too? Maybe he was the body on the floor.

God, I was way too old to be waking up hung-over in a hotel room surrounded by twenty-somethings, sleeping in until... "Fuck!"

Three of my four roommates jolted awake.

"What's wrong?" Scott asked, a yawn escaping his lips.

I was already out of bed and tossing my belongings into my suitcase. "It's noon. My flight leaves in forty-five minutes."

He rubbed his eyes and laid back down. "Where you going again? Toronto? Yeah...you're not gonna make it."

"What do you mean 'I'm not gonna make it?'"

"You'd be lucky to get to the airport and through security for a domestic flight in that amount of time. Even though it's only Canada, you're still flying over an international border. You need to be there at least two hours before, minimum."

"So what the fuck am I supposed to do?"

This was not happening. I couldn't be stuck here. I half expected Karma to appear and laugh at me. "You stupid bitch! You're too old to be staying out 'til all hours of the night with people you just met."

"Don't worry." He sat up and slipped his feet into his sneakers. The girls were up and taking turns with their first morning's pee.

"What? I have to worry about this. I need to be in Toronto, like in a couple hours."

"I know."

"Again, what the fuck am I supposed to do?" My patience with his lackadaisical attitude was fading. Add in my pounding head. Thanks

Karma. As if the missed flight wasn't enough, let's add some pain. I got it, okay. It was dumb to do what I'd done.

"Get your stuff all together."

"And what am I gonna do with it?"

"I'll put your suitcase in my car and we'll drive you there."

"Where? The airport? What if they can't change my ticket, or what if there's not another flight to Toronto that will get me there in time?"

"Lexi, relax. We're gonna drive you to Toronto."

I stared at him and blinked a few times. "What do you mean?"

"Me and Jo don't have to work today. It's only a two-hour drive. You gotta hurry, though. Not sure how bridge traffic will be, and I gotta drop Jaime and Aaron back at Hardware first. He's not allowed in Canada anymore." He grinned down at his friend, who had somehow managed to sleep through my mini-meltdown.

"I can't believe you would do that. You just met me."

Joleene came and put her arm around me and rested her head on my shoulder. "Yeah, but we really like you."

How in the world had I gotten lucky enough to make new friends, and not even twenty-four hours later, they had volunteered to drive me to another country?

I called Rich once we got on the highway. "Hey, how's everything at home?"

"Are you okay?" His voice was a mixture of worry and anger.

"I'm fine. Great, actually."

"I left you half a dozen messages this morning. Where were you?"

"Oh, um, I was sleeping. I must have been so out of it I didn't hear it ring."

"Even at eleven? Why were you still sleeping? Shouldn't you have checked out of the hotel by then? And how are you calling me now? Aren't you in the air?"

"Yeah, about that…"

The prior evening's events flashed through my head. Shots at the club, dancing, a venue change, more shots, more dancing. The night ended with a four AM breakfast at Denny's.

"You're joking, right?"

"I'll admit, I got a little carried away. But Scott and Joleene and Jaime and Aaron are really cool. We had such a fun time."

He sighed. "I'm glad you enjoyed yourself. Where are you now?"

"On my way to Toronto."

"How is that possible?"

"I'm with Scott and Joleene--they're driving me there."

Silence.

"I know what you're thinking."

"No, Lexi. You don't. How do you know these people aren't going to drive you somewhere and kill you?"

"You watch too many movies. And besides, the people here aren't how you think. They're not psychos. Trust me, okay?"

"I do. It's them I don't trust."

"Well, you'll have to trust my judgment."

"I love you. Will you please be careful?"

"I will. Can I talk to Preston?"

After a few minutes of baby talk and listening to him babble on the other end, I hung up. We still had an hour and a half before we arrived in Toronto. I laid my head back and closed my eyes for a much-needed nap.

* * * *

The rest of the tour was fun, though not quite as much fun as Buffalo. Then again, I hadn't allowed myself to get sucked into after-hours debauchery. I'd made it through the Toronto signing without keeling over in exhaustion and couldn't wait to get to the hotel and it's queen-sized bed. The other stops had been pretty similar and by the time my plane landed back at JFK, I was more than ready to step back into my normal lifestyle.

The cab dropped me in front of our building and when I walked into the apartment, no one was there to greet me. I knew my men would all be at their separate places of employment, but I had hoped my baby boy would be there. Oh, Thursday. Playgroup at the Central Park Zoo. Nicole and Preston wouldn't be home for another hour.

I rolled my suitcase into the bedroom with no desire to empty it. I stuck it in the corner where it would sit at least a week, until it needed to be emptied and refilled with honeymoon attire.

Yep. Just over two weeks until the big day. My heart fluttered just thinking about it. After being gone during this pertinent planning time, it was probably best to get on top of all these last minute things. There was a pile of stuff on my dresser: wedding-related messages, reminders from Kevin, an activities brochure from the resort in Oahu.

I yanked my laptop from its case and set it on the small desk in the corner. Had to check my email before continuing with my day. While I waited for it to boot up, I noticed a small note written in Rich's handwriting.

Meet with Amy Simon

9-23 Koffee Kafe at 1

That woman again--from the "realtor's office". Why would he be meeting with *her*? I checked the clock. 12:52. Even though I'd vowed never to do the spy thing again, I couldn't help myself. I changed out of my traveling clothes and started the five block walk to the cafe.

It was past one when I got there, and as inconspicuously as possible, I peered inside. I didn't see them at first, but there they were. Way in the back corner--cozy table for two. Rich smiled, a huge toothy one he saved for when something truly amused him. And the woman, though I couldn't really call her that, sat across from him, deep in animated conversation. She was much more of a girl, with a stick thin figure and a short spiky hair-do, but cute and youthful, not butchy. Rich said something to her and she threw her head back with laughter.

I did not like the look of this. And I was going to put a stop to it.

"Hi, honey." My mock excitement shone through as I appeared next to their table.

"Lexi, oh, um, hi." Rich jumped up and hugged me. "You're back from your trip."

"Yes, I am. I saw a note on the desk saying you'd be here, so I came." I wasn't going to lie and say this was a chance encounter.

When he pulled away, his coffee companion rose. "This is Amy Simon." He turned to her. "From the realtor's office."

"Um, yes, the realtor's office." She stuck out a hand to me. "Nice to meet you."

"Likewise."

"You'll email me those listings later on, right?" Rich asked, urging her to leave.

"Uh, yes. I'll email you later."

"Thanks." Rich played it all cool when she left. "How was your flight?"

"Fine." I sat on Amy's vacated seat, still warm from her skinny ass.

"I have a bunch of listings Bill sent over the other day and we'll have some more tonight. I'd like to go through them with you. Maybe we can make some appointments for this weekend."

"Sounds good." I could have drilled him with questions, accusations, but decided to let it go--for now.

* * * *

"Okay, people, we have two weeks left," Kevin started the second we sat to eat dinner on Friday. "We need to go over the song list for the reception. Have you guys picked something for your first dance? We

Stephanie Haefner

have, but we're keeping it a surprise. What about your rings? Have you had them sized yet?"

Rich and I shook our heads.

"Well, you better do it soon. You should go tomorrow. Marcus and I will be shopping for attendants' gifts. And our honeymoon documents are in. Yours should be too. You should come with us. Make a day of it--a fun-filled day of wedding prep. We need to pick up the favors and stop by the florist. I need to drop off a few things to be added to the centerpieces. Do you have a handkerchief you want wrapped around the handle of your bouquet? Definitely bring it."

I only heard half of what Kevin said.

"Lex, *hello*? You still recovering from your book tour?" He laughed.

"Oh, no. I'm fine."

"You better get a good night's sleep tonight. If we have time tomorrow, I'd also like to plan the bridesmaid's luncheon. It is next Sunday, after all."

Rich cleared his throat. "Lexi and I have plans tomorrow."

"Oh, well…when? Can we meet up and take care of some of the wedding stuff together?"

"We'll be gone most of the day. Can we do it Sunday?"

"The florist is closed on Sunday and so is the travel agent." His cheeks reddened. "And we have our own personal plans that day--brunch with Jess and Wes."

"I'm sorry, Kevin. We can't switch our Saturday plans."

"Fine," he huffed and continued eating his meal.

I felt the need to say something, try to smoothe things over. I didn't need Kevin pissed at me, again. "I promise, we'll get everything done the beginning of next week."

* * * *

Even though we hadn't lied, it still felt like we were two kids sneaking around to do something we weren't supposed to. Marcus and Kevin had never asked what our plans were, but Kevin focused solely on the fact that we were unable to do what he thought we should. We needed to do those things, but Rich was so adamant we look at apartments.

Rich and I took Preston with us this time--I knew asking Marcus and Kevin to take him was a no-go. We met the realtor, Bill, at the first place, pretty close to where we were currently living, but a simpler brownstone.

"This one is empty," Bill began as we climbed the front steps. "Three bedrooms, one and a half baths, galley kitchen, but the dining room is pretty large. The current owners made a lot of changes and upgrades to the place over the years."

"Any clue why they're selling?" Rich asked.

"Sick of the snow and cold. They're originally from out west and are itching to get back. They've listed the place at a great price, hoping to sell and close before winter gets here."

"Oh." Rich's eyebrows rose. "That's great."

"And lucky for you, no one else has seen it yet. Just came on the market yesterday."

We took the stairs to the second floor. No elevator, but I'd deal.

Bill opened the door into a wide open floor plan, gleaming hardwood at every step. We walked past the "galley" kitchen--which wasn't small at all--filled with stainless steel appliances. The main wall in the living room-dining room combo was exposed brick. We walked around as Bill talked and pointed out various things. The one con was the size of the bedrooms. But how much space did we need in a bedroom anyway?

We ended the tour at the bay window in the living room and the only word that came to my mind was *perfection*. The glimmer in Rich's eye said the same thing.

"What's the price again?" he asked Bill.

It was the same as the crime scene-esque apartments we'd seen last time.

While Preston tested his new walking ability in the furniture-free living room, Rich squeezed my hand. "What do you--"

"I love it!"

His smile said it all. This was going to be our home.

"Bill, can you call the seller's realtor now?"

"Are you sure?"

Rich looked at me once again and I nodded my head furiously. "Yep."

Bill pulled out his cell and made the call. We agreed to pay asking price, and within minutes, had written and handed over a down payment check.

"Congratulations." Bill shook both of our hands. "You're on the road to officially being home owners."

Chapter 26

Rich, Preston and I celebrated our apartment hunting success with lunch. We even ordered champagne.

"To us and our new home." Rich clinked his glass to mine.

I smiled and sipped my champagne, but it wouldn't wash away the fear in my gut. Marcus was not going to like this.

"Who should we tell first?"

I hated to wipe the shine off his face. "Is it okay if we keep it to ourselves?"

The smile faded.

"Just a little while?"

"Lexi, why would we keep it a secret?"

"Well…"

"It's Marcus, isn't it? I agreed to stay quiet while we were searching, but things have changed. We bought an apartment. And you heard Bill. The sellers want to close fast. We could be moving in a month."

"I know. I need time to think of a good way to tell him."

"I know a good way. 'Marcus, we're moving out.' He can't seriously think we'll all live happily ever after under the same roof 'til we're old and gray."

"Actually, I kinda think he did."

Rich shook his head. "I'm sorry, I can't do that. I thought you agreed with me."

"I do. I can't wait for it to be just you and me, no distractions. But can you please give me some time? It's going to break his heart."

Maybe it had sunk in. Maybe now that Rich was planning his own future as a father, he understood why I was so scared to tell Marcus.

"Okay, but please, can you tell him before the wedding?"

"I promise." That left less than two weeks to find the right words.

* * * *

The weekend was over, and I desperately needed to get some wedding stuff done. Rich had to work. He wouldn't be able to take off any more days before we left for New Paltz.

I stopped by the travel agency to pick up our documents and finished shopping for our honeymoon clothes. I bought engraved silver bracelets for the bridesmaids from Tiffany's, and while waiting for the engraver, made a list of song requests for the reception.

My last wedding errand that day was the bridal shop for my final fitting. Misty, the consultant, had left a dozen messages while I was gone on my book tour and at least a dozen more before that.

"Where have you been?" she asked the second she saw me. "I've been calling you for weeks."

"I'm sorry. I was out of town and really busy. I know I don't have an appointment today, but is it okay I stopped in?"

She flipped through her appointment book. It was a Monday afternoon. How busy could she be?

"Well, you're lucky you came now instead of in an hour. Come on in back."

She helped me into my dress. Its fabric fit every curve like it had been sewn to my body. Misty walked around me, assessing the gown in various spots.

"Thankfully, everything looks good." She tugged at the skirt and fluffed it. "Have you purchased a veil elsewhere? I don't have one listed on your paperwork."

"Oh." I'd totally forgotten headwear. "I haven't. I'm not into that sort of thing, though."

"A lot of modern brides aren't. You can do a simple veil, no tiara." She left and came back with a long piece of shimmery fabric. "This is just tulle on a comb. It's a cathedral length veil. Your dress doesn't have a train and something like this will work nicely. How are you wearing your hair?"

Oops. Something else I hadn't thought of yet. "I hate up-dos, so I might leave it down. I don't know."

Apparently my laid-back attitude worried her. "You really should decide. Most veils won't work unless your hair is pulled back at least partially. You need to figure it out soon."

Story of my life. I was getting pretty sick of people telling me what I *needed* to do regarding this wedding. Thank God it was almost over.

* * * *

"Lex?" Marcus approached while I set the table. "We need to talk. Can we go grab a coffee after dinner?"

"Yeah, sure."

My insides swirled though our meal, making me unable to even eat. Why did Marcus need to talk to me--and away from the apartment? It was something he didn't want Rich or Kevin to hear. Did he know about the apartment hunting? Oh God. Something worse? Was he going to sue me for custody?

We walked to the coffee shop, wind whipping around us as it chased the first fallen leaves of autumn. Marcus said nothing until we were seated with our chosen beverages.

"I want to do a DNA test."

Where the hell had this come from? "Why? I thought you decided Preston was yours, no questions."

"I did. But I've been thinking--a lot--and it's wrong."

"Uh, I have to disagree. You are the father of my child. That's what I want and that's how it will be."

"Lexi, I can't live with questions in the back of my mind. And I can't keep a man from his son."

"You're not."

"I might be."

"No. You are Preston's father. End of discussion." I sipped my mochachino.

"What if it had been reversed? What if you thought all along Zak was the father, and one day it occurred to you it might be me? What would you do then?"

"Well, of course I would do a DNA test."

"Why is that any different from what's happening now?"

"Because I love you and you are the best father for Preston."

Marcus set down his cup and took my hand. It trembled in his and I forced myself to look at him through watery eyes.

"I need to know."

* * * *

Never had I thought I'd need a test to determine the paternity of my child. Those tests were for afternoon talk shows featuring rednecks with missing teeth or strippers who too often let their jobs get personal. Not for me.

I walked into the clinic with Marcus and Preston, all eyes on us. Or at least that's what it felt like. "Another skank who doesn't know who knocked her up." I'd thought I knew. Maybe I was no better than those women on TV.

A nurse called for us and Marcus wheeled Preston's stroller to the exam room. She instructed Marcus to roll his sleeve and drew a small vial of blood. We sat in silence as she then came over to Preston and stuck him with the needle. He wailed and I held him tight, tears in my eyes too. But not only for my baby's pain. I hated this. Marcus was my son's father, DNA match or not.

"The results will take a few days and will be mailed to you in a plain brown envelope, no return address."

Marcus thanked the woman while I held Preston, his cries subsiding.

"This is it. Soon we'll know for sure." He took Preston and held him tight.

I hoped it wouldn't be their last embrace as father and son.

* * * *

I told Rich about the DNA test, and he thought it best to forget about it until the results came in the mail. I told him I'd try. There were enough things to worry about. Like my mother, who called at least five times a day.

"Make sure you get your rings sized."

"Have you packed Preston's bags yet for his week with us?"

"Ask the bridal shop to steam iron your dress before you pick it up."

"Don't forget about the bridesmaid's luncheon on Sunday."

"Have you written your vows yet? Marcus and Kevin already have."

What's wrong with the same vows people have used for hundreds of years? Love, honor, trust…that's all I needed. Well, and great sex. Would it be okay to add *unlimited orgasms* to our vows? I could already see my mother's ghastly expression. We could film it and send it to *America's Funniest Home Videos*. If she fainted, we'd be a shoe-in to win the hundred thousand dollar jackpot.

And on top of all that, I had Amanda in my ear too, already planning her wedding. She'd asked me to be her Matron of Honor. And I truly did feel honored to do the job. But could she at least let me get through my own wedding first?

Apparently not.

She guilted me into a trip to the bridal shop with her. Which was fine. I had to pick up my dress anyway. On Friday, after her last class, she met me at the dress shop. My mother and Abby already waited there.

After a million squeals, giggles and hugs, I asked, "So why are we doing this now?"

"There's barely nine months to plan the wedding. Amanda needs to choose her dress soon."

"Oh. I didn't know you'd set the date."

"We did! I really want a summer wedding, so June twenty-third it is. The first Saturday of summer."

"What about your mom? Doesn't she want to be here for this?"

"Well, of course, but she understands. She can't fly into the city every time I go dress shopping. That's why I have my mother-in-law and sisters-in-law-to-be."

The consultant assigned to us walked over to our group. "Hello, ladies, I'm…Oh, Lexi. Hi," Misty said. "I'm sorry, I have an appointment right now. I can't take care of you."

"I know. I'm here with your appointment, actually."

"Oh, okay." She smiled. "Everyone follow me."

An hour later, we made it into the dressing room. Amanda had at least two dozen dresses to try on and even more bridesmaids' dresses. And with Abby's stomach way too big for modeling duties, it was all on me to try on every horrible frock. Yippee.

Against my wishes, I was up first. Amanda, Mom and Abby sat and watched as I strutted out in each dress, eliminating many of them before I even took five steps. As difficult as those things were to get into, the least they could do was give them more than two-point-five seconds of consideration.

When the thirty had been narrowed down to five, I was instructed to put each on again. Amanda nixed one and Abby another. Misty wrote down the three remaining dresses in Amanda's file.

Now it was Amanda's turn. It felt like an hour had passed, but when she finally appeared, she floated like a princess at a fancy ball. Strapless and beaded from bodice to hem, with a poofed skirt and long-ass train. She even had the cathedral-length satin gloves. Misty set a jeweled tiara on her head with a long, flowy veil, trimmed with even more sparkling gems.

"Oh, Mandy," Abby cooed. "You look amazing."

Mandy? Where'd that come from?

Mom stood and moved closer for inspection. "Simply breathtaking."

I watched Amanda take in her reflection, eyes filling with tears. "Do you think Andy will like it?"

"Of course," my mother and Abby squealed in unison and pulled in for a cozy group hug.

What the hell were they doing to my BFF? Where did my sassy Amanda go? It had taken me a long time to mold her into my likeness.

When they pulled apart, she turned to me. "What do you think, Lexi?"

"I like it. It's pretty and it suits you."

She asked Misty to add it to her file and went in for the next dress.

Two hours later, I'd fielded calls from all three of my men, wondering where I was. I told them to have dinner without me. Mom had already made dinner plans for the four of us girls.

As we sat into the cab, I asked Amanda which dress she was going to buy.

"Oh, I don't know. I still have at least four more shops to visit."

I choked on my saliva. "What?"

"I have to be certain there isn't anything else I might like."

"Absolutely," Abby chimed in. "I must have tried on a hundred dresses before deciding."

"I bought the only dress I tried on."

"And that's the difference between you and Mandy and me."

Again with the Mandy shit.

"We both like everything to be completely perfect." They shared a giggle.

Was I imagining things, or was my sister totally trying to steal my best friend? I was not going to let this happen. After we were seated at the restaurant, I asked Amanda to go to the bathroom with me. Luckily, Abby stayed put, which was amazing, since she had peed pretty much every ten minutes the entire time we were at the bridal shop.

"So I'm just gonna put this out there…no dicking around. Are you and my sister BFFs now?"

"Lexi, don't be ridiculous. You know I love you best." She turned to the mirror and dusted on some powder.

"Well, I get the feeling you guys are getting kinda cozy."

"We do hang out more, now that I spend so much time at your parents' house and at the restaurant. It's only natural we've become friends."

"And what's up with this 'Mandy' shit?"

"Oh." She giggled. "Abby thinks it's cute, Andy and Mandy. She's the only one who calls me that."

"And it doesn't bother you?"

"No." She walked to a stall and closed the door behind her. "Which bridesmaid's dress did you like best? I thought the taffeta strapless with the dropped waist and pick-up skirt looked nice on you."

"Huh?"

The toilet flushed and she reappeared, a condescending smile on her face. "The lilac one with the scrunched skirt."

"Oh. That one itched."

She washed and dried her hands. "Ready? I'm starved."

"Uh, yep."

Chapter 27

Knock. Knock. Knock.

Giggles erupted behind the door and I knew who was there without even checking the peephole.

I'd left bachelorette party planning to Abby and Amanda. It didn't even matter to me if I had one or not. Rich had decided not to have a bachelor party. He just wanted to get trashed on his friend's dime--a last guy's night out. Not that he had to stop doing that anyway. Even after we were married, I still planned on having girl's night every once in a while.

When I opened the door, a rhinestone encrusted tiara was shoved on my head and a sash looped around my body reading *Bride-to-Be*. To top the ensemble off, a hot pink feather boa, matching the ones every bridesmaid wore--including Sheila. I burst out laughing when I saw her.

"None of this was my doing," she said when I met her eyes.

"The limo is waiting." Amanda led us to a pink stretch limo.

Yeah. It was friggin' pink. And inside, more pink, and filled with test tube shooters, plastic penis straws, and a *Bachelorette Party Checklist*.

"We are doing everything on this list, ladies," Abby giggled. "Get ready for a wild night."

I scanned the list. Oh my. Wild night, all right.

> *1. Get a guy to buy you a drink.*
> *2. Get a guy to give you a condom.*
> *3. Get the bartender to laugh at something.*
> *4. Dance with two guys at once who don't know each other.*
> *5. Show a guy your bra.*

The list continued. Yeah, this had been a typical night out in my single days.

The first stop was a mix-your-own body lotion shop. Had to be Abby's idea. Each girl mixed her concoction and when we'd finished, the sales woman wrapped them in pretty boxes.

Abby handed me the bag. "These are all for you, Lexi."

"Oh, thanks." What the hell was I going to do with six bottles of lotion? It'd take me forever to use it all.

Our next stop was a dance club with hardly anyone in the place. What did Abby expect at eight-thirty? We had a few drinks and being the only ones in the place, getting the bartender to laugh wasn't very hard. Our group convened on the dance floor and shook our asses to a club remix of an old Madonna tune.

We then headed to a karaoke bar. Good Lord.

Abby grabbed the song list. "Mandy, what should we sing?"

Yuck. There it was again. *Mandy*.

"If there's any justice in the world," Sheila whispered in my ear. "They won't find anything."

I laughed and Sheila ordered two gin and tonics.

"Lexi, what do you want to sing with us? There's *Girls Just Wanna Have Fun*, or *It's Raining Men*, or even better, *We Are Family*." Abby was way too chipper for five and a half months pregnant.

"Um, I'll pass."

"Nooo!"

"Party pooper!"

"You guys go have fun, okay?"

I sat with Sheila as Abby, Amanda, Jeanette and Stacey took the stage to sing *Girls Just Wanna Have Fun*. It took them a few minutes to sync together and actually sing the words in time with the music, but it did look like they were having fun. Maybe I could belt out a tune or two.

First, another drink.

The girls returned and Amanda ordered a round of blow job shots. For Abby, a shot glass of OJ with whipped cream on top.

A resounding "Woo!" erupted after the shots had been downed.

"What are we doing next?" Sheila asked.

"We'll stay here a bit longer and then I thought maybe we'd hit The Dessert Bar for some late night goodies." Abby answered.

"That's it?"

"Well, it is getting late and we have the bridesmaids' luncheon tomorrow."

Sheila checked her watch. "I have somewhere a bit more exciting in mind." She slipped off her barstool and downed the rest of her drink. "Come on."

We followed her to the street and everyone piled into our pink limo. Sheila had a chat with the driver, and half an hour later we arrived at Peppermintz.

"Oh, I haven't been here in years!"

Decade-old memories flooded my brain. Man, those were some good times. Federico had always been my favorite.

"Where are we?" Abby asked. "It looks fun."

The half-drunk girls, and the pregnant one, followed me and Sheila into the club.

"Now this is more like it."

Abby's eyes bulged so far out of her sockets, I though for sure they would plop onto the floor. On stage was a tanned hottie in a red g-string and a fireman's hat.

Sheila smiled and led us to a vacant table near the stage, where a tall, dark, and handsome waiter informed us of the two hundred dollar tab on the table.

"Oh, nevermind…" I started to say.

Sheila whipped out two hundred dollar bills and handed it to the scantily clad server.

He tucked it into his Speedo, took our drink orders, then turned toward the bar.

Sheila patted his ass as he passed by.

My jaw dropped.

"What?"

"Nothing. Just amazed at this side I've never seen."

We sat at our front row table and watched Mr. Firehose finish his set. He had lost the g-string, or maybe it had incinerated.

Abby sat down next to me. "We should leave."

"Are you joking?"

"No."

"Why? This is fun."

"Lexi, you're about to get married. I'm a married woman, and pregnant. Amanda is engaged to our brother. We shouldn't be in a place like…*this*."

"Abby, would you please pull the stick out of your ass for a couple hours and live a little?"

A figure walked toward us and a smile spread across my face.

"I know how to have fun, but this is not appropriate for women who are--" Abby noticed the suede-covered penis gyrating very close to her face. She screamed and jumped. "Oh my God!"

The cowboy drawled a, "Howdy, ma'am," put his rope around her and pulled her closer to him.

"Eww! No! I'm a married woman. Can't you see I'm pregnant?" She hesitantly touched his mounded pectorals with the tips of her fingers and pushed him away.

"Okay, darlin'." He flashed a thousand-watt smile and released her. "I see someone here who isn't hitched…yet." He wrapped his rope around my waist and led me to the stage.

Our table hooted and hollered, except Abby, who sat at the seat farthest from the stage, a pout on her face. A chair appeared and I sat as Mr. Cowboy's first song started, *Save a Horse, Ride a Cowboy*. There'd be Wild West dreams for weeks.

* * * *

It had never been the plan to attend my bridesmaids' luncheon hung over, but at least I wasn't the only one. We couldn't let Sheila's two hundred dollars go to waste. And it hadn't been our fault the drinks were cheap and we'd had to order more to use up the money.

After my trip down south to Cowboy Heaven, Amanda had bought me a lap dance with a policeman and Stacey had paid for a body shot from the navel of a very buff construction worker. All I'd needed was a biker, a Navy guy, and a Native American for the complete Village People fantasy.

"You ladies look like you were out late last night."

Why was my mother yelling? She never yelled. Or maybe it just seemed like she was yelling.

"I tried to get them home earlier," Abby started, always the nark. "But they kept saying, 'One more song.'"

When I was huge and pregnant at her bachelorette party, did I once complain about babysitting her and her drunk, skinny-ass friends? No, I didn't.

She sneered at me, then continued with her tale. "That place was disgusting. It was nothing but big, sweaty men dancing and shaking their genitalia."

"Aww," Kevin whined. "Why wasn't I invited?"

I patted his back. "Sorry, it was ladies only."

I took my seat at the round table in the private dining room at Magnolia. Each of the bridesmaids filtered in, probably wishing to be home in bed, just as I was.

Mom began the luncheon by handing itineraries to the bridesmaids, Kevin and his mom. Geez. I thought this was going to be a relaxing meal, not a lecture on wedding weekend events.

"I expect all of you will be to the Inn at Harbor Hill by three PM on Thursday, allowing plenty of time to familiarize yourselves with the property and freshen up before the Welcome Dinner."

A chorus of "Umm-hmms.

"As you can see, Friday and Saturday are pretty well planned. I expect you'll get plenty of rest before the wedding."

"Yes, Mother, don't worry. No one will be hung over for the wedding."

The waiter brought us rolls and butter and suddenly I was famished. I scarfed one down and reached for another.

"Alexandra, don't eat too much. You have a fitted gown to wear in only seven days."

Had she seriously told me not to get fat before my wedding?

Our salad course arrived and the room quieted, with only the muffled sounds of greens being chewed.

My mother cleared her throat. "Alexandra, wouldn't you like to say a few words before our entrees are served?"

Not really. I was tired. I just wanted to eat and leave.

"Sure." I wiped my mouth on my napkin and stood. "Um, well, thank you, all of you, for being a part of our wedding. It means a lot to me and Rich, to have the most important people in our lives be a part of this day."

I sat back down.

"Dear, aren't you going to hand out your gifts?"

Gifts?

"Your appreciation gifts for the bridesmaids?"

"Oh, those. I, um, didn't bring them."

"But it's the entire point of a bridesmaid's luncheon."

"Abby didn't give gifts at her luncheon."

"She did. You weren't there."

Oh, yeah. I'd skipped that pre-wedding party. I'd gotten out of a lot of stuff the last month of my pregnancy, claiming hemorrhoids or nausea, or ligament pain. That was my favorite.

"I'm sorry. I forgot."

"It's fine," Sheila said. "Who needs an engraved photo frame anyway?"

I smiled at her. Leave it to Sheila to save me with her sarcastic wit. "Actually, they're engraved bracelets. I do have presents. I just forgot to bring them."

"Oh, much better." She winked at me from across the table.

Chapter 28

My last Monday as a single woman--a few more days of work and normal life before all our lives changed forever. If I could call this normal life. Kevin constantly ran around the apartment, freaking out about some wedding mishap. I was not into that drama and couldn't wait for it to be over.

I worked on copy edits, then took a break. It had been a while since I'd surprised Rich at work with lunch. I bundled Preston and gave Nicole the rest of the day off. We picked up some sandwiches and headed to Big Apple Records. Now that he was a few steps up the ladder, he had an office instead of a cubical. I knocked on the door despite the voices inside. Hoped this wasn't a bad time.

Rich answered the door and when he saw me, his eyes widened and a moment of sheer panic surged through his body. "Lexi. What are you doing here?"

"Surprise!" I said and held up the take-out bag. I looked past him, concentrating on the figure in the chair, and recognized the spiky blond hair. I wheeled Preston's stroller into the room, almost running over Rich's feet.

"Um, you remember--"

"Amy, right? From the realtor's office?"

She stood without saying a word.

"She, um, just stopped by to give me some paperwork."

"For the apartment?" I asked, eyebrows raised.

"Yep, the apartment."

Bullshit. I turned back to her.

"How nice of you." If looks said anything, mine was telling her to back the fuck off.

"Let me know if there's anything else you need," she said and made her way to the door.

Yeah, I don't think so.

Rich closed the door behind her. "What's for lunch?"

"What was that all about?"

"I told you. Paperwork." He reached inside the bag I'd set on his desk and took out sandwiches wrapped in deli paper.

"Nice try."

His eyes met mine for a milli-second. "That's all it was. I'm sorry you don't believe me."

The surprise lunch didn't exactly go how I'd planned. Instead of talking and laughing and playing with Preston, we ate in silence. Until I reprimanded Preston for throwing a piece of ham across the room and he wailed like I'd slapped him. My attempts at calming him proved pointless, and I left before I'd finished my meal.

Halfway home, he stopped crying and fell asleep. But that left my brain clear to think of what I'd walked in on at Rich's office. There weren't any telltale signs of an affair, but something didn't jive. I hated to think he was lying to me, days before our wedding, but I couldn't shake the weird feeling.

Still flustered, I fetched the mail and flipped through the huge pile as I waited for the elevator. Until a plain nine-by-thirteen brown envelope stopped me dead. No return address. The elevator opened and someone stepped out. I didn't acknowledge them. My eyes were too focused on the thing in my hands--the paper that could change our lives forever.

Preston woke just as we pulled up to our door. I took off his coat and hat, changed his diaper, and popped in a Baby Einstein DVD. A good mommy would have sat and played with him, but my brain and nerves were shot. I poured myself a glass of wine and relaxed on the couch, the envelope on the coffee table in front of me.

Should I open it? I could read it and tell Marcus he was Preston's father, even if the paper said otherwise. But, of course, he'd ask to see it. Surely I could make something up.

No. I'd promised Rich I was done with stupid stories and lies.

My wine was gone, but the nerves still haywire. One more glass. I filled it and returned to the couch. My son sat mesmerized by the shapes, colors, and music before him. How could I take away the only father he'd ever known?

Suddenly my stomach flipped around. I set down my glass and rushed to the bathroom, just in time. It was my own fault. I'd barely eaten a quarter of my sandwich at lunch, and then to come home, as upset as I was, and drink a glass of wine? Stupid.

I brushed my teeth and pressed a wet washcloth to my face. Preston's giggles floated in from the other room. It must have been his favorite part of the DVD. I walked in, and instead of him dancing along with the kids on screen, he was at the coffee table, red liquid all over it and him and the brown nine-by-thirteen envelope. He smacked his hands in the puddle and laughed when it splashed all over.

"Preston!"

His little body jumped and he immediately stopped, twisting his head in my direction. He burst into tears before I even got to him. I didn't mean to scare him again. The mess could wait. I cradled my baby, kissing his tears away. He calmed down and I changed his clothes, then returned him to the living room to watch his show, like nothing had happened.

And there sat the DNA test results in a puddle of merlot, soaked all the way through. I took it to the kitchen and dried it, but nothing was going to help. I opened the envelope, paper disintegrating in my hands as I tried to peel it away from the envelope. No way to decipher any of it. It was completely ruined.

Marcus was going to be pissed.

But wait. I could tell him I read it before Preston spilled wine on it. I could tell him they were a match. This would be my last lie. Promise.

It would work. It had to. Thank God for spilled wine. Or was this Karma's doing? Thank you, Karma. She knew how much this meant to me.

Marcus, Kevin and Rich came home, and we went through our normal after-work routine of prepping and cooking dinner. I had to tell Marcus about the DNA results. But should I bring it up casually--a hey-by-the-way conversation? My stomach churned as I concentrated on my task of slicing an onion for our stir fry. Marcus stood next to me with the more difficult chore of mixing the sauce.

"Did the test results come today?"

Was he freakin' psychic now? "Oh, um, actually they did. " My hand began shaking--not a good thing with a sharp knife in said hand.

He took a deep breath. "And, where are they?"

I needed cool, calm, and collected. Or he'd see right through my lie. "I had to throw them away."

He stopped and turned to me. "What?"

"Preston spilled my wine on the envelope and it was destroyed."

"Are you kidding me? We have to go do it again?"

"Oh, no. I read it before it was ruined." I hoped my acting skills portrayed complete confidence. "You're a match!"

His eyes met mine and I smiled as big as I could, hoping to mask my lie and the nausea. He pulled me to him and hugged me tight.

"It's all over," he spoke into my shoulder.

"Yep. Everything is exactly how it should be."

When we pulled apart, we both wiped away tears and continued with our tasks. I threw the onion into the skillet and turned toward the kitchen island to grab the red pepper. I jumped a foot when I saw Karma sitting there, shaking her head at me.

"You okay?" Marcus asked.

I turned back around to him. "Yeah, fine."

Karma was gone when I looked again. Weird. She'd helped me earlier today. Why was she now shaking her head? Oh well. I didn't have time to worry about it.

*   *   *   *

"We need to tell Marcus about the move," Rich said while we packed our honeymoon suitcases the next night.

"I know. We will."

"When? You said you'd do it before the wedding."

"I will," I repeated, counting underwear as I packed them in the suitcase.

"Lexi, do you know what day it is? It's Tuesday. Only two more days until we leave for the wedding."

I knew what day it was. And was I stalling? Most definitely. If I waited, we'd be too busy with wedding events to sit down for a chat. Then we'd all be gone on our respective honeymoons, delaying the inevitable for another week.

"You promised me."

I did, didn't I? Grabbing a few dresses from the closet, I avoided his eyes.

"I talked to Bill earlier today. The sellers have everything in line. We're set to close two days after we come home from Hawaii." Rich closed his suitcase and zipped it. "I'm sorry, you're out of time."

I dug through my jewelry armoire, selecting necklaces to bring along.

"Lexi, are you even listening to me?"

"Yes. I'll talk to him tomorrow, okay?"

"I think you should do it tonight. Right now, actually."

I finally met his gaze, terror zipping through my body. "Now? Do I have to?"

"Yes."

"But--"

"Lexi, please." His hands went to his face, then slid through his hair. "This is really starting to piss me off. You tell me our new life together is important to you, but you're not ready to let go of your old, easy life."

"*Easy* life? What the hell is that supposed to mean? Nothing in my life is easy."

"Oh, yes it is. You have three grown men to take care of you. And you love it. Admit it--don't want to give that up."

What woman wouldn't want all those hands to help? But it wasn't about that. "This is about Preston, not me."

"The new place isn't far. Marcus can see Preston whenever he wants. Hell, he can walk down every night and tuck him in if he wants." He paused, his tone a bit softer. "We're going to be husband and wife in a few days. Does it matter to you at all what I want?"

Nice guilt trip. He was starting to irritate me. "Fine. I'll go tell him we're moving, and rip his heart out with my bare hands while I'm at it. That work for you?"

I stomped out of the bedroom, my heart thumping double time, as I called for Marcus. I had no clue what I was going to say; no carefully prepared words that would deliver the blow gently.

"Shhh." Kevin closed Preston's bedroom door behind him. "Marcus went to the office. He doesn't think he'll have enough time tomorrow to get everything done before we leave."

Relief filled me. "Okay, thanks."

Rich followed me back to our room. "One more day of reprieve."

"Yep." I grabbed a few pieces of lingerie. "You wanna pile on some more guilt now that you have time?"

He walked around the bed, took the lacy things from my hands, and set them down. His arms wrapped around me tight.

Tears streamed down my face.

"I know how hard this is. I'm sorry I got so crazy. But you have to understand how I feel too."

"I do. And I so badly want the life we've dreamed. But getting what I want is really hard to do when I know it will crush Marcus."

We went to bed after that, but it didn't matter. I lay there awake, completely exhausted, thinking of what to say to Marcus. And when the nausea returned, I told it to go away. It didn't listen. As I rested my head on the toilet seat, I prayed that once the stress of telling Marcus about the move was gone, I'd stop hurling.

Chapter 29

My entire day passed without seeing Marcus. He'd left before I'd gotten up, and as I filled the dishwasher with dinner dishes, he still hadn't come home. Not good.

While Rich gave Preston a bath, and Kevin packed some last minute things, I sent Marcus a text.

comin home soon?

A few seconds later.

Just grabbed a cab

He was on his way. He'd be there within minutes. Oh, God. Wine... now.

I tried not to chug. It wouldn't end well.

"Lex, you okay?"

Kevin must have heard my mad dash for the bathroom.

"Um, fine. Thanks."

"O...kay."

Maybe tea would help. I nuked a mug of water and threw in a bag of my favorite chamomile.

Back on the couch, I kept looking at the clock. How the hell was I going to do this? I couldn't even think about it without barfing.

The ding of the elevator rang in my ear like a cathedral's bell. My back stiffened. The door opened and Marcus walked in, shoulders slumped and eyes half-closed. Great.

"Hey, Lex. How's everything?"

He dropped his briefcase by the door and removed his coat, taking much effort to do it.

"Um, fine."

"Good." He walked past me. "I'm exhausted."

Now or never. "Marcus, wait."

He turned in slow motion.

"We need to talk."

"Can it wait 'til the morning?"

I'd love to wait forever to have this conversation. But I'd risk being left at the altar. "Well, no. It can't."

He trudged back and dropped onto the arm chair. "Shoot."

Oh, God. This was it. My stomach twisted and I told the vomit to stay put. Time to put my big-girl panties on.

"I have something to tell you."

Marcus stared at me, silently willing me to proceed. When his eyelids closed for more than the allotted time for blinking, I started again.

"Um, Rich and I…we decided to, um, like, get our own place."

Did I forget how to speak?

Marcus just sat there, staring at me. Did he fall asleep with his eyes open?

"Did you hear me?"

He nodded.

"Are you okay with that?"

He rubbed his eyes and blinked a few times. "When did you decide this?"

I hadn't anticipated that question. "Uh, a couple months ago. When Rich got his promotion."

"You decided this a while ago and didn't say a word to me?"

"I should have, I know. But I was scared to tell you. Are you mad?"

"Lexi, have you thought about what you're doing to me and Kevin?"

"Of course I have. But Rich and I are getting married. We can't live here anymore."

"Why not? I thought you liked being one big eclectic family. I thought you were happy here."

"I am…I was. I mean, it's time for us to have our own place."

"You mean, *Rich* thinks it's time to have your own place."

"He's going to be my husband. We need to start our own life."

"Without me. What about my life, my child? How are you going to leave and take him away from me?"

There it was. The question that had hammered at my mind ever since Rich had proposed we move. "That's not what we're doing. You can see

Preston whenever you want--you know that. We'll be close by, only a few blocks away." Rich's words tumbled out of my lips.

"Oh, so this is already a done deal? No discussing it with me. You've already found a place."

"We close two days after we come home from Hawaii."

"Unbelievable." He closed his eyes and shook his head. When he reopened them, his soft blue eyes had been replaced with something else. Something I didn't recognize. "After everything we've been through, *this* is how you treat me?"

"I'm sorry."

"Sorry? Lexi, you've done some fucked up shit in your life and I've always stood by you. I loved you, no matter what. I can't believe you're doing this to me."

"What about me and Rich? You can't seriously think we'd live under your roof forever."

"What, Rich isn't man enough to live in a place where his name isn't on the deed?"

Now he had crossed a line. "It's called pride, Marcus, and living in a home you've earned. Yes, it was Rich's idea to get our own place, but I agreed with him. We need our own space. We need to start our married life on our own. If you can't understand that, maybe you don't love me at all."

"Just like it's always been, everything is about you. Not one care to anyone else's feelings."

That was bullshit and he knew it. "I'm done with this conversation." I stood and started toward my bedroom.

"Not so fast." Marcus grabbed my arm. "I'm not gonna let you do this."

Kevin came in the living room. "What's going on out here?"

"You have no say in what I do." I yanked from his grasp. "I've done so much for you. You have no fucking clue how much I love and care for you."

"You have a real funny way of showing it."

I wanted to smack the smug look off his face.

"Can someone please tell me what's going on?" Kevin asked again.

"Lexi and Rich have decided this apartment isn't good enough anymore and have decided to move out and steal Preston away from us."

"That's not what we're doing and you know it!"

I felt Rich's hand on my back. Finally, I had an ally.

"You can say whatever you want Lexi, but it's all a bunch of bullshit."

"That's enough, Marcus." I'd never been so thankful for Rich's voice. "Lexi had a real hard time with this."

"Now your boy-toy is gonna defend you?"

"Hey--"

I stopped Rich. There was no point in bringing him into this ridiculous argument. "I can't take this anymore. Please get me out of here."

He nodded. "We're already packed. I'll grab our bags. You get Preston."

"Oh, no you don't. I don't give a fuck where you two go, but there is no way I'm letting you out of this apartment with my son."

Rich turned back. "I'd like to see you stop us."

"Don't test me." Marcus was eerily calm. I'd never heard him talk like that before. "If you even try to walk out the door with Preston, I will do whatever I have to. I can call in favors with judges all over this city. I'll have full custody by midnight and maybe throw you both in jail just for fun."

I envisioned myself pummeling him, ripping that sneer off his face. "You're a fucking asshole." Tears burned my eyes as my stomach once again began its raucous churn. If I didn't escape the insane drama, there'd be puke all over the floor.

"Call me whatever names you want, you're not taking my kid."

"He might not even be your kid!" I screamed, amazed at the instant relief of the statement.

"What's that supposed to mean?"

"I lied, Marcus! I didn't read the DNA test results before Preston ruined them. I told you Preston was yours, but I lied. And right now, I'm wishing I would have read them. Maybe then I'd have the joy of telling you Zak is his father and not you."

His eyes softened and the superiority faded. "But...you said we were a match."

"I lied. To protect you. To keep you happy. If I'd known you'd be such a fucking jackass about us moving, I would have changed my lie." I glared at him, despite his glossy eyes. "Don't worry. Tomorrow morning I'll be on the phone with the lab, begging them to send me a new letter as soon as possible."

His face went white and now looked like he wanted to puke.

"We'll stay the night. And you better spend some quality time with Preston. It might be the last you ever have."

Chapter 30

I managed maybe three hours of broken sleep, between the crying and vomiting. I'd never known what it was like to lose a best friend, but hacking an arm off seemed like it would incur less pain. Marcus had been in my life every minute since I was born. How was I going to survive without him?

Rich. That's how.

But what about this crazy wedding weekend, an event that was supposed to be one of the happiest times of my life? How would I stand there, next to someone who clearly hated me, and share in a marriage ceremony?

I couldn't think about it. We'd have to take it one day--one hour--at a time.

After calling the lab and getting a manager to agree to send the results overnight to the inn, I threw the last few items into my makeup case. The buzzer rang at noon. We'd booked the car service months ago to take all of us to the wedding. It was going to be just lovely sharing a nine-passenger van with Marcus and Kevin for a two-hour drive.

Nothing we could do now. It was our only way there.

The driver took the suitcases to the elevator as Marcus and Kevin brought more to the door. Rich wheeled ours out, too. The room felt like a morgue, with no one making eye contact. The silent vibe followed us into the van. Rich and I took the back seat, where we'd buckled Preston's car seat. Marcus and Kevin took the first row, leaving an empty row between us.

The drive would have dragged, but I spent the first hour on my phone, fielding calls from my mother and answering texts from Abby and Amanda.

Enough of that. I shut the phone off and snuggled against Rich for a nap.

When we pulled up to Kevin's aunt and uncle's place, The Inn at Harbor Hill, I hoped I was still asleep and dreaming. But oh, no. There really was a gigantic banner spanning the front porch.

Congratulations Alexandra and Richard & Kevin and Marcus!

I half expected it to light up and play *Here Comes the Bride.*

The door to the inn opened and my mother trotted out. "They're here!" Time to plaster on the happy face.

She hugged each person, then pulled us inside, her mouth rambling faster than a square dance caller. The inn was more like a millionaire's mansion, with its grand foyer and staircase, ballroom to one side, casual dining rooms to the other. After showing us where the ceremony would be, she finally took us to our suites.

"Okay, give Preston to me and I'll leave you alone so you can freshen up. Make sure you review your itineraries. The Welcome Dinner is at six sharp."

I closed the door behind her and plopped onto the bed, face first. Rich came over and rubbed my back.

"Still tired?"

"Exhausted. Can I take a nap?"

"We have like three hours before dinner. I don't see why not."

"Sounds fantastic." I closed my eyes.

Knock. Knock.

Rich went to the door.

"Is Lexi here?" Marcus asked.

"She's sleeping."

"Oh." He truly sounded disappointed. "Please tell her I stopped by."

He'd gotten almost halfway down the hall when I made it to the door. "Wait."

He faced me, looking almost as distraught as I felt.

"What do you need?"

"I was hoping we could talk."

Rich put his hand on my back. "You don't have to talk to him if you don't want to."

"No, it's okay." I turned back to Marcus. "Come on in."

He walked past Rich into the suite, my soon-to-be husband's eyes burning a hole into his back.

"I was hoping we could talk alone."

"Oh, no. You're out of your friggin' mind if you think I'm leaving her alone with you."

I rubbed Rich's arm. "It's fine."

"Not after the way he talked to you last night."

"I said a lot of terrible things, too. Trust me. I'll be fine."

He did not want to go. "I'll have my phone on me. Call if you need anything." He gave Marcus one last glare before leaving the room.

We both sat quiet. What did he want? Hadn't we said it all the night before?

"I'm sorry to bother you." He fidgeted with his fingers. "I needed to tell you something."

"Okay. What?"

He looked up, bloodshot eyes staring back at me. "When those papers come, if Preston and I are not a match, you'll never have to see me again." His voice was strained.

I nodded my head and he continued.

"If we are a match, we'll arrange a fair custody agreement. I love my son and I want to be in his life as much as you'll allow me." His last few words came as a whisper.

Marcus rested his elbows on his knees and covered his face with his hands, his shoulders trembling.

God, was he crying? I couldn't handle that. I'd done everything in my power to keep my eyes dry all day. No way could I sit here with Marcus; not like this.

"Lexi, I'm sorry. I'm so, so sorry." Forget keeping my eyes tear-free. His face was red and moist. "I hate the way I treated you last night. I don't know what came over me. I'm disgusted over the things I said to you. You have every right to take Preston and never let me see him."

The floodgates of my eyes opened. "You know I would never do that."

"I deserve it. Only a complete dickhead would treat the mother of his child the way I treated you. Maybe I don't deserve to be his father."

"Please stop. Don't beat yourself up like this. I was there too. I said some awful things. You were tired and stressed, and I should have told you months ago about us moving."

"Don't make excuses for me." He spoke more calmly now, his tears under control. "I completely overreacted. You were right. I can't expect newlyweds to live under my roof and play house as one big family. Rich deserves to have his own life and his own family, with you. You both deserve a new start."

"You and Kevin deserve a happy life too. And Preston will be a big part of it."

He forced a laugh. "Yeah, if he's even mine."

My heart broke all over again and reminded me why I had kept everything a secret. Marcus loved that boy with everything in him.

"I promise. We'll make it all work, somehow."

"I know." He stood and pulled me to him. "You're the closest thing I've ever had to a sister and I love you more than most of my family members. I can't lose you."

"You won't." And before I could control my vocal chords, they uttered a phrase I was unable to take back even if I'd wanted to. "We'll stay."

"What?"

I pulled back and looked into his wide eyes. "I can't take Preston away from you. And I need you too. We'll make it work."

He lifted me and spun around, his laugh in the curve of my neck. "Thank you Lexi! You don't know how happy this makes me."

"I do know. When you said you'd take him from me, I imagined what my life would be like, and I was heart-broken."

"I can't believe I said that to you. I hope you know it was the hurt talking. I would never ever have followed through."

"I know. But it made me realize it was exactly what I was doing to you. And I can't do it."

His jubilant smile faded. "What about Rich?"

"If he loves me like he says he does, he'll have to accept this."

"Lexi, I promise, we'll make it better than it was before. I'll do whatever Rich wants, anything, to make him happy and keep our family together."

"Me too."

A knock came at the door and Rich's head peeked in. "Everything good in here?"

Both Marcus and I smiled. "Better than ever."

Chapter 31

After Marcus left, I felt refreshed and ready to start this amazing wedding weekend. I was so deliriously happy I dragged Rich into bed and did lots of naughty things to him. He reciprocated, of course, and after two orgasms each, we lay spent, fighting for breath.

"We need to get ready for the Welcome Dinner."

"We can be fashionably late," I said as I conjured a bit more energy. My lips traveled down his chest, yet again. I needed one more taste of him.

"At this rate, we won't make it at all."

Even though I thoroughly enjoyed my head-giving, my mind started to wander. What was I going to wear to dinner? I needed to save something fabulous for tomorrow's rehearsal. Luckily I'd brought a dozen dresses with me, most of which were for romantic dinners in Ohau.

I had to tell Rich about canceling the move, but I would do it later. Or maybe the conversation was best had while deep-throating his cock. It wouldn't be a pleasant conversation, but maybe if I did it in between licks of his penis, it would soften the blow, pun totally intended.

Rich loved me. I'd make him understand why we had to stay put.

I wimped out on bringing it up, but the knock on the door and my mother's "Hello, you two," was a quick way to end our sexcapade.

"Can I come in?"

We answered with a resounding, "No!"

"Oh, okay. Dinner is starting in five minutes. Don't be late."

Yeah. Considering we were both naked and sticky and my hair was pointing in ten different directions, we were not going to make it in time. Oh well. She'd just have to deal with it.

* * * *

Rich and I walked in to the Welcome Dinner at six thirty-five, the fastest I'd ever showered, dressed and applied makeup. Surely it showed on our faces that our tardiness was due to hours of love-making. We had that *sex look* about us.

Kevin ran to us and hugged me tight. "Thank you! You don't know how much this means to me...us."

Before he could spill any of the beans, my mother stepped to us.

"Where have you been? I spoke to you over a half-hour ago."

"I'm sorry. It took us a while to get ready."

"I thought you were ready when I knocked. Were you naked or something?" She giggled at her joke, then caught my expression. "Oh, dear. Were you *actually* naked?"

"Mother, trust me, you don't want that answer."

I steered her away and after grabbing a glass of champagne from a silver tray, I mingled with my mother, chatting with the wedding party and welcoming the guests who had arrived early for the wedding.

The announcement was made to take our seats.

Kevin's father stood, microphone in hand. "I'd like to say a few words before our meal is served."

The room quieted, all eyes on him, which was no difficult task. He was pretty hot for a sixty-something year old--exactly what Kevin would look like someday, and Marcus was a very lucky man.

"A parent spends years, hoping and praying their child will find love. A true love. And it's painful to watch them make mistake after mistake with all the wrong people. But we sit back and continue to hold hope. And the moment we met Marcus, we knew. Kevin had found his soul mate. He'd found the man who would complete his life and make him happy. This road hasn't been easy. But that only makes this occasion more wondrous. I get to watch my son marry the man he loves, and for a parent there is only one event that tops that." A quick glance at both Marcus and Kevin. "And I hope to experience the joy of seeing my son with his own child one day, too!"

Their eyes met and exchanged smiles. I hadn't thought of Marcus and Kevin having a baby together. But why not? Marcus had enough money to hire the surrogate of their dreams.

"So, let's raise a toast to my son and his groom-to-be."

The room clinked and silence ensued while everyone sipped.

"And let's not forget Lexi and Rich. I can't thank you enough for accepting my son into your family. I look forward to our future and spending it together as one giant family. To Lexi and Rich."

Clinks again.

The salad course was placed in front of us and our guests dug into their strawberry Caesar salads. Every person I loved was right there, faces illuminated, and not just from the candlelight and wall sconces. They were happy. If I could have taken that moment and relived it forever, I would have.

"Anyone want anything from the bar?" Rich stood and set his napkin on the table.

I asked for another glass of champagne and mom needed a refill on her ginger ale.

While he was gone, the unmistakable rock ringtone of his cellphone sounded. I looked around the table. It had to be there somewhere. I found it under his napkin.

The caller I.D. listed *Simon, Amy.*

It was after seven. Why would she be calling now? She had to know we were away for our wedding weekend.

Rich returned with the drinks and took his seat. I downed half of mine in one gulp.

"Something wrong?"

"No, not at all." I downed the rest and narrowed my eyes. "Your phone rang. It was that Amy Simon."

His face went pale. "Oh. Um, sorry. She shouldn't be calling now. Maybe I should call her back, find out if something's wrong."

"Yeah, you go do that."

Three drinks later, I'd shaken off the call from Amy. I told myself he wasn't cheating on me, but something was definitely up.

* * * *

The phone rang on my nightstand at eight the next morning. Who the hell was calling me so damn early?

"Good morning," an automated voice greeted me. "This is your wake-up call. Have a lovely day at the Inn at Harbor Hill. Good bye."

I had not arranged a wake-up call and was not happy about it. Closing my eyes, I tried returning to my dream world.

Rich's hand moved across my back. "We should get up."

"Why?"

"Didn't you read your itinerary?"

Crap. Forgot about that thing.

"Breakfast is in..." Rich paused and lifted his head. "Fifty-eight minutes."

"Ugh. Can't we skip it?"

"Fine by me. I'm not the one who's gotta deal with your mom."

I groaned and threw the comforter off. "I so don't need that drama."

We showered and dressed and made our way to one of the dining rooms, where a breakfast buffet had been laid out. By then I was starved and the sight of steaming chafing dishes made my stomach growl. I piled a waffle and a pancake on my plate and topped them with strawberry sauce and whipped cream. Rich followed me to a table where Preston was already sitting with a plate of cut-up fruit and waffle.

Before I could even get a bite in, Marcus sat down next to me. "Have you checked with the front desk yet?"

"No." I shoved some pancake in my mouth, not needing to ask why.

"I haven't either."

I moved my gaze from my giant plate of delectable yumminess to his face.

"I'm scared, Lexi."

"I am too." I reached for his hand and squeezed.

"What am I going to do if we're not--"

I stopped him. "You're a match. After breakfast, we'll go to the front desk and get the test results. They should be here. It will all be over and we can enjoy this weekend."

He squeezed my hand this time. "What would I do without you?"

He'd never have to know.

While Rich chatted with the chef about the rehearsal dinner menu, and Kevin tended to something wedding related with my mom and his, Marcus and I walked to the front desk.

"Hello. We're expecting a letter today. Has it arrived?" He gave the clerk his name.

"Um, I don't see anything here, Mr. Wells. I can call your room when it arrives."

He nodded. "Thank you."

I walked with him outside to the garden, where tables were being set up for our rehearsal dinner.

"I have a bad feeling about this," Marcus said.

"Why?"

"I don't know. I just do."

"Well, I know everything is going to be great. Look at where we are. Is there anyplace more beautiful than this?" I opened my arms wide. "Everything is going to be perfect. And if it's not, they'll answer to me."

That got a smile out of him.

He pulled me into a hug. "Can I tell you again how sorry I am for the other night?"

"It's not necessary."

"I'm ashamed at what I almost threw away."

I stared him in the eyes. "It's done and over with. I don't want to ever talk about it again, okay?"

He nodded and smiled. "Message received."

"Good, 'cause I gotta get going. I have a strict schedule to stick to today."

"Oh, I think we all do."

An hour later, I sat with my feet in an invigorating foot Jacuzzi and my hands in a paraffin wax dip. Amanda was on one side, Sheila on the other, gabbing and laughing. Ahhh. What a life! Even my mother was being semi-normal.

Everything was perfect.

Except we still hadn't gotten the letter from the lab.

And I still had to tell Rich I'd changed my mind about moving.

Chapter 32

"Places, everyone!" Mom sang as she twittered around the garden.

The sun had begun its descent, but the garden was lit with candles and twinkle lights. Gold, burgundy, and orange chrysanthemums lined an aisle leading to an arbor, covered in shades of fall. I'd been told the flowers were dahlias, amaranthus, celosia, Chinese lanterns, kangaroo paws and curly willow. No clue what any of those were, but they were gorgeous all together.

I linked arms with Dad behind a long line of bridesmaids and groomsmen.

Kevin stood in front of me, both his parents with him. He turned around and winked at me.

The harpist began her rendition of Pachabel's *Canon in D*, while Amanda and Andy began the procession.

When my turn came, I walked down the aisle, imagining the chairs filled with smiling faces. And when I spied the face at the end--the biggest, brightest smile of them all--I fought tears. My dad placed my hand in Rich's, my other clasped a bouquet of ribbons and bows.

The minister spoke and explained how the ceremony would go, but I wasn't listening. My mother and everyone else were. They'd fill me in later. My eyes stayed on Rich's. In less than twenty-four hours, I would be his bride, his wife. And I couldn't wait.

The harpist played her jubilant exit music, and Rich and I led the procession to the rehearsal dinner area beside the ceremony. Waiters circulated with trays of fancy drinks and I snagged one and took a long sip. A few of my relatives and some of our out of town guests had joined the party. I pulled Rich over and made the introductions.

As we made our way to the bar, I saw my mother chatting with Mrs. Wells. Preston was in her arms, and the two old friends fawned over his cuteness.

Rich and I mingled some more and when I turned to place my empty glass on a tray, I caught the faces of my four newest friends.

"Ahh!" Joleene and Jaime screamed as they ran and hugged me.

"You guys weren't supposed to be here 'til tomorrow."

"I know, but you know Scott, he likes to get in the car and take a drive." I reached and hugged the guys.

"You must be the Buffalo crew."

They laughed. "That's us."

"Guys, this is Rich."

He put a hand out as I introduced each person, ending with Scott. "Man, I can't thank you enough for driving Lexi to Toronto last month."

"No problem. I figured we owed her for making her stay out so late with us."

"Yeah." Rich turned his grin to me. "I'm sure you had to twist her arm."

Ding. Ding.

My mother's voice boomed over the outdoor sound system. "Could everyone please take their seats?"

Screeching feedback from the mic reverberated through the area as she handed it to my dad.

"Sorry, folks." He cleared his throat. "Mr. Jacobs had his turn last night, so now I guess it's mine."

The crowd laughed.

"Lexi has always been the child to give me heartburn. She was first born and first in trouble." More laughs. "But I always knew she could take care of herself. We did still worry, hoping she'd make something of herself and find what made her happy. For a while there, we thought for sure she'd marry Marcus."

More chuckles.

"Lexi, honey, I wish you all the happiness you deserve. Rich, I know you'll take care of my girl."

Rich squeezed my hand and kissed it.

"Marcus, you've been like one of my kids, and I wish you and Kevin the same happiness." He reached for his beer. "Everyone, please raise your glasses and toast to the happy couples, Lexi and Rich and Marcus and Kevin."

Servers filled the tables with platters and bowls brimming with Southern cuisine. I'd been dreaming about this for months. Who could resist a saucy BBQ'd rib and a fresh baked corn muffin? Certainly not me.

"Ahem. Excuse me." Mr. Wells had taken over the microphone. "I'd like to say a few words, if I could."

The crowd hushed.

"Not many of you know who I am. I'm Victor Wells, Marcus's father. My wife and I are very honored to be here today. Over the last few weeks we've gotten to spend time with Marcus and Kevin and we see how happy our son is. There really is nothing else a parent can ask for. We wish them the best and we welcome Kevin into our family." He lifted his glass. "To Marcus and Kevin."

I raised my glass at Marcus. "Here, here."

His eyes were glazed with tears as he stood and walked to his father. The two embraced in the only hug I'd ever witnessed between them.

Looking around, our guests had returned to their plates, devouring the luscious feast. I nudged Rich's arm. "Told you this would be a hit."

He nodded and took another bite of his corn on the cob.

Just when I thought I'd burst, dessert was set on the table--a big steaming platter of apple cobbler with scoops of vanilla ice cream melting on top. Guess I could make a little more room in my stomach.

After filling a bowl for myself, I turned to Rich. "You want some?"

His eyes were on his phone. "Huh?"

"Dessert?"

"Oh." He pulled his gaze away. "No thanks."

"Suit yourself. It smells amazing."

I dug in while he twisted in his seat. Was he nervous or something?

"You okay?"

"Yeah, fine." He checked his phone again.

"Expecting a call?"

He looked at me, not realizing I had been watching him. "Oh...no. Just checking the time."

"Got a hot date?"

He smiled and kissed my cheek. "Only you."

"Not tonight. You have strict orders to bunk with Andy, remember?"

"Aww. I did forget. Why are we doing that again?"

"My mother insisted we spend our last night as single people in separate beds."

Another phone check. Now I was getting curious.

"Can you believe it?" Kevin came up behind and put his arms around both Rich and I. "By this time tomorrow, we'll be happily married and dancing the night away."

"Yes we will."

"I am so happy! And after Marcus told me the great news, it made the whole weekend even more perfect."

I shook my head at Kevin as Rich asked, "What great news?"

Apparently Kevin had missed my hint.

"Silly, about you guys staying with us instead of moving."

"What?"

Oh. That was not a face I liked on Rich. He turned from Kevin to me. "What is he talking about?"

"Um, well…"

Kevin put both his arms around me tight. "Lexi is just the best!"

"What the hell is he talking about?" Rich's eyes burned into mine.

I pushed Kevin off me, and he noticed the glare on Rich's face.

"Oh, dear. What have I done?"

"Did you tell Marcus we'd stay?"

"Oh, uh, kinda."

"Fuck!" Rich stood. "How could you do this? And without even talking to me."

"It just kinda happened. And it's not even definite. Only if Marcus and Preston are a match."

"Lexi, we agreed. We put money down and signed a contract."

"I know, but…we can cancel it, right?"

"So this is how it is? No discussion?"

"Well…no, but--"

"Don't even bother."

He walked away as the screech and burst of a bright blue firework exploded above our heads. A red one followed, transforming to gold.

"Rich, wait." I jogged after him, not an easy feat in four-inch heels on grass. "Let me explain."

"There is no explanation. Marcus's happiness is obviously more important to you than mine."

He turned to keep walking, but I grabbed his arm. More fireworks boomed and sparkled in the night sky, with oohs and aahs from our guests.

"That's not true and you know it."

"No Lexi, I do know it. I will never be your priority. And…" His gaze dropped to the ground then back at me, the reflection of a green explosion shining in his glossy eyes. "I can't live my life like that."

He walked off toward the inn and I followed him to our room. Once there, he grabbed his suitcase and threw clothes into it.

"What are you doing?"

"I'm leaving."

"What?" I'd stayed calm the entire time, but the severity of the situation had now slapped me across the face. "You can't. Our wedding is tomorrow."

He met my eyes once again. "I'm leaving."

No. This was not happening. I was not going to let the man I loved walk away the night before our wedding.

"I love you. Please don't do this." Forget holding my composure.

"I know you do, but I think you love Marcus a little bit more." He zipped the suitcase and hauled it to the floor.

I shook my head violently for emphasis. "No."

He wheeled his suitcase toward the door. "And just so you know, Amy Simon is an events planner who helped me arrange the fireworks as a surprise for you."

I couldn't form words.

He grabbed his jacket from the coat rack. "Goodbye."

Chapter 33

I'd thought losing a best friend was the worst feeling in the world. Nope. Dead wrong on that. Being practically left at the altar was.

Hot tears cascaded down my cheeks as I threw myself on the bed in a *deja vu* moment. This wasn't the first time Rich had walked out on me. But the other was a lifetime ago, and this was far more devastating.

A knock came on the door and it creaked open.

"Rich?" I quickly wiped my face with the back of my hand.

"Are you okay?" Marcus asked. "You ran off, and then Rich got in a car with his best man and tore out of here."

I erupted in a bawling mess of tears. "This is all your fault!"

"What happened?" he asked and cradled me.

I pushed him away. "If you hadn't flipped out over me and Rich moving, none of this would be happening right now."

"Lexi, calm down."

"No, I will not calm down. You fucked everything up. You guilted me into staying and the kid might not even be yours. Rich will never forgive me for choosing you over him."

"Is that what this is about? He's mad you told me you'd stay?"

"Of course he is. Why did I ever think it would work?"

He pulled me to him again and this time I let him. "It's gonna be fine. I'll call Rich and tell him we changed our minds. You can move out. We'll make it work."

I shook my head. "It's too late. I chose you over him and he thinks I don't love him enough."

"You were put in an impossible situation. And you were right. It is my fault."

This was not how I'd wanted the night before my wedding to go-- sobbing hysterically, imagining the rest of my life as a spinster. There were even a few dozen cats in this nightmare.

Marcus smoothed my hair. "I'll make it right. I promise."

He tucked me into bed and pulled out his cellphone. He left a message for Rich, begging him to call. After kissing me on the forehead, he clicked off the light and closed the door. As if I could actually sleep.

I grabbed my cellphone from the nightstand and called Rich, leaving the same pleading message.

I called back and told him how much I loved him and couldn't live without him.

And after more crying, I called again and promised to do anything he wanted if he came back.

"Lexi." Amanda's soothing voice echoed in the room.

"Please go away."

She came and sat on the bed, moonlight shining in through the window. "What can I do?"

"Unless you can make Rich come back, and still marry me tomorrow, there's nothing you can do."

She pulled the covers back and climbed in next to me.

"You don't have to sleep here."

"Yes I do. It's the night before my best friend's wedding. We were supposed to have a gal's night."

"I'm not much company, and besides, with no wedding, there's no night before the wedding."

"He'll come back."

My incessant sobs started again. I wanted to believe her, but she was so wrong. I'd fucked it up for the last time.

* * * *

"Lexi, Lexi, Lexi."

I opened my eyes and there stood Karma in my wedding dress, shaking her head at me. Bright autumn sun shone on her perfect skin and frizz-free hair.

"Get out of here. And take the dress with you."

"You can fix this. It's not too late."

I sat up and stared her down. "You come in here, punishing me for everything I've done the last few months, and now you want to help me 'fix' it? Sorry if I don't jump up and kiss your feet."

"I haven't been punishing you."

"Yeah? What do you call it?"

"Lexi, you make your own decisions and must deal with the repercussions."

"Gee, thanks for sharing your ingenious wisdom with me. Now, I'd really like it if you could leave so I can sleep through my ruined wedding day."

"I told you, it's not too late. Everything can still work out." She stepped out of my gown and laid it at the foot of my bed.

"I don't know what to do." Tears that had been clinging to my lashes released and trailed down my cheeks. "Please tell me what to do."

"You know I can't."

"Then what the hell good are you?"

She smiled and waved, disappearing into the full-length mirror.

The phone next to my head began ringing, jolting me awake. God damn wake-up call. I picked up the phone and slammed it right back down, closing my eyes.

Knock. Knock. "Lexi, it's Mom. I have your breakfast cart."

Oh. My. God. I looked at the clock. That hour went by fast.

"Go away."

"There's a long day ahead of you. You need to eat."

Without permission, she opened the door and wheeled the cart of food in.

"Mom, Rich left. We're not getting married."

"Oh, I don't believe that. He just needed to run an errand."

Was she seriously this stupid? Sometimes she only understood pure bluntness. "Please get the fuck out of here."

She continued, ignoring my statement. "I saw Amanda this morning. She's having breakfast with Andrew."

Oh yeah. Amanda was here when I fell asleep.

I sat up, bringing myself back to my disaster of a reality. "Will you listen to me, please?" And she actually did. "I fucked up. Rich is gone. He's not coming back." My voice caught at the last statement.

She sat, wrapping her arms around me. "I don't know what's going on, but it will all work out."

For once, I wished she was right.

"You better eat. The hair stylist will be here soon." Her gaze moved to the end of my bed and she gasped. "Why is your dress laying like that? It's going to get wrinkled."

She hung it back on its padded hanger, then walked to the door. "I'll be back with some compresses for your eyes. Can't have such puffiness on your wedding day."

For some odd reason, her smile made me feel better.

I flopped back on the bed and closed my eyes again, but the smells of cinnamon and sugar rose and made their way into my nostrils, and my stomach growled. I grabbed a piece of French toast from the platter and took it to the window seat overlooking the front of the property. People everywhere delivered boxes and toted chairs and tables and other wedding related items. Had anyone told them only half of the wedding was happening today?

I thought of calling Rich again, but would it make a difference? Was there anything else I could say? I'd already left him a bunch of messages, telling him everything I could think of to make him come back.

Why not make one last-ditch effort?

"Rich, I hope you listen to this. I know how bad I fucked everything up. But I love you and I want to spend my life making you happy." I tried to contain my tears. Wasn't going to happen. "Please marry me today."

I hung up and checked the clock. Four hours before the ceremony. He still had plenty of time to get back to the inn.

Yeah. Whatever.

Another knock on the door. Marcus poked his head in. "Hey, how are you this morning?"

"Still miserable."

"Well, what I'm about to tell you isn't going to help. The letter from the clinic still hasn't arrived."

"Does it even matter at this point?"

"No, I guess not. Any word from Rich?"

I couldn't even answer him.

"There's still time."

Knock. Knock.

Would there be no peace today? This time it was Amanda, followed by the hair stylist.

Marcus gave me a quick hug and disappeared.

"Ready to have your hair done for your wedding?" the stylist asked with bubbly exuberance and a hundred-watt smile.

"No."

Her perky face deflated.

"She's kidding," Amanda said and turned back to me. "Right, Lexi?"

"Whatever."

Amanda pulled me toward a chair and forced me down.

"I don't see the point."

"You can't get married with hair like this."

"Did you get whacked on the head and forget everything that happened last night? I'm not getting married today."

She ignored me and spoke to the stylist. "She wants something pretty and simple, some of it pulled back. No crazy tight up-do or she'll slit your throat."

The stylist giggled.

"I'm not kidding."

As the skinny blonde applied some product to my frizzy hair, Amanda rummaged through my things, producing the silk gardenia hairclip I had bought in lieu of a veil.

"Here," she said and handed it over. "Work this in, too."

Amanda quick kissed my cheek and told me she'd be back.

Not two minutes later, my door opened again. Just prop it open and let everyone at the inn pay me a visit.

This time it was Sheila. She sat on the bed across from me. "You know, if he doesn't show today, I will hunt him down and hack his balls off."

I fought a smile, but lost. "I know you will. Thank you."

The parade of people kept on coming and by twelve-thirty my hair and makeup were done and my dress was on. The bridesmaids and my mother had congregated in my room, laughing and smiling, snapping pictures. Stacey finally made an appearance. I'd gotten the feeling she'd been avoiding me all day.

I met her gaze. "Have you talked to him?"

"Um, well, I…"

"He called you?"

She sighed. "Yes, this morning, but I'm not supposed to tell you I talked to him."

"What did he say?" My hands were on her elbows and I restrained myself from shaking her. "Is he coming?"

"Uh…he didn't say."

"Then what exactly *did* he say?" This time I did give her body a little jerk.

"He asked if he could stay at my apartment."

Well that was it. The end. Finito. He definitely wasn't coming back.

"Can everyone please leave?"

No one said a word. A couple people headed toward the door. A couple more asked if I needed anything. I shook my head and held back tears. I'd wait until they left before letting the dam break.

Amanda was last and put a hand to my shoulder. "Do you want me to stay?"

"No, thanks."

Before the door had even clicked shut, tears burst through my ducts like a flash flood, rushing down my cheeks. I curled up on my bed and let them keep coming. There was no point in even trying to stop them.

Chapter 34

A knock at the door. What did they not understand about "Leave me alone?" But the knocker was persistent.

"Go away."

"Lexi, we need to talk."

The voice was familiar, but my brain would not let me figure it out.

"No, leave me alone."

"Please. I have to tell you something."

Finally it clicked. Zak was outside my door. Why?

I stood, my dress all kinds of wrinkled, and opened the door a crack. "What?"

"I'd rather talk in the room instead of the hallway."

"Fine." I pushed the door open and shuffled back to the bed.

He closed the door behind him and turned to me. "You look like shit."

"Yes, thanks. That's what every bride loves to hear."

"What's going on? Why are you in tears?"

"My groom left and the wedding's off. Life as I know it is over and... wait, why the hell am I telling you this? What do you want?"

"Can I help?"

"No. Just tell me why you're here."

"Okay. I talked with Ruth yesterday, about the night you broke in. She told me the conversation you two had that day."

"And? I'd rather not relive it. I'm miserable enough."

"Why did you ask about my vasectomy?"

No reason to keep it a secret now. "Since your wife was pregnant and it happened so fast and easy, I thought maybe you'd had a reversal or it had reversed itself naturally."

"What would that have to do with you?"

"I thought Preston could be yours."

He laughed.

"Thanks, that's exactly what I need on my ruined wedding day."

"Lexi, it's funny 'cause there's no way it could be possible."

"Well, there's no other explanation for how your wife got pregnant and I couldn't help but think there was a chance you'd impregnated me instead of Marcus."

He crossed the room and sat on the bed next to me. "You should have come to me. I could have told you I had sperm on ice."

"What?" Please let me have heard him right.

"The prerequisite to having the vasectomy done without having any children was that I had to keep some frozen, in the event I ever did want to have kids."

Thank you God, Buddha, Allah, Karma! Whomever there was to thank.

He continued. "And I'm so glad I did. I can't imagine my life without my baby girl."

I nodded. "I know what you mean."

So all this time, and all these problems, because I'd jumped to a stupid conclusion. What was wrong with me?

He put an arm around me and gave me a squeeze. "Can you believe where our lives are now versus what they were when we were together?"

"Yours is great, mine is in the shitter."

"What happened?"

"Same as always. I fucked up. Rich got sick of me choosing Marcus over him."

"Yeah, I know how he feels."

Again I found myself in shock.

"Why did you think I couldn't stand Marcus when we were together? You were always asking his opinion on everything. We couldn't even go to the movies alone without you asking him which one we should see. Made me feel pretty useless."

God, he was right. I did do that. I'd lost some of it when I got together with Rich, but I still did it. A lot.

I turned to him again, eyes with fresh tears. "What do I do to fix it?"

"I don't know. When I met Meg, she made me feel needed. I can't pinpoint how. She just did."

"Well, that's a real help."

He pulled me tight to him again. "You'll figure it out. I could see how much Rich loves you."

"Yeah, well, not anymore."

Someone knocked on the door again. Marcus popped his head in, dressed to the nines in his custom-made Armani tux, doing a double take when he saw Zak.

I stood and rushed to him, tears flowing, but this time, from joy. "Preston is yours.

"What? How?"

Zak stood. "My vasectomy is still one-hundred percent effective."

Marcus hugged me tight and whispered, "Finally, it's over." He turned to Zak. "Thank you."

"No problem." He patted Marcus on the back. "I've gotta go. My girls are waiting in the car. Congratulations on your wedding."

"Please stay. You drove all this way, the least I can do is feed you."

Zak smiled. "Thank you. Let me go talk to Meg."

He left and Marcus and I were alone.

"He's really mine?"

I shook my head and forced a smile. This was going to be the best day of Marcus's life. He hugged me again and joy radiated from his body.

"How are you holding up?" he asked when we parted.

"While my life is crumbling around me?"

"I talked with Stan, the maintenance guy, and he said Rich was at the apartment this morning."

"Did he take all his things?"

"Didn't say."

I nodded my head. Time to accept my life as it was. And grow up. "I think I'm gonna look for a place of my own. Is that okay with you?"

"Yes, if that's really what you want."

"I need to do it. I know we never wanted the every other weekend kind of custody thing, but I think it's time I live on my own. I hope you understand."

"I do. And I'll help in any way you want."

"Thank you."

We stood in silence for a moment until he cleared his throat. "I came here for a reason. I, um…"

What bad news could possibly come next?

"The ceremony is due to start in half an hour. You're supposed to be my, um, Best Woman."

"Oh my God. I completely forgot. Marcus, I'm so sorry."

"I know. It's okay. I came to ask if you mind that Jeff takes your place."

I'd fucked up this whole day for myself, and now I was messing it up for Marcus too. "Yes."

"Okay. I'll go talk to him."

"No, I meant yes, I mind. You've been my best friend since forever and I need to put my own bullshit aside and stand by you."

"Lexi, you don't have to do that. You'll have to face all those people."

"So what? I have to stop being so selfish."

"I can't even tell you what this means to me." He pulled me close.

I let him hug me for two-point-five seconds, then pulled away. "If I'm gonna do this, I have to fix myself so I'm not so hideous."

The reflection in the mirror was horrid--puffy, red and bloodshot eyes, frizzy hair with a smooshed silk gardenia in it. "I think I have enough time to beautify, somewhat."

"You always look beautiful to me."

"Thanks, but I don't want to scare people away."

I reached for my makeup bag and did what I could. Then noticed my dress. "Shit. I can't wear this."

Marcus checked at his watch. "We kinda need to go…now."

"Okay." I rubbed some product over my hair and smoothed it down. "I paid a crapload of money for this dress--might as well let people see it."

When we made it to the garden, the wedding party had already assembled for the procession. Guests were in their seats and the harpist plucked the last few notes of her piece. Amid gasps and whispers, I took my place next to Marcus at the end of the aisle. I held my head as high as I could and kept my gaze above the guests'.

I wore Kevin's wedding band on my thumb and rubbed my forefinger over it. The symbol of everlasting love and devotion. Fighting tears, I shook off my sadness and forced a smile. I turned my attention to the procession.

Most of the guests watched the bridesmaids and groomsmen, but my dad looked at me. He was so handsome in his black tuxedo--his "monkey suit"--and now it was a waste. Our eyes locked and he told me he loved me.

The day was perfect. Glistening sunlight beamed with a light wind that rustled the trees, occasionally sending a crimson or amber leaf to the ground. The bridesmaids were beautiful in their black dresses with autumn floral bouquets popping in contrast.

Andy took his place behind me and for the first time--I think ever--put a warm hand on my arm, asking if I was okay. I nodded.

After Jeanette and Jeff took their places, my little man came bouncing down the aisle. My heart burst with pride as he smiled and flirted with every camera. He saw me and yelled "Mama" and rushed over. I squatted down and hugged him, unsuccessful at keeping my tears back. But I limited them to only a couple.

The music changed and the guests stood. There was Kevin, chic as ever in his white tuxedo. His smile nearly touched the bright sky above us. Marcus's eyes were completely glazed.

Kevin's parents walked him to the end of the aisle and the music faded, silence surrounding us. I was supposed to be walking down the aisle at that exact moment, my arm linked with my dad's, Rich's adoring eyes on mine.

It took every ounce of strength to keep my feet planted. I couldn't control my tear ducts as well.

"Dearest family and friends, we have been invited here to share with Kevin and Marcus a very important moment in their lives. Their love and understanding of each other has grown and matured, and now they have decided to live their lives together as husbands."

The minister turned his attention to Kevin and his parents.

"Who gives this man to be wed?"

"We do," they replied, then kissed Kevin and joined his hand with Marcus's.

The minister continued. "Marriage should not be entered into unadvisedly or lightly, but reverently, discreetly, advisedly and solemnly."

My eyes were on Marcus, Kevin and the minister, when the low hum of whispers started once again. What could they possibly be saying now?

The ceremony continued, but I blocked out all sounds. I was standing there, about all I could handle at that moment. Until Marcus said my name.

I shook out of my daze, the minister staring at me with his palm outstretched.

"The ring, please."

I pulled Kevin's wedding band from my thumb.

After a blessing, Marcus pushed the sparkling band onto Kevin's ring finger. "With this ring, I thee wed." Kevin then did the same.

Surprised at my composure, I actually smiled when the minister exclaimed, "I now pronounce you husband and husband."

Marcus and Kevin kissed, then turned to the crowd of guests, accepting cheers and clapping. They practically skipped down the aisle.

I stepped forward, unsure of what to do. This wasn't how we'd practiced it. I was supposed to be down the aisle already, happily married. The harpist continued with her jubilant exit music and I stood there. The guests were staring, but their faces blurred together. I put my head down and took another shaky step. God, was there anything more pathetic than a bride walking down the aisle, alone, at the end of a wedding ceremony?

Someone took my arm. Even through a layer of tears, I recognized the leather jacket and messy-on-purpose hair.

Chapter 35

We'd reached the end of the aisle before my tears dried enough to let me see that Rich was physically there, his arm looped with mine. He wasn't some bizarre hallucination caused by my heartache.

The wedding party headed toward the patio for cocktail hour, but Rich led me inside the inn. He'd come back, but was he there for the reasons I'd hoped and prayed for? Did he still love me? I couldn't let my heart read too much into it. For all I knew, he was back to get the engagement ring. We walked in silence and he led me to the library. Once inside, he let go of my arm and closed the doors behind us.

I stood there, heart racing, stomach churning, as Rich stepped toward me. He hadn't said a word. His face showed nothing. Did he know how badly he was torturing me?

Before I knew what was happening, his lips had pressed to mine with pure urgency. He'd pulled me to him and wrapped his warmth around me. My body reacted the only way it knew how, and I kissed him back, winding my arms so tight around his neck I thought I might break it.

"I'm so sorry I left," he said when his lips released mine. "Please forgive me." He held me tight, the dampness of his tears on my shoulder. "I love you."

I pulled back and put my hand to his face, light stubble pricking my finger tips. His sad, ocean-blue eyes pleaded with me.

"I thought I'd never see you again."

He nuzzled his cheek into my hand, another tear trailing.

"Why did you come back?"

"I can't live without you. I was so stupid last night. Please forgive me." He moved my hand to his lips and kissed it.

"But Stacey said you asked to stay at her place."

"I did." Guilt crept into his eyes. "When I left, I didn't know what I was doing. I was so confused. I slept at Gryz's and then I called her this morning, but not even five minutes later, I knew there was no way I could leave you. I hate myself for what I did to you last night."

"You're not the one who's to blame. I did this. I'm the one who screwed it all up."

"Lexi, you are who you are and that's why I fell in love with you. It was wrong to force you to change."

"But it's not all about me. I need you to be happy too, and I can't ask you to sacrifice for me. I decided to move out, even without you, and already talked to Marcus. We're going to arrange shared custody."

"Are you sure that's what you want?"

I nodded. "An old friend kinda smacked me in the face with some truths about myself that I never realized before."

His eyebrows rose. "Like what?'

"It doesn't matter." I smiled at him. "You're the one I love, and who I want to spend my life with. You matter most to me, and I never should have let myself forget that."

He moved a stray hair from my face and wiped the tears from my cheek. We kissed again.

"I think we can work it all out."

I nodded. "I go where you go. It's only a few blocks away. It will be perfect."

"Lexi, I cancelled the sale on that apartment."

"Oh." How stupid I'd been to think we were getting back together so easily and skipping off into the sunset. Of course he'd want some time apart. After everything that had happened, we couldn't just jump back into our old lives. My gaze fell to the floor. "I understand."

"I found something even closer to Marcus and Kevin."

"You did?"

"What do you think about next door?"

Huh? I did that confused head-tilt thing that dogs do.

"The last day we looked at apartments, Bill told me about a new listing. I said no. Back then I wasn't remotely interested. I called him this morning and it was still available. Lexi, it's right next door to Marcus and Kevin."

"The Bernsteins?"

"They're retiring to Florida. We can even open Preston's room into the new place. There can be access to it from both apartments."

I jumped and covered him with kisses, sending him stumbling back.

"I didn't want to do anything without talking to you, but to make sure no one else could have it, I had to get some cash to the realtor. That's why

Stephanie Haefner

I was so late. But I wanted to be here." He held my cheeks in his hands. "You shouldn't have had to face everyone alone."

"I don't even care about that now. You're here and I love you and it's all going to be perfect."

He drew my lips to his, connecting us and bringing us back to that perfect place with me and Rich, where no one else mattered.

He pulled away, all traces of tears and sadness gone. "So, are you ready to marry me?"

"Even more than the first time you asked."

We burst through the library doors, not even sure where we were going or what exactly we were doing, and almost hit Sheila and Amanda with them.

"Holy shit! I'm so sorry," I said and laughed.

"Geez. I knew I was risking my health when I agreed to be your bridesmaid, but I didn't think I'd get a broken nose."

I hugged Sheila.

"Is everything...okay?" Amanda asked.

"Better than okay." I looked to Rich, then back at her. "Wedding's back on."

"Oh my God!" She did a little jig. "Now?"

We hadn't really thought it through. "Um...well. I don't know if--"

"The sooner the better," Rich answered.

"Okay," Sheila clapped her hands together. "Me and Amanda will herd the guests back to the garden. You two go and fix yourselves. You look like hell."

They trotted off down the hall.

Rich squeezed my hand and pressed another kiss to my cheek. "I'll meet you at the end of the aisle."

* * * *

I'd just finished reapplying some makeup when a knock came at my door. Dad peeked his head in. "You ready?"

I stood from the vanity, fighting my happy tears. "Yes."

He handed me my bouquet--pure while calla lilies and roses. "You are beautiful. I hope he knows how lucky he is."

"I'm the lucky one."

I looped my arm through his and we stepped over the threshold. When we reached the garden, the bridesmaids and groomsmen were already in their places. No need for another procession. With a hand signal from my father, the harpist once again played *Wagner's Wedding March*, and our guests stood a second time. The long aisle was lined with smiling faces, but the only one I cared about was at the end.

The minister re-welcomed the guests, then turned to my father. "Who gives this woman to be wed?"

"Her mother and I do."

He kissed my cheek and took my hand and placed it in Rich's. We stood there as the minister spoke, but I wasn't even paying attention. My dreams were coming true, when an hour earlier, I'd thought they were lost forever. Rich squeezed my hand, a warm reminder he was still there, and would always be.

The minister asked us to face each other and I handed my bouquet to Abby to hold. One at a time, we recited the vows we'd chosen together.

"I, Lexi, take you, Rich, to be my friend, my lover, the father of my children and my husband. I will be yours in plenty and want, in sickness and health, in joy and sorrow, in failure and triumph. I promise to cherish and respect you, to care and protect you, to comfort and encourage you, and stay with you, for all eternity."

By the time I'd finished, fresh tears trickled down my cheeks, matched by the ones ready to fall from Rich's eyes. I held his hands tight as he recited the same lines to me, then brought my hands to his lips.

The minister then asked for our rings. Both Abby and Gryz stepped forward with shimmering platinum bands. After a short prayer, he offered his hand to us and we each took one ring.

"Repeat after me. I give you this ring as a symbol of my love and commitment."

I looked at Rich, my hand shaking, and pushed his wedding ring onto his finger. "I give you this ring as a symbol of my love and commitment."

He did the same, and a wave of euphoria surged through my body. The minister hadn't said it yet, but we were officially married. I stared at Rich, an uncontrollable giddy smile on my face.

The minister opened his arms wide. "By the power of your love and commitment, and the power vested in me..." He glanced from me to Rich. "I now pronounce you husband and wife. You may kiss the bride."

Finally.

Cheers erupted around us and I planted my lips on Rich's, my tongue diving deep inside his mouth. Yeah, not the understated sweet kiss we'd talked about for that moment. But I couldn't help it. Any semblance of control had long disappeared. I even heard a howl and a "Go Lexi," come from the back of the garden. Had to be those crazy Buffalo kids.

We pulled apart, laughing, and I collected my bouquet.

"For the first time, may I introduce, Mr. and Mrs. Richard Taylor."

More cheers as we exited the garden, millions of camera flashes sparking at us. We ran inside the inn for a moment of peace while guests filtered back to the patio for an extended cocktail hour.

Rich kissed me again and pulled my body into a tight hug.

"I can't believe we're standing here--married."

"Thank you for coming back," I said to him, swallowing a sob.

"There is no need to thank me. I should be thanking you for still agreeing to marry me."

Rich nuzzled my nose and placed one last kiss on my lips. He traced the edging of lace that formed the deep v of my neckline, his fingertip leaving a trail of goosebumps on the inside of my breast. "This dress is really sexy."

Hunger and desire heated my core and I saw it in his eyes, too.

"Mmm-hmm." I nibbled at his neck.

"We should probably get out there, huh?"

"Yep." My kisses traveled to his earlobe.

"Maybe we should freshen up before the reception."

"Definitely."

Rich grabbed my hand and ran toward our room so fast I could barely keep up. He didn't remove his tux jacket. We didn't even take my dress off--just hiked it up for a crazy quickie.

While I fixed my hair, he readjusted his shirt and tie.

"Is my wife ready to party the night away?"

"As long as my husband is on my arm."

Chapter 36

Rich and I entered the ballroom and mingled with guests, gave hugs, and received words of congratulations. My mother ran over when she saw us, her burgundy gown shimmering in the glow of crystal chandeliers.

"Oh, I'm so glad you kids worked it out." She hugged me, then Rich. "I knew you would." She pulled away. "Now make sure you greet every guest and thank them for coming. Dinner is starting in twenty minutes, so I suppose that's impossible. But there will be time later. And make sure your Best Woman's toast is ready and--"

"Mom," I interrupted her oral instruction manual.

"Yes dear?"

"Can't we just enjoy ourselves and go with the flow, for once?"

She smiled. "Yes. Go have fun."

I gave her a quick hug before continuing our sweep of the room. Sheila stood near the bar, a balding man on her left, at least six inches shorter than her.

I hugged her, even as much as she tried not to let me. "Thank you for getting everyone back to the garden."

"No problem."

I turned to the man next to her. "You must be Paul." I held out my hand.

"Pleasure to meet you."

"This is my fian--I mean husband, Rich."

They exchanged handshakes.

"Let me get you both a drink," Paul said, and asked our preferences.

He took his place in line at the bar and I noticed Sheila staring at Rich.

"You're lucky, you know," she finally said.

"Yes, I am." He reached for my hand and brought it to his lips.

"Not because of her. I meant the pair of scissors I have with your name on them."

I laughed as Rich's brow furled in puzzlement.

"Huh?"

"Be happy your balls are still attached."

Paul presented us with our drinks, a glass of wine for me, and a Jim Beam and Coke for Rich. He took a long swig as Amanda bounced over.

"I'm so happy for you guys!" She hugged us both. "I saw Rich walk out to the garden, but you didn't see him, and then when he came up like that and escorted you out, I almost burst into happy tears."

Andy shook Rich's hand and even hugged me. First time for everything.

The announcer asked us to take our seats. Rich and I took our spots at the head table next to Marcus and Kevin. It was the first we'd seen of them since entering the ballroom. I quickly hugged them both before sitting down.

The *maitre d'*, and emcee for the night, handed me a cordless microphone. "Whenever you're ready, go ahead."

The toast.

Of course I'd given thought to what I'd say, but not within the last week. I'd been too caught up in the drama of my life to finalize what I'd say. I'd be winging it.

I stood with the mic to my mouth. "Um, welcome...everyone, to this really wonderful and really odd event." Several chuckles. "My apologies for the double ceremony that ended up being split into two completely different ceremonies. I guess we didn't want to share the spotlight after all."

More laughter. Good. I found Rich and then Marcus and Kevin, all beaming at me. I continued.

"I've known Marcus my entire life. We've seen each other through pretty much everything imaginable. But one thing I've learned over the last few days is that true friends are rare, and we should always treasure them."

I turned to the newly married couple. "Marcus and Kevin, you've shown me what real love looks like. What a responsible relationship should be, and it's given me something to aspire to and model my own actions after. Love is always worth it, no matter what the obstacles are, and we all have our obstacles. You've both become so important to me, especially over the last year and a half. We share a special bond and I truly cherish our wacky new-age family unit."

I picked up my champagne flute. "I wish you a lifetime of happiness and love. And I'm excited to share the next fifty-plus years with you. Cheers!"

Everyone drank and I kept the microphone in my hand.

"And before I turn this over to Keith, I'd like to say a few words to my new husband." I turned to Rich and right away fought tears. "I never knew what I was missing until I met you. You changed my entire world. And I thank you for that. You surely know I am not perfect, but I hope you also know how hard I will try to be the woman and wife you need."

A tear rolled down my cheek as Rich stood.

"I love you."

He kissed me right there in front of a ballroom full of people, like it was just the two of us.

After a resounding "awww" we took our seats and listened to Gryz's toast, clinking glasses when he'd finished.

* * * *

"And for their first dance as husband and wife, Mr. and Mrs. Richard Taylor."

Rich squeezed my hand as he led me to the middle of the dance floor, pulling me close as the singer belted her rendition of *At Last*. Camera flashes sparked all around us like paparazzi, but we hardly noticed.

"A few hours ago, I never thought I'd see you again, let alone be in your arms, dancing as husband and wife."

He pulled me in closer and I nuzzled his neck.

"I love you, Lexi. And I promise to spend my life proving that I deserve you."

The photographer stepped close for a shot. I smiled at him and snuggled close to Rich. The camera flashed a brief second, and over his shoulder I caught a familiar face in the crowd. I'd recognize that head of curls anywhere.

Karma nodded and smiled. She brought her hand to her stomach, rubbing a small protruding bump.

I looked at Rich, then back at her, but she'd already disappeared. My hands crept up behind his neck and pulled him to me for a kiss.

"What's with the goofy grin?" he asked, blue eyes glittering at me.

My cheeks hurt from how wide I was smiling. "I'm pregnant."

Meet the Author

What is life without love and laughter? If you ask Stephanie Haefner, she will say, "A whole lot of nothing!"
Combining a love story with comedy is what a good book is all about for Stephanie. She is always on the lookout for the next story that will have her aching from laughter one minute and her heart fluttering the next. She hopes to convey those same emotions for her readers.
As the mom of two amazing little people, Stephanie finds it hard to imagine life without some comic relief. When the house is a war zone, the kids have tied each other up, and the hubby is asking where dinner is, what else is there to do but laugh? Well, a toddler-esque fist-swinging tantrum is an option too…but who is that really helping?
And a world without love, passion, romance… If that ever happens, better stick her in a mental institution.

Stephanie's Website:
www.stephaniehaefnerthewriter.com
Reader email:
Stephanie_Haefner@yahoo.com

www.ingramcontent.com/pod-product-compliance
Lightning Source LLC
Chambersburg PA
CBHW031418250626
47155CB00004B/1533